SINS
of the

FATHER

BESTSELLING AUTHOR
ISABEL LUCERO

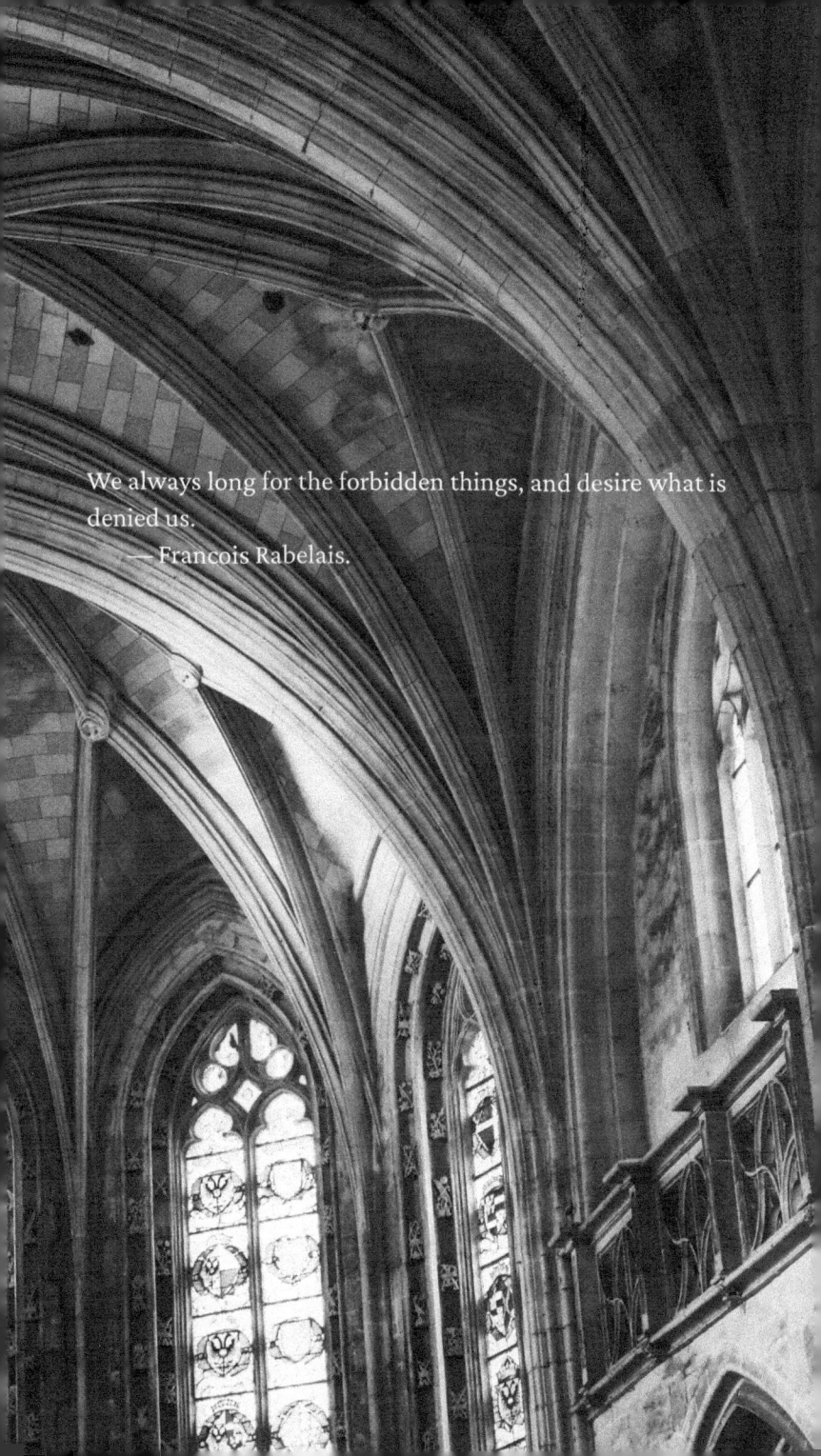

We always long for the forbidden things, and desire what is denied us.
— Francois Rabelais.

WARNINGS:

Sins of the Father isn't a very dark book, but it does have dark elements such as violence and murder. There's also discussion about faith, and lack thereof, so you can expect some blasphemy and sacrilege as well as depictions of grief, loss, and homophobia. If you'd like more details on any of these, please feel free to reach out to me.

FROM THE AUTHOR:

This book features commentary on religion, and as I am not Catholic myself, I conferred with a Catholic friend about a few things. However, I'd like to remind you that this is a fictional story in a fictional setting, and therefore, there are times where I had to take liberties and bend the rules in order to move the story along in the way it needed to. This does not relate strictly to the religion aspect, but in general. Things might not happen the way you've read in a different story, and that's okay. That's why every book is unique.

Now, I'd like to mention a couple things for perhaps two different types of readers.

For those who aren't religious, I'd like to note that in no way am I being "preachy" in this story. I am not a religious girl, so I am not trying to sell or force religion on anyone. The main character is a priest, so he will say priest-like things. There will be some discussion on religion and faith, but not in an over-the-top kind of way, and there will be scenes that take place in a church.

For readers who are religious, please be aware this story deals with a priest struggling to keep his vow. In writing this story, I did not try to mock religion. Though there are characters who are not believers. Before I continue, I'd like to warn that, while I'll do my best to keep it vague, reading this note further could potentially spoil a scene or two for you.

.

.

.

If a priest doing very un-priest-like things, possibly in his cassock and collar might offend you, I offer you the chance to turn back now.

PROLOGUE

He pulls the trigger, the bullet flying from the chamber and crossing the room to meet its target.

Dead.

When I glance to my left, I watch as he slowly lowers his arm to his side. His gaze finds mine.

Murderer. Sinner.

I see nothing behind his eyes. No guilt. No remorse.

CHAPTER 1

Every day I come to work and feel like a hypocrite. I preach the importance of being honest while hiding behind my own lies. I condemn sexual immorality while suppressing the sinful desires I harbor. And I promote forgiveness while clutching onto resentment.

Nobody's perfect. *"For all have sinned and fall short of the glory of God."* But if anyone should be close, it would be a priest, and yet some days, I feel furthest of all.

In the small town of Crest Haven, it's hard to keep much a secret, so it's best to abstain from any and everything that could be found out. I moved here a couple of years ago for this position, leaving my home in Pennsylvania after completing my time at St. Mary's Seminary.

However, you could say moving to Massachusetts was a homecoming. Too bad there wasn't anyone here to be excited about my return. Growing up, I lived about three hours from here, much closer to Boston. I enjoy Crest Haven though. Less trouble to be found in a small town. At least that's what I tell myself.

I'm the priest of the only Catholic church in town, sharing the duties with another priest who travels into town on the weekends.

I make my way to the confessional booth and await the parishioners who will show up.

Someone enters the other side, proven by the sound of their steps and the long sigh that follows. When they don't say anything, I speak up.

"Welcome."

"Not sure what to say. Forgive me, Father?" he questions. "Do I have to do something specific here?"

"Did you make the sign of the cross?"

There's another brief hesitation before he says, "Yeah." He either just did it, or lied about doing it at all.

"Bless me, Father, for I have sinned. That's what you say."

"Oh. Well, Bless me, Father, for I have sinned." His words drip with skepticism.

Sensing he's never been or not been in a while, I guide him through.

"How long has it been since your last confession?"

He chuckles. "Probably two decades. I haven't been since I was around ten."

"Okay. What are your sins?"

"Too many to cover in one session, Padre."

"Talk to me," I encourage.

"To be forgiven?"

"God forgives those who repent."

"To be honest, I'm not here seeking absolution. I'm aware of my actions, but I don't see them the same way others do."

"What do you mean?"

"I know right from wrong. It's not about that. But not

everyone can live in such black and white. Everyone sins. Even you, I'm sure."

I swallow and clear my throat. "You're right. Nobody is perfect. We make mistakes, but we have to learn from them."

He snorts. "Mistakes. Yeah, well, they say it isn't a mistake if you do it more than once, right?"

"What's bothering you the most right now?" I ask.

"I'm not really a religious person. My mom brought me to church when I was a kid. I haven't stepped foot in one of these in a long time."

"Something obviously drew you in. What are you struggling with?"

He huffs. "It doesn't matter. Again, I don't know why I'm here when this is no place for me."

"Everyone is welcome here."

"Don't give me the bullshit speech, okay?"

His hostility catches me off guard, but he's clearly wrestling with something. "Are you—"

A phone blares from the other side, cutting me off. With a sigh, he says. "Never mind. I gotta go."

"Wait."

But he's gone. I hear the rustling of his clothes as he gets up, and then the sound of his footsteps as he rushes away.

That's not the first time that's happened. There's a lot of people who get nervous when it's time to confess their sins. Afterall, it's hard to reveal the truth to ourselves, let alone someone else. I just hope they find their way back.

I glance at my watch and see that it's almost six-thirty, so I leave the wooden confessional and walk in front of the mahogany pews to my right. I come to a stop in front of the altar, taking a moment to gaze upon the opulence.

The arched, stained glass window is massive—perhaps nearly twenty feet tall. The images etched into the glass in a variety of colors reflect on the exquisitely waxed hardwood floor. Large marble pillars stand tall on both sides, the gold accents on the tops match the double chandeliers that hang right above the steps to the stage.

It's stunning, and I try to take a moment every day to appreciate that I'm here. Especially on the days I feel like I don't belong.

In the sacristy, I remove my vestments and gather my belongings, taking a moment to stare at my reflection in the oval mirror on the wall.

My brown hair is perfectly combed and coiffed to appear as though I simply ran my hand through it. I have to look put together, considering I still struggle with feeling like I am. My face is clean shaven, though I prefer a little facial hair, and it's something I may change in the future. I think I'm still clinging to some of my father's habits, hoping, in some childlike way, that the commonality between us will mean something. I adjust the glasses on my face, wishing they weren't clear, so I wouldn't see the discontent threaded through the brown irises every time I look at myself.

Turning away, I decide it's time to head home, but the mysterious penitent from today lingers in my head. And even after I'm home and decide to go for my evening run, his words chase me on my route.

Everyone sins. Even you.

CHAPTER 2

S hortly after a young lady leaves the confessional, I'm ready to depart as well, since it's already past confessional hours. I'm opening the wooden door when it's suddenly pushed back, closing me in.

"One minute," a man's voice says.

I glance at the lattice and watch someone stand on the other side.

"Hello," I say, almost like it's a question.

"I came back, but nobody was here."

I slowly get to the bench and sit down. "When did you come?"

"I don't fucking know. Two days ago, maybe."

"I have specific confessional hours."

"Well, you should have them posted on the fucking door or something."

My lips twitch. "We have them on our website. Or you could have called."

"Or you can just tell me now."

"Monday, Tuesday, Thursday, and Friday I'm here for confessions from eleven in the morning to eleven forty-five.

21

And Wednesday from twelve-thirty to one, and six to six-thirty. On Saturdays it's from ten to eleven and again from four to five. However, there are times when there are two of us here, taking confessions."

"Jesus Christ," he huffs. "I didn't know I'd have to write it down. Why can't it be the same time every day?"

"Well, we have—"

"Never mind. It doesn't matter."

He's rude and brash, but I stay quiet to see if he'll open up more this time. Instead, several long seconds go by with both of us just sitting in silence.

"Did you always know you were gonna be a priest?" he asks, once again, catching me off guard.

"No. Not always, but for a long time."

"You sound fairly young."

"I'm thirty."

"How long did it take to become a priest?"

"About eight years."

"So you devoted your life to this right after high school? Through your twenties you learned about Jesus instead of, I don't know, drinking and fucking and doing shit young people do?"

I shift in my seat. "Well, we all have different paths."

"Ain't that the truth." He pauses briefly. "You ever regret it? The path you chose?"

"Not yet."

He chuckles. "You need to work on your believability." With a sigh, he continues. "I don't think there was any other path laid out for me than the one I'm on. I didn't have a choice. Sometimes doctors raise future doctors. A guy in the Army is gonna have kids who go to the Army. You know? You do what's expected of you—what your dad wants you to do. But hey, I guess I shouldn't complain. I have a fairly good life. I don't want for much, and I'm good at what I do."

"And what is it that you do?" I question.

He laughs again, but it's not authentic. "Oh, Father. We aren't there yet."

"Are you here to confess anything?"

"If I confess, then what?"

"I'll give you a penance."

"What's that gonna be?"

"Depends on what your sin is."

"Could the penance be to tell me to turn myself in?" he asks with a laugh. "Because I don't think I'll be doing that, Father."

His statement leads me to believe that whatever he's referring to isn't just lustful thoughts or drug use. In his hesitations and omissions is a confession I may not want to hear, but honestly, it piques my curiosity more than it should. Who is this man on the other side of the lattice?

"I cannot go to the police myself," I tell him, "But I—"

"Is this like that doctor/patient confidentiality thing? What I tell you, you can't repeat?"

"Correct. The sacramental seal is inviolable."

"But you would still judge me."

"It is not for me to judge anyone. I could maybe encourage you to make the right decision."

"That's the problem, Father. Your right and my right are two totally different things. You live to obey your Lord and Savior, but I'm my own savior. I have my own rules to abide by, and they don't fall in line with the laws of your God."

"Then why are you here?" I ask, knowing it's not what I should question. "Why come to a confessional and not confess?"

"Is it not a process? Am I on your timetable, Father?" he bites, frustrated with me.

"Forgive me," I say. "You can continue to come here as often as you like."

He snorts. "Right. Well, I guess I'll be going."

"I'll be here Saturday," I say before he can leave.

"Yeah. Ten to eleven and four to five, right?"

"That's right."

He doesn't say anything else, I simply hear the door open and close followed by his heavy steps as he leaves the church.

For the rest of the evening, I kick myself for questioning why he's here. It was the wrong thing to say, and I hope he comes back. I hope he gets to a point where he can confess, if not for anything but to maybe make himself feel a little lighter.

But again, something tells me I may not want to hear it.

CHAPTER 3

"Thank you, Father," Lucy says as we stand between the pews. "I appreciate you taking the time to talk to me."

I give her a slight nod and smile. "Of course. Anytime. Stay safe out there."

She grins and gives me a small wave before taking quick steps toward the front door. I notice a figure in the narthex, lingering just outside of view. Lucy spots him as well, rushing through the front doors, letting the sunlight in. It shines on him briefly before the heavy wooden door closes.

He's wearing dark sunglasses and a hat underneath the hood of his light jacket. I can't tell for sure, but I think he's looking in my direction, however he's not attempting to come farther inside.

I assume it's the man who's visited me twice. Based on his disguise, he doesn't want to be seen or recognized. It's the beginning of August, and therefore not too cold just yet, so the jacket and hat aren't for warmth. I stare back for a few seconds, lifting my hand before I walk across the room toward the confessional booth and settle inside.

A few moments later, footsteps draw closer, and then the door opens and closes.

"I didn't realize you were wearing all that."

I look down at my black cassock and purple stole and think this is one of the plainest outfits I wear in the church.

"Did you think I was wearing jeans and a T-shirt?"

He laughs a little. "I don't know. Do priests ever just wear normal clothes?"

"Sure."

"Do you always have that collar on?"

"Not always."

"I've been doing research."

"Oh? What about?"

"That sacramental vow or whatever you said."

I smile. "The sacramental seal. What did you want to know?"

"Just how sacred it is. Some people say that priests can break the vow and tell the police."

"Some might, but they'd likely be excommunicated for doing so."

"So I guess it just depends on the person and how righteous they're feeling."

"Are you afraid I'd break the seal?"

"I don't know. I don't know you."

"What do you want to know?"

"Why did you become a priest?"

"That's a long, complicated story."

"I have some time."

I chuckle. "Well, I suppose it's very similar to what you said before. We do what our dads want us to do."

"Is your dad a priest?"

I hesitate. "No."

"But he wanted you to be one?"

"Yes."

"And you just said, 'okay'?"

I laugh. "No. We fought quite a lot about that, and many other things, but eventually—"

"You did what he wanted."

"Yes."

"You close to him?"

"No."

He snorts. "Makes sense."

"What did you want to do? What did young Carlo Gallini want to be as a kid?"

"You know my name."

"Yeah, well, I picked up one of those pamphlet things. Had your name in there."

"Are you gonna tell me yours?"

"Probably not, Padre."

"I see. Well, to answer your question, as a kid I obviously wanted to be a superhero. When I turned seven and realized I couldn't do that professionally, I eventually came to the idea that I wanted to be an artist."

"What kind?"

"A painter."

"Are you any good?"

"I thought so."

"That's pretty different from what you do now."

"Yeah, but we need both priests and artists, and I think we're lower on priests than artists these days."

"Hmm."

We sit in silence again, and as soon as I'm about to open my mouth to say something, he beats me to it.

"So, you're married to Jesus, huh?"

My eyes widen, surprised at the question. "Well—"

"I mean, you can't get married, right?"

27

"Right."

"And you don't fuck either?"

I shift, straightening my back. I've never had anyone come to a confessional and talk the way he does.

"No. If I were married before I became ordained, that would be okay, but I was single, so I must remain celibate."

He barks out a laugh. "What the hell? That's the craziest rule I've ever heard of, and I've had some pretty strict rules. So, again, in the beginning of your twenties, you chose to live the rest of your life without ever getting your dick wet?"

I cock my head. "You know, your language—"

"Is vulgar? Yes, I know, and to be honest, I'm really toning it down in here. Forgive me, Father." The last part oozes with sarcasm. "But come on, how does it keep you from doing your job? That's probably why you're low on priests. These rules are asinine. Tell me, though, did you do everything you wanted before you were ordained? Did you sow your oats?" He gets closer to the lattice, but he's still wearing his hood, so I can only make out part of his jaw, lips, and chin. "Confess, Father," he teases. "Did you get your fill of pussy before you cut yourself off for life?"

I don't answer, struck dumb. Scalding hot discomfort claws at my neck, because this stranger...this man who comes in here and all but admits to committing crimes so unfathomable, God wouldn't forgive him, is now questioning me, a priest, about my sex life. Most people would have enough sense to know you can't come in here and talk like this to a priest, but this guy doesn't seem to care about anything.

"Father." His voice comes through the lattice, low and teasing. "Father." This time there's less teasing, but his tone is an octave lower. "You're thinking about it, aren't you? All the sins you committed? Tell me one."

I clear my throat and tug at my collar. "I'm not here to confess."

"If you tell me something, maybe I'll tell you something."

Temptation conflicts with my job. Part of me wants to join him in this tit-for-tat strategy, not only to hear what he has to say, but for the ability to tell him something about myself. To tell anyone. But that's not why I'm here.

"I don't get anything out of that game," I lie. "People come to me to confess. To seek absolution. You come here to question me about my personal life. I'm a priest. I'm here to help others."

"Doesn't mean *you* don't need help. I think you're too stiff. Your voice is practiced. Your tone lacks warmth. It feels like you're trying too hard to be something you're not. Maybe you're afraid the past isn't far enough behind you. I've met a lot of people, Father. Some good, most bad, all of them sinners. I know you have skeletons in your closet. We all do."

Once again, he knocks me off kilter a little bit. Perhaps he's hitting a little too close to home, and that's probably why I react the way that I do.

"You should leave. It's well past confessional hours, and I need to go home."

He sighs before he lets out a humorless chuckle. "All right, then."

I see his figure pass the lattice, and then the door opens and closes before he walks away.

He was right, though. The skeletons in my closet have been waiting to be freed.

CHAPTER 4

I know I shouldn't let the opinions of others affect me, but for the rest of the night, all I can think about is how I don't come off as authentic. He said I sound practiced. I lack warmth. That's the last thing a priest wants to hear. I wonder if everyone I talk to feels that way. I thought I've been doing a good job.

My phone rings as I'm taking my dishes to the sink. When I glance at the screen, I do a double take, because it's an unknown number. I don't get many calls as is, but anyone that does call is programmed in my phone.

"Hello?"

"Hey. It's your dad."

My brows lift. "Oh. What's going on?"

"I just thought I'd let you know I have some work business going on. I uhh…" There's some rustling on the other end before he speaks again. "I'll be leaving town."

"For how long?" I question.

"Don't know. Probably not long," he says.

"Why tell me? We haven't spoken in—"

"It's been several months. I know. Just thought you should be aware in case, I don't know, you needed me."

I swallow down the words that would question why he'd think I'd need him. "Okay."

"Anyway," he says, still making noise in the background. "I got something you might want. Johnny will hold onto it until he can get it to you."

"What is it?"

"Not much. Just check in with Johnny when you're ready."

I hesitate, feeling strange about his sudden reappearance and now gift. "You okay?"

He laughs that snarky laugh of his. "I ain't got cancer or nothing," he says.

"All right."

"Yeah, anyway. You doing okay? You good?" His questions come as an afterthought. Something he needs to ask right before he hangs up.

"Uh, yeah. I'm good."

"All right. Well, I'll let you know when I'm back."

"Yeah. Sure."

"See ya, kid."

The phone call ends before I can reply.

Considering our relationship, or lack thereof, his call has curiosity climbing up my back. I quickly press some buttons on my phone to bring up Johnny's number, but when I call, he doesn't answer.

I spend the rest of the evening thinking about my relationship with my dad. It would be a lie to say I don't think about him fairly often, even though we don't speak. I'm a priest because of him. Every day that I don my collar, I'm reminded that I didn't have a choice.

When I was seventeen, my father walked in on me

kissing a boy from school. Dad made it clear he wasn't happy about what he saw, and it would not be tolerated.

I rebelled, as most teenagers do. I acted out and did everything he explicitly told me not to. Kissing boys in my room wasn't the only thing I was doing, I was flaunting it. I kissed them on the front lawn of our home. I snuck them into my room. I wanted him to know. I wanted him to accept it.

Instead, my plan backfired. By my nineteenth birthday, I knew I'd be joining the priesthood.

My dad didn't play around, and I should've known better than to test him, but I was young, stupid, and full of hormones.

There came a night when he saw me out at a restaurant with a guy. When I got home, he was waiting for me with an ultimatum. I'd go into the priesthood or I'd move away and be cut off from him and his money.

Because I was still young, I definitely thought I'd move away, because I'd be damned if I let my dad control my future. The truth is, he's always been in control.

My mom died when I was a baby, so it had only been my father and I my whole life. Don't get me wrong, I had nannies, because Dad had to work, but he was there as often as he could be. He makes decent money, and I never had to beg for anything. I always had the nicest clothes, shoes, and electronics.

It wasn't until I was well into my teens that I started to understand more about the sacrifices he was making for us to live the way we did. As kids, we simply expect things. We don't have the burden of worrying about electricity and food, let alone the extras. We anticipate they will always be there without us having to do anything.

Because of my dad, I never had to work. Not a real job,

anyway. Sometimes he'd have me do things for him—errands, if you will. I was paid for my work, but I never really needed to make my own money.

So when the threat of being cut off, and forced to move was shoved in my face, I knew I didn't really have a choice. Without his money, I wouldn't even be able to go anywhere. Without the car he bought me, the money he gave me, I wasn't going to be able to drive or fly to another state. I wasn't going to be able to rent an apartment or go to college. I was completely under his thumb and he knew that.

My life was set as long as I stopped being gay, so I went into seminary school, which he paid for. I lived there for five years, became a transitional deacon when I turned twenty-four, and before I was twenty-six, I was a priest.

Don't get me wrong, I don't hate it. Not too much, anyway. It's not like I didn't believe in God. I just didn't want to be a priest, because I knew it would keep me single. Celibate. And that's the main reason my father wanted it for me. He hasn't gone to church in years, so it's not like he simply wanted his son to be a holy man.

My father is the boss of the Esposito crime family. It's a fairly new title for him, but he's been in since before I was born.

My father didn't want his gay son to be in the family business, so I was ousted and forced to the church. I guess that's more acceptable to mafia families, considering they all show up to mass and pretend they aren't violent criminals or adulterers.

I call Johnny one more time before I go to sleep, and this time when he doesn't answer, I leave a message.

CHAPTER 5

A week goes by before the mystery man full of sin and brash language shows back up. I thought maybe he'd given up for good, but once again, right before my confessional hours are over, he sits in the booth across from me.

He's quiet, forcing me to speak first.

"How long has it been since your last confession?"

"I've never confessed to anything in my life."

"Then I imagine you have a lot to repent for."

"Yep," he says without regret. "This will likely be the last time I'm here, Padre."

"And why is that?" I ask, curious and somewhat disappointed.

"Coming here doesn't help me. You were right before. I have no reason to show up if I'm not going to confess. And," He hesitates. "Well, it doesn't matter."

"Are you just looking for someone to talk to?"

"In my profession, I'm not paid to talk. In fact, it would be the opposite, if anything."

"So you come here to talk to someone who can't repeat

anything. It seems to me like you want to confide in someone without the threat of consequence."

He chuckles. "Oh, is that what you think?"

"If that's not the case, tell me what is."

"You're not ready for my confessions, Father."

"Try me."

He snickers again, like he's amused by me. "What's the worst thing someone has confessed to you?" he questions.

"In here?"

"Yeah."

"Those are private and personal confessions."

"I'm not telling you to give me their full names and addresses. What do I give a fuck what people do? I'm not one to judge."

I sigh. "Common confessions are lying, stealing, lusting, having affairs. Harboring thoughts of revenge."

"Lusting? You mean to tell me people aren't allowed to lust after anyone?"

I ignore his question. "So, what are your sins?"

"Well, Father," he says with a small laugh, "I can tell you I've lied, I've stolen, I've lusted, and I'm currently harboring thoughts of revenge."

"Are those all your mortal sins?"

"No."

"You must confess all of your mortal sins. Get on your knees and confess them all so I can absolve you."

"On my knees, huh?" he questions. "That's what this little cushioned bench is for?"

"Yes."

A few seconds go by and I'm sure he's about to leave, but then I see his face at the lattice as I sit back in my seat. He looks at me through the small holes, his eyes hidden behind dark glasses. I can't make out any discerning features—the lattice doing its job to obscure faces in the dim lighting of the confessional booth.

"We'll be here all night, Father."

"That's fine."

"You want me on my knees all night?"

Something in his tone sets me on edge.

"Go ahead and start."

"If I tell you everything right now, you'll never see me again. I won't come back."

"Will you continue to sin?"

"Yes."

"Then you'll need to come back."

"Sounds like you want me to be a sinner, Father."

I hesitate. "Are you ready?"

"I'm not going to bore you with the sins of my life. We don't have that sort of time, but I'll confess some recent ones."

I sit up a little straighter. "Go on."

"There's blood on my hands, Father." He pauses, waiting for my response, but my tongue is dry and stuck to the roof of my mouth. "Lots of it."

When I finally come down from the shock of this particular confession, I speak. "Was it self-defense?"

"I'd say so. Self-defense is to protect yourself or family from harm, right?"

"Were you in immediate danger? Could this have been avoided?"

"Immediate? Maybe not. Could I have avoided it? No."

"Do you regret it?"

"No."

"You have to be able to say you are sorry for all of your sins."

"That would be a lie."

"Then I cannot absolve you."

"That's fine. I don't need to be absolved of something I plan on continuing to do." He stands up. "Goodbye, Father."

"Be safe out there. Be conscious of the lives you affect with the decisions you make," I say before he's gone.

"I'm well aware."

I can't help but feel like I didn't do a good enough job with him, but it's clear he's not sorry for what he's done, and has no plans to change who he is.

I'll pray on it. Maybe he'll come back and I can do more for him.

CHAPTER 6

"Sorry it took so long to get back to ya, kid," Johnny says from the other side of the phone. "It's been a little busy around here."

"I left you a few messages."

"I know. Look, your father told me you'd be calling. It's just a goddamn circus these days. I gotta watch who I'm talking to and who I'm around. Now, what's going on?"

"Nothing. My dad said you had something for me. Where do I need to go to pick it up and when?"

"Right. I have it over at Kat. You gonna be okay to be seen over here, Father?" he asks with a slimy laugh.

"It'll be fine," I tell him. I haven't seen Johnny in a long time, but he seems exactly the same. "When?"

"I'll be there around ten o'clock."

"Okay, I'll meet you there. Have you heard from my dad?"

"No. He's under the radar, kid. You know. I'm sure he'll pop up like he always does. We can talk later."

"Okay."

I look at my watch and see that it's already nine-fifteen.

The drive to Kitty Kat—the topless bar my dad works out of sometimes—will take about forty-five minutes.

After changing into a pair of black jeans and a white T-shirt, I slip on some white sneakers and head to my car.

It's been a week since my father left and told me he had something for me. Johnny didn't reply to any of my calls until now, so I've been sitting on pins and needles, wondering what the hell this package could be.

Yesterday, a man confessed to murder in my confessional booth, and today I'm walking into a nudie bar to talk with the underboss of a crime family.

I say a little prayer and make the sign of the cross as I drive. The sins of my father are not mine. The sins of that man are also not mine.

That's not to say I don't have my own, but I'm not taking on anyone else's.

After I park, I pocket my keys and make my way over the thick cracks in the sidewalk that lead to the front door.

Inside, the bass of the music thrums through the room, and two women on a small stage in the back sway their hips in front of a handful of men who sit and watch.

"I.D.?" a voice to my right questions.

"I'm looking for Johnny," I tell him as I reach into my back pocket.

"Oh yeah? Is he looking for you?"

I pull out my wallet and hand him the Pennsylvania license I didn't relinquish when I got my Massachusetts one. I told them I lost it, but I wanted to hold onto it as it's the one with my real last name. Not what I go by now. Not Gallini. When I came back home, I changed my name to allow distance between my father and I. However, in a place like this, my last name holds power.

"Yeah, he told me to meet him here."

He takes my license, but only continues to scrutinize my face. "And who are you?"

My brows furrow as I gesture to the card in his hand.

His small, dark eyes aim daggers at me before he gazes down at it. After just a second, those beady eyes flicker back up at me, a bit larger this time.

"I see. I'll show you to the office."

I take my ID back and follow him to a small hallway that houses the bathrooms on each side, and the office at the far end.

He gestures at the dark green door before turning around and walking away. I continue on and knock, waiting to be told to come in.

The door opens, and a man with a large belly and a scowl etched on his face stands there staring at me like I've made a mistake.

"I'm here to see Johnny."

He runs a hand over his slicked back, black hair, looking me up and down before angling his head over his shoulder. "You expecting someone?"

Johnny's head pops over. "Oh, yeah. Let him in. I'll talk to you later, okay?" he says, effectively dismissing the man who seems hesitant to let me in considering he hasn't budged.

"Yeah, okay," he finally says, opening the door a little wider and brushing past me.

"Come on in, kid," Johnny says, making his way to a messy desk.

"People around here seem friendly."

He snorts. "Don't worry about them. Everyone is kinda on edge right now."

He shuffles through some papers before finding a key, and then unlocks a drawer at the bottom of the desk.

I gaze around the room, noticing a lot of my father's stuff on the walls—old pictures I remember seeing growing up, a wooden sign hoisted behind the desk with our last name carved into it.

"Why is everyone on edge?" I ask as he continues to unlock drawers, seeming a little frazzled himself.

"Oh, you know. Ah, here it is."

"I actually don't know. Does it have anything to do with my father being gone?"

Johnny wipes sweat off his forehead before huffing out a breath. "What do you know? Or care? You ain't in this life, kid. Your father hardly talks about you, and I don't say that to hurt your feelings, but it is what it is."

I cross my arms over my chest. "What's going on, Johnny? Honestly. This isn't new to me," I say, gesturing around the room. "Just because I haven't been to this particular business doesn't mean I haven't been in others. I grew up with him. I'm not naive."

He watches me carefully. "Yeah, but you're—" Johnny gestures around his neck, referring to my clerical collar, which I don't even have on right now.

"It's not like I'm a cop."

He shrugs before falling into the leather chair. "Someone wants to take your dad out," he says simply. "He's only been the boss a few years, and he's made some waves lately that some people aren't too happy about." His shoulders rise and fall again. "We think we know who it is, but we're moving carefully."

I slowly fold myself into the chair opposite his, the news of my dad having a target on his back taking me out at the knees.

"Well, what...I mean, is there something I can do?"

He barks out a laugh. "You? I guess you can pray."

"I'm serious, Johnny."

"Me too," he says. "What else you gonna do, huh? You a hitman now? You got pull with some other family? I doubt it."

"What if he's already dead?" I ask. "How would you know?"

"We'd know. Don't worry."

I let out a deep breath. "All right, well, what did he leave for me?"

Johnny picks up the small box and holds it in my direction. I get up and take it, wanting to dig into it right now, but I restrain myself.

"Thanks."

"If you need anything, kid, you got my number."

I nod. "If you hear anything..."

"I'll let you know."

With the box in hand, I leave the office and head straight for the bar. I don't drink often, but right now feels like the perfect time to at least have one.

The bartender—a man with a clean-cut face and thick eyebrows—comes to a stop in front of me. His black shirt is snug around his muscled arms, and I find my eyes lingering a little too long on his body before I snap out of it and meet his gaze.

"Uh, Gin martini, please."

He doesn't say anything, instead simply getting to work. The drink is in front of me in no time, so I hand him a twenty and tell him to keep the rest. After he takes the bill, he helps a customer a few seats down.

I slowly enjoy the drink, knowing I won't get another one. I busy myself with my phone as I eavesdrop on a conversation taking place next to me. Apparently the man to my right doesn't care if everyone knows he is currently mad at his girlfriend for wanting him to spend more time with her and that's why he's here. He then goes on to talk about how hot the dancers are.

Relationships aren't for everyone. Maybe it's best to be a celibate priest. At least I won't have to worry about my significant other going out to a bar and talking shit about me while checking out someone else.

When I take another sip of my drink, I lift my head and look around, noticing a man across from me. He's holding a glass of amber colored liquid, swirling it around as his eyes focus on me. I glance away before letting my eyes wander back to him, only to find he's still staring.

I wait to see if he'll notice and look away, but he keeps watching me, his face stripped of any emotion. My brows furrow as I continue the staring contest. He smirks like I amuse him and then downs the rest of his drink before putting the glass down. After dropping a bill on the counter, he gets up and walks toward the bathroom.

This is why I typically avoid bars. There's almost always a man who wants to act tough or feels like he has something to prove. I'm not afraid of those guys. They're usually all bark, no bite, but it's best to avoid situations that can cause trouble. And I'm just now remembering which bar I'm in. Anyone in here could know the workings that go on behind the scenes, which means they're connected in some way.

I get up from the stool, leaving my glass mostly full, and pocket my phone before grabbing the box I got from Johnny. When I push open the door, I make my way around the corner to get to my car, but immediately spot a man at the edge of the building. His back is to me as he lights a cigarette. I think it's the same guy who stared at me from across the bar. He must've exited through a back door.

While my feet falter at first, I keep moving.

I expect to hear him say something to me, but he doesn't. I force myself to not look over my shoulder, and instead get to my car. When I drive past the building, he's still outside, this time closer to the street with a phone pressed to his ear. He watches me as I pass him and a cold chill runs over me.

CHAPTER 7

Whn I get home and open the box, I find myself looking at old pictures of me and my dad. Some are just of me at different times in my life—my first baseball game, my sixth grade graduation, as well as my college graduation. There's some birthday photos, and the day my dad bought me a car. A lot of the important moments in life were captured.

As I continue to dig, I find letters I wrote to my dad when I was a kid—one saying he was my hero.

I'm surprised that he kept all of this, but also confused why he's giving it to me. Unless...I don't want to think about why, because the only thing I can think of is that he doesn't believe he'll be coming back.

I step away from the box, choosing to take a shower and get to bed. I might need to talk to Johnny again. I'm starting to think this situation my dad is in is a little more serious than they're letting on.

✝

FOR THE NEXT WEEK, work occupies a lot of my time. On top of my normal duties, I've had to perform last rites for a member of my parish, two baptisms, and counseling for an engaged couple.

I've only reached out to Johnny once but it took him a day and a half to respond, and he only said there was nothing to update me on.

I've called my dad numerous times, but it's clear his phone is turned off. My concern grows until it's almost all I can think about, so on a Friday evening, I make my way back to the bar and hope Johnny is there.

The same man with the beady eyes and thinning hair takes my I.D. He doesn't have anything to say this time, just a cursory glance at the license before his narrow-eyed gaze lands on me again. With a slight jerk of his head, he lets me know I'm free to go.

My eyes scan the room before I make the turn into the hall that leads to the office that my dad occupied until recently.

Before I knock, I lean in and listen, because I hear raised voices.

"I don't fucking care. He shouldn't have information I don't," Johnny says.

"What am I supposed to say? He's not talking."

"Figure it out."

"All right."

The voices get a little lower, or the customers get a little louder, because now I only catch a few words here and there.

"He doesn't know who...but he's not happy... looking for Cortez."

Johnny responds. "Fuck." That word comes through

loud and clear. "Haven't heard...but if he finds him...don't let..."

I nearly press my ear to the door, unconcerned if anybody sees me. They mentioned my dad. Someone's looking for him, but who? The one who wants to kill him? Someone else?

"He's furious...won't stop. We have to get..."

I lean a little too close and my body hits the doorknob, causing it to make a noise. I silently curse myself before quickly knocking.

The door swings open, and Johnny stands there with a vicious scowl on his face.

"Holy fuck, kid, you better be careful whose fucking doors you're bumping into."

"Sorry. Can we talk?"

The guy inside with him gives me a head-to-toe once over, his hand slowly coming around from his back. I don't doubt he was reaching for a gun that's hidden there.

Johnny sighs. "Fine. I don't have much time." He looks at the other guy—a short, stocky man that's definitely younger than me. "Remember what I said."

He nods. "Got it, boss."

Once the door closes, Johnny sits down with a sigh.

"You're the boss now?" I question.

His eyes flash in my direction. "Someone has to step up."

A memory runs through my head. I was young—maybe fourteen, and Johnny was hanging out with my dad. They were laughing and talking about what they'd do if they were the boss.

At that time, I had a good idea what my dad and Johnny were into.

Mistrust runs through my blood.

"That's something you've wanted for a while, right?" I ask.

Johnny narrows his eyes at me, his jaw clenching. "You watch your fucking mouth. I'm tolerating this one time, because I've known you your whole life and I respect your father, and it's the latter that's keeping me from cutting your tongue from your fucking mouth. Don't you let those words spill from your lips again."

I hold up my hands in surrender, my heart racing in my chest, though I try not to let on. "I was just asking."

He huffs out a breath, and when I study him, I see the bags under his eyes and his messy hair. He's stressed and worried.

"I need to know more about what's going on," I tell him. "Dad leaves me this box of sentimental memories, and you know him, he's not a sentimental man. He's now MIA without his phone, and you're in here looking like you've aged five years since I saw you last. And before you try to lie or downplay anything, I overheard part of the conversation you were having in here."

Johnny sighs again. "You know, you're gonna get yourself killed. Listening in on conversations and running that mouth of yours."

"Who's looking for him?" I ask, getting back to the point.

"Just a triggerman. He's working for another family."

"He's not *in* the family?"

"No."

"Someone has to know where my dad is. Someone has to be able to go check in and make sure he's still fine."

"Sure, someone knows."

"Okay, and?"

"And what, kid? You some mafioso now? What're you gonna do with all this information?"

"I want to go see him."

"Absolutely not," he says, shaking his head. "And you shouldn't even be here."

"Why?"

"Because." He leaves it there for a minute, but when I continue to stare at him, he continues. "It's not safe. You got your little life all set up. You're good. Keep it that way."

I swallow down my anger, knowing it's fueled by fear and shouldn't be aimed at Johnny. I stand up. "I want updates. I want to know how close you are to finding this guy who's looking for my dad. I want to know when it's safe for my father to come back."

His brows lift slightly. "Okay, *Father*," he says, emphasizing the title. "You want me to alert you when the problem has been *dealt* with?"

"Yes."

Johnny looks slightly amused. "Sure thing. Anything else?"

Now he's just humoring me, so I stand up and get ready to leave.

"Oh." I stop and turn around. "Last week, there was a guy here. He was staring at me from across the bar. Then he was outside as I was leaving. He watched me as I drove off, but he was on his phone. Is that something I need to be concerned about?"

Johnny's brows knit. "What did he look like?"

"Tall. Dark hair. Angry demeanor. Five o'clock shadow."

"He have any tattoos?"

I shrug. "He was covered up."

"He never asked you anything?"

"No."

"It's probably nothing. I'll look into it, but hey, don't talk to anyone about this place. Your dad. Anything."

"I know, Johnny. I remember the rules."

He dips his chin. "I'll be in touch."

I leave, no longer sure if I want to hear from him or not. I won't know if he's calling with good news or bad.

CHAPTER 8

When he shows up again, it's over two weeks after the last time he was here, but this time, he speaks from the shadows of the trees between the church and the rectory. I was ensuring the house was locked up since it's being worked on by a maintenance crew when I heard the snap of twigs nearby.

"Father," he says simply.

I turn my head in his direction, finding only a dark figure leaning against a tree trunk maybe twelve feet away. The sun has already dipped well below the horizon, and the clouds in the sky make it darker than it normally would be at this time. He's wearing a baseball cap pulled down low.

"Hello," I reply. "Wasn't sure you'd come back."

"Yeah, well, desperate times." His voice is low and rough, the words sounding like they've gone through a shredder first.

"You okay?"

He pushes off the tree, grunting. "Shit." His hand goes for his side, alerting me of an injury.

"Do you need help?" I ask, stepping forward.

51

"Is that house open?" he asks, jerking his head toward the rectory, his voice strained.

"I have the key."

"Anybody in there?"

"Not right now. It's being worked on."

"Can we go inside?"

I hesitate. I don't know anything about this man except that he's likely killed a lot of people. It's not smart to go inside an empty house with him without letting anyone know what's going on or where to find me.

He takes a step forward and grunts, clutching his side. After another step, I'm not sure he'll be able to stand much longer.

"Dammit," I say under my breath, rushing to the house.

I unlock the door and push it open before I make my way back toward him.

"I got you," I say, my arm wrapping around his waist from his non-injured side.

He curses the whole way, grunting with each step until we're inside and I get him to a chair.

"I don't have my phone with me," I tell him. "Do you have yours? I can call an ambulance."

The man shakes his head slightly, his head lowered so I can't properly see his face. However, I can still tell he's in a lot of pain.

"No," he states, reaching into his hoodie pocket.

I step back, fear climbing up my spine, but then I see what's in his hand. A small, plastic box.

"What's that?"

"Suture kit," he says through gritted teeth. "Swiped it before I came over here. Can you?"

"I think you need a doctor."

"Nah," he says, standing up and reaching for the zipper that'll open up the hoodie he's wearing.

Grimacing and cursing, he eventually gets both arms free from the sleeves, the material dropping to the floor, leaving him in a black tank top. Though it's dark, I still immediately spot the wet, blood-soaked section of his shirt.

"What happened?"

"Could you just—" He doesn't finish, instead he grunts and gestures to his injury.

"Lie down," I say, pushing the small coffee table away from the loveseat.

He finds his way over, lying across the cushions with one leg dangling over the arm, and the other one planted on the floor.

"This couch is rough as fuck."

"It's old. I'll be back."

I rush toward the linen closet to grab some towels, then I go to the kitchen for a bowl of water.

At the couch, I drop to my knees and lift up his shirt. His arm is across his eyes, lifting his cap off his forehead, and his mouth is set in a firm line.

I take one of the cloths and dip it in the water before gently wiping away the blood that's covering the wound.

"Is this a stab wound? Bullet? Anything lodged in there?"

"No bullet."

Once I find the cut, I start questioning whether anything I do will actually help. It's fairly long, but I'm not sure how deep.

I hand him a dry washcloth. "Might wanna bite down on this."

He ignores it, but as soon as I start inspecting the laceration, he starts yelling.

"Fuck!"

I open the kit and get what I need. "It's been a while since I've had to do this. I still think a hospital is a better option."

"Just do it."

With the needle holder, I grip the suture and press the tip of the curved needle into his flesh.

"Goddammit!" he curses, bringing his fist to his mouth.

"Sorry."

With the tweezers, I grab a hold of the skin and puncture through the other side before tying a sloppy knot. I repeat the process all the way down the length of the cut, which has to be at least six inches.

It feels like it takes forever, but the man stays conscious throughout the experience, biting down on his hand or yelling into the room. I take a wet cloth and clean it once more before looking around for something to cover it with.

"Hold on."

"Not going anywhere," he grunts.

I make my way to the bedroom and rip a pillowcase from the pillow. I fold it in half and then get back to my knees next to the couch and cover the wound. I tuck the end under his body, and let the rest lie over his stomach.

"To keep any dirt or anything from seeping in there," I tell him. "I don't think we have any medication in here."

"I'm guessing you don't have any hard liquor either."

"No."

He attempts to sit up, groaning in the process.

I put my hand on his shoulder and push him back. "Take it easy. You can stay here for the night."

The man looks at me then, and I realize it's the first time

I'm studying his face. I'd been so focused on taking care of the wound that I never took the time to see the person I was caring for.

His hair is like onyx, and his eyes are nearly as dark. They're narrowed on me, studying my face like I'm the one to be suspicious of. His square jaw is covered with hair, like it's been a couple weeks since he's shaved.

He's handsome. And scary. Tattoos wrap around his throat and arms, but his torso is free of ink. It allows me to see just how fit he is.

Familiarity sparks somewhere in the back of my head.

"You said this place is being worked on."

I ease back. "They don't work on Sundays. You'll be left alone tomorrow."

He eyes me again, like *he* can't trust *me*. "Do you live here?"

I shake my head. "No. I'm...far away," I say, being vague, lying about how close I actually do live to the church. His stomach growls loudly. "I can go get you some food. This place isn't stocked since nobody's living here."

"It's fine," he says.

I stand up. "I'll be back. I'll also grab some pain medication."

"I said it's fine."

"And I'm not listening to you. You clearly make questionable decisions."

I think I hear him snort out a laugh as I make my way to the door, locking it before I close it behind me.

What the hell am I getting myself into?

CHAPTER 9

When I open the door to the house, the man whose name I still don't know jolts up slightly, his arm extending, and in his hand is a gun pointed directly at me.

I freeze in place, but he quickly adjusts, using the back of his gun-wielding hand to rub his eyes.

"Sorry."

I step inside and kick the door closed before taking the bags to the kitchen. I return to lock the deadbolt before heading back to unload my purchases.

"Is someone looking for you?" I question.

"Probably."

After I put away almost everything, I make my way to the living room where I set down a bottle of Gatorade and a convenience store sandwich wrapped in plastic.

"There's a little variety in the fridge. Also," I place a bottle of ibuprofen on the table. "There's these."

"Thanks," he grunts, attempting to sit up fully, a grimace marring his face.

"Hold on." I go back to a bag in the kitchen and remove

the sterile wound dressing I picked up at a CVS. "Let me properly cover the stitches."

"You don't have to do that," he says with a sigh as he lies back.

"It could get infected."

He peeks at me from under the arm he has draped over his forehead. "Fine."

I open the box and then peel open the wrapper. I found the largest one they had, and place the padding over the wound while pressing the adhesive edges to his skin.

When I'm done, I stand up, unsure what to do next and still trying to determine why he looks familiar.

"Do you need anything else?"

He glances at me before sitting up. "You've done plenty." Reaching for the sandwich, he says, "Unless you're asking if I need to confess."

"Well, I'm sure you do," I tell him. "But I'm not holding my breath."

His lips twitch. "It's been a rough couple of weeks, but hey, I'm alive. Can't complain."

"You've been stabbed. That's probably worth a complaint or two."

He snorts before taking a big bite of the sandwich. Before he's done chewing, he starts talking.

"I know you said the confessions are confidential, and considering I haven't had cops on my tail, I can assume you've kept what I said to yourself. But this right here," he says, gesturing between us. "This is confidential too."

He's not asking me if it is. He's telling me I need to keep this encounter between us.

"I won't say anything." I go silent for a few seconds before adding, "But you can't keep putting me in a moral dilemma."

He peers up at me, his eyes no longer suspicious, but perhaps a little amused.

"Oh, I think you're always in a moral dilemma, Father."

His eyes pin me in place, his tone teasing but with an underlying thread of knowledge.

When he doesn't break eye-contact, I feel sweat prickle under my arms. I play it off.

"I think we all struggle with our morality. It's part of being human."

"Nah. That's not what I mean. I mean, *you* specifically."

My head tilts slightly. "What are you talking about?"

"You tell me," he says between bites.

"I have nothing to tell," I say, straightening my spine.

He finishes chewing and wipes at his mouth before standing up, swiping the gun from the table. The movement hurts him, and makes him a little slow, but he still approaches me, his body coming within inches.

I force myself to keep my footing, my arms in front of me, hands clasped. He inspects me closely, dark eyes roaming my face. I feel his breath on my lips as he cocks his head, leaning in even closer, moving toward my neck.

I suck in a breath and then he's back in front of me, staring into my eyes. His tongue wets his lips and I track the movement before meeting his gaze again.

He reaches for my collar, tugging on the white material. I stumble just slightly, my hands brushing against his crotch.

I hastily step back, clearing my throat and turning my head. "I don't know what you're doing, but—"

"I pull a gun on you when you walk in, and you hardly react. I bring it over here and you don't even pretend to be afraid." He erases any space between us, and my pulse spikes. "I get close to you and you can't control your breathing or your wandering eyes."

My brows knit together at his implication. "That—"

"You go to a titty bar and don't look at the women once."

I cock my head, brows furrowing even further. "That was you. At the bar. Outside."

He makes his way back to the couch now. "I'm just doing my research, Father. I need to know who I'm talking to."

"And who do you think you're talking to?" I ask, afraid he's aware of my connection to Johnny. To my father who owns that bar.

"Someone who has something to hide. A sinner," he says with a smirk, gazing up at me.

"Well, I'm sorry to disappoint, but I'm simply a man of God who doesn't think to lust after women, whether they're clothed or not."

He snorts. "I see." After taking a sip from the bottle, he leans back on the couch. "So, tell me, Father. Why go to that sort of bar at all? You do know what it is, right? Did you get lost?"

Fear claws at my throat. Not because I think he's going to do anything to me, but because I'm afraid he's getting too close to knowing too much. I don't have an excuse for driving all that way simply to have a drink.

"I have to go," I tell him, turning toward the door. "I'll make sure nobody disturbs you, and I'll come back tomorrow to see if you're okay. After that, you'll need to find another safe house and leave me out of whatever it is you have going on."

"You have nothing to confess, Father?" he asks.

I ignore him and unlock the deadbolt.

"That bar is pretty far, isn't it? I mean, you have to pass at least three to get there. I'm unsure why a holy man like yourself would go to such a place."

I put my hand on the knob and turn, but before I leave, I make the mistake of looking back at him.

He smirks, his eyes informing me he knows I'm not on the up and up. His finger runs across his bottom lip, and I can't help but focus on it for a second too long. Then I leave, slamming the door behind me.

CHAPTER 10

Three days after I left that man in the rectory, I have yet to see or hear from him. When I showed up the next day, he was already gone, but his words continue to stay with me.

I wonder what all he knows, or at least presumes about me. And I wonder why he cares.

It's five after ten at night when my phone rings. Johnny's name on the screen has my heart picking up speed.

"What's going on?" I answer.

"Hey, kid," he says, defeat in his voice.

"What is it?"

"Your dad isn't... We've been looking for him, but—"

"What do you mean? You said he was safe. You said nobody knew where he was! What did you find? Blood?"

"Calm down, calm down. I don't wanna talk on the phone."

"I'll be there soon."

I end the call and quickly shove my feet into my shoes. I was already in a pair of gray sweats and a white Tee when he called, so I don't bother changing. My foot presses down hard on the gas the whole way, getting me there twelve minutes faster than usual.

I rush in this time, bypassing the man checking IDs. I'm halfway down the hall that leads to my dad's office when I hear footsteps approaching from behind. I ignore the man's demands to stop, violently shaking the door knob when it doesn't open for me.

Johnny opens the door, a scowl on his face. "Good god, kid. Get in here. It's fine, Lou," he says to the man behind me.

"What do you know?" I ask, not bothering to sit down.

"We had someone go out there to check on him, but he wasn't there. Doesn't look like there was a disturbance. Definitely nothing that would raise any flags, but he's gone."

"Who's the person who knew he was there? Have you questioned him?"

"Of course," he says. "He doesn't know anything. He wasn't staying with him. Your dad didn't want that. He was just checking in from time to time."

"How do we know he wasn't followed?"

Johnny sighs. "Look, we're working on it. We're gonna find him."

"Do you know anything else about this triggerman? This guy who's apparently been hired to kill my dad?"

"We know who he is."

"And?"

"It wasn't him. He's been captured on CCTV the last few days. He's been around town, and where your dad went, it wouldn't have been possible for him to have gone out there and been back in town at the times he was seen. He's been in bars, restaurants, and coffee houses."

"I'm sure they have more than one person who can get the job done."

"I'm just letting you know where we are because I told you I would. Now, we're still workin' on some things. I'm not worried yet. When I am, you'll know. Your dad is a smart man. If he thought he needed to leave, he would've. I'm sure he'll get a message to us soon, but if you hear from him first, let me know."

I exhale, rubbing my forehead with my fingers.

"Who's the other family?" I ask.

"You don't need to know."

"Tell me, Johnny," I spit, my voice rising.

"No. You don't need that information. You're already comin' in here talking reckless. I don't need you to go gettin' in trouble."

"Goddammit, Johnny! That's my fucking name on the wall, too!" I yell, pointing at the sign behind my father's desk that reads *Gallo*.

His brows go up, taken aback by my outburst.

With resignation, he shakes his head and lets loose a sigh. "The Bonetti Family."

I give him a single nod before I leave. My anger has me seeing in tunnel vision. I don't notice anyone around me, bumping into a couple people on my way out of the building. I start up the car, and the whole way home I think about what I could do with the information I have.

Johnny's right. I'm not connected. Knowing it's the Bonetti Family technically doesn't mean anything. I've heard of them, but what am I going to do? I'm a priest. Not a capo. Not even a soldier.

I need someone's help.

The mysterious man pops into my head. He's a killer.

He's not afraid of a fight, based on the knife wound he came to me with. Could I use him?

As I'm pulling into my driveway, I'm suddenly hit with another thought. One that has my chest tightening.

What if he's the one who's after my father?

CHAPTER 11

T wo full weeks go by before I see him again. In those two weeks, I get zero information from Johnny. There's been no updates on the where-abouts of my father.

The only information I have about the Bonetti Family is rumored areas they have businesses. It's not like I'd be able to convince anyone with power to talk to me—a random citizen without any obvious ties to another family.

So when I see him sitting in the back of the church toward the end of my sermon, my pulse spikes. I hope he stays because it's not like I can stop and chase him out of the church if he decides to get up and leave.

He's in his typical garb when he comes here—a black hoodie with a cap and dark sunglasses. Considering the type of guy he is, I doubt he cares about church etiquette.

"So, we need to look past our own needs," I continue. "We shouldn't focus on only our own comfort. We need to reach out to family and friends who are struggling. Even strangers. Sometimes it's just a kind gesture, a prayer, or a shoulder to lean on. Listen to their struggles. Offer a helping hand. As God has compassion, we too must show our own. Let us leave here today with a renewed commitment to helping someone else. Now, more than ever, our world needs love and compassion. Echo God's love with your actions. Now, we'll pray."

Before I begin the prayer, my eyes find him still sitting in the pew, and I hope that when I open my eyes he'll still be there.

When I'm done, I invoke the Trinity and dismiss everyone. My eyes travel to his seat and relief floods me as I realize he hasn't left.

While most people quickly make their way to the exit as the recessional hymn plays, there are some people who linger to talk. I tell Deacon Erick that I have something to address, and I quickly make my way toward the last pew.

"Hello," I greet.

"Father," he says, taking his glasses off just long enough for me to see his eyes rake over my garments.

"Can I speak with you please?" I ask, glancing around.

He doesn't move. "Is this gonna be some sort of kinky Catholic discipline?"

"What?" My brows knit together as I look down at him. "Why—never mind. Could you please join me?" I nod and smile at people walking by. "Why are you here anyway?"

"Learning about Jesus, obviously," he says with a smirk on his lips.

"Follow me."

I walk off and hope he's not being stubborn. I calmly make my way to the side aisle that takes us out of the nave and leads to a hall that will take us to the sacristy. This is where we prepare for Mass and store our vestments and furniture, but nobody should be coming back here anytime soon.

"I've done some research," he says before I can even fully step inside the sacristy. "Self-flagellation. You guys still do that?"

I close and lock the door once he's inside, turning to face him. "No."

"It's kinky, don't you think? I know what they say it's for...but, the scourge is nothing but a flogger. You think it was the priests that discovered pleasure in pain?"

"What's wrong with you?" I ask, my brows furrowed as I cross my arms in front of my chest.

He finally takes his glasses off. "Plenty. You know that, though."

"Did you come here for any particular reason?"

"Did you invite me back here for any particular reason?" he questions, his expression lascivious—eyes drinking me in.

"Yes."

His brows lift and his lips curl into a smirk. "Oh? And which one of us is getting on our knees?"

I cut him a look. "You're clearly into...illegal things." His eyes quickly flicker around the room. "There's no cameras in here," I tell him.

He leans on the vesting table, casually crossing one foot over the other. "What are you about to ask me, Father?" he questions with a slight grin.

I clear my throat. "Do you know the Bonetti Family?"

He stands up straight, his face losing his previous playful expression, turning dark and serious. "I suggest you get to your point. And quick."

"What if I needed your help?"

His eyes narrow slightly. "My help with what?"

My confidence wanes and I'm suddenly doubting myself. Maybe I shouldn't be talking to him about this.

"Never mind," I say quickly, heading toward the door.

He reaches out and stops me, his fingers wrapping around my wrist. "I know that family."

My eyes meet his.

"Do you work for that family?"

His expression barely changes, but I see a twitch of his brows, and I don't know what that means.

He lets go of my wrist. "Are you in trouble with them?"

I shake my head. "Just forget it."

"If you get on their radar," he says, hesitating briefly. "Well, you don't want to be. They're one of the most ruthless families out there. Even I try to avoid them."

I nod once, slightly relieved to know he doesn't work for them. "A parishioner mentioned them to me," I lie. "He might be in trouble. I'll counsel him. Anyway, did you come see me for a reason?" I ask, getting off the subject.

He studies me for a few seconds before answering. "I wanted to thank you for helping me."

"That's what I do."

He grins. "And I just wanted to see you again."

I cock my head. "Why?"

His shoulders lift and fall. "That's the question, isn't it?" He pauses for a few seconds. "Do you want to see me again?"

I study him—my complete opposite. He's a criminal, violent, vulgar, and likely a sinner beyond saving. I'm a priest who strives to live my life with obedience, and in a way that Christ would. But I'm also a priest with secrets and demons, just like anyone else. I know I should say no. But I don't want to.

I tell myself it's because I need more information. I want to know why he came to me in the first place. I want to know more about what he does. I want to see if maybe he can help me with my father.

I ignore the thoughts that say I want to see him again because I'm attracted to him—to the lifestyle he has that could've been mine.

"Where?" I ask.

His smile grows. "I got the perfect place."

CHAPTER 12

Turns out the perfect place is a hole-in-the-wall Mexican restaurant that boasts lively music, friendly employees, and minimal customers. After we parted ways at the church, I went home and debated my decision-making capabilities. Ultimately, I decided I wanted to meet him, but didn't delve too deep on why.

"You ever been here?" he asks as the waitress drops off our drinks.

"No."

He nods, lifting the glass to his lips. His gaze stays trained on me the whole time, causing me to break eye contact first as I pretend to find interest elsewhere in the colorful room.

"So, what have you got yourself into?" he questions.

"Me?" I say, brows going up. "I haven't gotten into anything."

"Yet you're asking about certain families and saying you need help."

"Let's not pretend that you're not—" I cut myself off when someone walks by. "You know…"

His lips curl up into an amused but dangerous smirk. He doesn't let me off the hook by finishing the sentence or even nodding like he knows what I mean. "I'm what?"

I tilt my head and give him a look. "Don't act like you haven't confessed to me."

His grin widens just a bit. "You still haven't forgiven me, Father."

"It's not me that...never mind. You clearly have a different life than I do. A dangerous one. I assume you have connections that I don't. And even knowledge that I don't."

He shrugs. "Maybe."

I shake my head, frustrated with his games. "Anyway, I told you, it has nothing to do with me." Before I can say anything else, the waitress is back with our food.

"¿Necesitas algo más?" she says.

"No. Gracias," he replies with a smile.

"What brought you into the church the first time?" I ask.

He watches me for a few seconds before turning his attention to his food. "I don't know. Existential crisis?"

"Is that true?"

"We all go through that, don't we?"

"Sure we do. For different reasons. What were yours?"

"Ah, you know. Questioning the meaning of life...or my place in it."

I can't tell if he's being honest or sarcastic. "Hmm."

"Are you trying to be my counselor?"

"Just curious is all."

"You said your father forced you to be a priest," he says, changing subjects quickly. "Did he know you were gay and that's why?"

My head pops up, my brows knitting as I quickly scan the room. I'm not wearing anything that would give away the fact that I'm a priest, but it's still not something I want overheard.

"What?" I ask simply.

"I saw you that night. At the bar with naked women you didn't even glance at."

"I'm—"

"A priest. Yeah, I know," he finishes. "But you're also a man. And I'm not blind. I see the way you look at me. I remember the way you reacted when I got really close to you."

His voice is low and his expression intriguing. Under the table I feel his leg brush the inside of mine.

"Are *you* gay?" I blurt, moving my leg so we're no longer touching.

He stares at me for several very long seconds. "I consider myself an equal opportunist. Guys, girls. I like what I like." My eyes widen at his reply. "Didn't expect that?"

After a while, I say, "I never know what to expect with you."

His lips twitch briefly before he swallows down a gulp of his soda. "So, moment of truth. Are you gonna answer my question?"

"I need something from you first," I say.

His lips curl into that flirty, smug smile. "I don't doubt you do."

"What do you do?"

"A little bit of everything."

"Who do you work for?"

"Why do you assume it's one person?"

I let loose a sigh. "You're not really giving me anything."

"And you're still keeping things from me."

"What's your name? Can I at least know that?"

He hesitates before answering. "Javier."

I nod. The name suits him. Strong. Sexy.

"Yes," I state simply.

It takes him a few seconds before he realizes I'm answering his question. He leans back in his chair and smiles, his eyes swallowing me up. He's looking at me like I'm a challenge that he's already accepted.

Dear God, give me strength.

CHAPTER 13

"You never told me why you went all the way to that bar," Javier says as we walk to our respective cars.

"I don't want to be seen by my parishioners," I lie. "I was out driving, thinking about life, and I came across it."

He eyes me like he doesn't believe me, and he'd be right not to, but I can't tell him the truth.

My phone vibrates in my pocket, so I reach in and pull it out, reading a message from Johnny on the screen.

Spoke to your dad. He's doin ok. Talk soon.

I HUFF out a sigh of relief. He's fine. Not dead. No longer missing. He's okay.

When I look up, there's a smile etched onto my face, and for the first time in a while, it feels genuine.

"You look happy," Javier says. I continue to grin, pocketing the phone with the plan to make sure I get more info soon. "In need of a celebration?"

Yes! My initial thought is definitely yes. It's been weeks of worrying that someone got to my father. I didn't realize I cared so much until the thought that he could be taken away was put in front of me. Facing mortality can change a person, even if it's not their own life at risk.

My father has been the source of my anger and frustration, and while I'm still unhappy over the level of control he's had over my life, I never wanted him dead. I can be relieved and know that we'll likely still never be close.

"Is that a no?" Javier questions, watching me.

"Maybe just a drink," I say with a grin.

His smile is wide. "Once again, I got the perfect place."

I give him a look. "Not anywhere where there's naked people."

He laughs. "Come on, Padre. What kind of man do you think I am?"

✝

I'VE BEEN FOLLOWING him in my car for fifteen minutes already, and with each second, I begin wondering if I should take a turn and go back home.

What will hanging out with him do for me? He's not someone anyone should hang out with. He's confessed to me, and yet I feel like I still don't know everything he's capable of. If my dad is fine, I no longer need his help.

Why am I going for a drink with him?

The devil on my shoulder whispers into my ear. *You know exactly why.*

I've been deprived.

I feel ridiculous even thinking that. I grew up with everything. More than I needed, at least materialistically. I had a good education, a warm bed, and a full stomach always. I should be grateful, and I am. Truly.

But my father basically banished me from his life—from the life I had come to know. He didn't want me in the business. He was too ashamed to have a gay son, caring more about what his other family would think. He forced me into a career that would keep me from exploring more of myself—from finding love.

I've been deprived of love and affection. Of excitement and thrills. And I want those things.

A few minutes later, we pull into the parking lot of a liquor store. Javier quickly gets out and holds a finger up, telling me to wait. A few minutes later, with a bottle in hand, he saunters back to his car and starts it up. We're on the road for another ten minutes before we arrive at a lake.

There's a small lot where I park my car, but as I'm getting out I watch Javier drive his truck over the grass, make a turn and back it up closer to the water's edge.

"What in the world," I mutter to myself as I head over.

He gets out of the cab and rounds the back before dropping the tailgate. "See, it's perfect," he says.

I look around, but the shadows swallow everything up. There's a couple lights in the parking lot, but nothing near the water. I can see the massive trees that seem to surround most of the lake, giving me an idea on how wide it is.

"Nobody will see you drinking out here," he says, hopping onto the tailgate and opening the bottle.

"That's all you got?" I ask, eyeing the Jim Beam.

"Do you not drink bourbon?"

"Not straight."

"Then you're not drinking it properly," he says, handing it to me.

I reach for the neck of the bottle, my fingers lightly brushing his in the exchange. After a couple seconds, I bring it to my lips and take a sip.

He laughs, extending his hand to take it back. I watch as he takes a sizable gulp before I sit on the tailgate with him, making sure to leave plenty of space between us.

"So, what are we celebrating?" he asks.

"Just something I no longer have to worry about. A weight has been lifted."

Javier hands me the bottle, and this time I take a bigger sip. I'm not a huge drinker, and I've never been one to drink anything straight, so when I swallow it I can't help but make a face.

He seems to find it amusing.

"Maybe if you do that another ten times, it'll equal a shot," he teases.

I roll my eyes. "I still have to get home."

Javier digs into his pocket and pulls out a pack of cigarettes. After removing one and rubbing it across his bottom lip, he pulls a lighter out of the half empty pack and lights it up.

As he's exhaling the smoke, he asks me a question. "Could you ever stop being a priest?"

I adjust the glasses on my face. "Yes and no. I'd have to request a laicization, which would strip me from my duties and obligations, but my ordination is permanent."

He's quiet for a minute. "Would you ever do that?

"And do what after? I spent several years studying to be a priest. I didn't focus on anything else."

A humorless laugh rumbles in his chest. "I'd fucking hate my dad if he made me do some shit like that."

"Well, I did."

"Do you still?"

I think about the relief I felt when I found out my dad was fine. I don't think I hate him, but I do hold a lot of resentment, and some days it does feel like hate. I struggle with my feelings toward him a lot. Can you both hate and love a person? I think the line between the two emotions is thin, and on any given day you can teeter more toward one side than the other.

"Not sure," I answer honestly.

"Doesn't that go against the Bible's teachings?" he asks in a teasing tone.

I turn and look at him. "I never said I was perfect."

His eyes narrow briefly as he studies me, smoke exiting his mouth and entering his nose—an action I shouldn't find at all attractive.

"Hmm."

I track every line in his face, noting the slight scar above his eyebrow, and one that cuts into the bottom right corner of his lip. His dark eyes are framed by even darker lashes, and his five o'clock shadow doesn't disguise the sharp line of his jaw.

My thoughts begin to spiral, so I look out toward the water. "And you? What led you to what you do, and would you do anything else?"

"Nah. I couldn't do anything else. There's something different in me, and doing what I do allows me to justify it. It's part of the job."

I'm struck silent. I don't know how there are moments where I forget what he's done. He told me he had blood on his hands. There's no other way to interpret that. The way he casually mentioned there being something different inside him sent a chill down my spine. I don't truly know who I'm sitting next to. And more disturbing than that, I don't know why I'm not in a rush to get away.

"Don't you find it weird that we're here together?" he asks, putting sound to the thoughts in my head.

"Yes."

"More weird for you, probably."

"Why do you want to hang out with a priest?" I question, reaching for the bottle to take another sip. "Hoping I can get you into heaven?" My lips curl into a smirk.

He grins. "Not sure I believe in it."

My brows lift slightly. "So, why?"

The silence stretches between us, but our eye contact remains connected.

"Maybe I'm intrigued by you. Maybe I'm suspicious of you. Maybe I'm confused."

I cock my head, wrinkling my forehead. "Suspicious?"

Javier shrugs, taking a sip from the bottle.

"What are you confused about?" I ask.

"Everything," he says, looking up at the sky.

I study his profile, noticing things I shouldn't. His neck and the tattoos that decorate it. The way his Adam's apple bobs when he swallows His lips, and how soft they appear to be for a man who seems anything but. The furrow in his brow like he's deep in thought, and the way I want to smooth it out.

His head slowly turns in my direction, his eyes firmly on mine. "What are you thinking about?" he questions.

I lick my lips. "Nothing."

His lips twitch. "I don't believe you."

I swallow and watch as he jumps down, his feet hitting the ground with a crunch before he comes to stand between my jean-clad legs. He tosses the cigarette away, and I swallow again as my heart thumps inside my chest.

"What are you doing?" I ask.

"Nothing," he replies, taking another swig from the bottle.

He then puts the glass opening on my bottom lip, pouring a healthy amount into my mouth. My eyes stay trained on his, but his gaze is focused on the way my lips wrap around the bottle.

When he pulls it away, I swallow, my face contorting before I swipe at my bottom lip with my tongue.

My breathing intensifies as he continues to stare at me in such close proximity. There's two very different parts of me that are at war with each other right now. One seeks pleasure, the other knows the rules.

"I should go," I say, moving to slide off the back of the truck.

He only steps back slightly, so when my feet hit the ground, we're still very close.

"*Should* go or *are* going?" he questions, eyes bouncing between my mouth and eyes.

"I'm going." The words come out softer than intended. They lack conviction and he knows it.

"You want me," he states simply. There's no teasing inflection in the words. He speaks them like they're fact. "You're aware of what I've done and still you want me."

"No," I say, my voice gaining some strength.

"I think I found something we have in common," he says, taking a step back. "We're both liars."

CHAPTER 14

I strip down to my underwear and kneel at the side of my bed, reaching under the mattress to grab the scourge that meets my skin more times than I'd like to admit.

Javier was right. I am a liar.

Self-flagellation is something I practice when temptation inches too close to action.

We're told masturbation is a sin, and I do my best to keep my thoughts from straying into lustful territory, but I'm only human.

In order to keep myself from reaching into my underwear and touching myself with thoughts of Javier—a man and a murderer—I swing the scourge over my shoulder and let the leather strips hit the flesh on my back.

Javier's face flashes in my mind, more specifically the expression on his face as he was pouring the liquor into my mouth. I swing again.

Flashes keep appearing.

His lips. I swing.

His hands. I swing.

The way my body reacts to him. I swing harder.

My cock remains hard and I fear the pain of the leather on my back isn't doing its job. I imagine he's doing the swinging, and I like the idea of him punishing me for the thoughts I'm having about him.

After what feels like forever, but was probably only twenty minutes, I drop the scourge on the floor and make the sign of the cross before delving into prayer. My back stings, but it's what I need—a reminder to stay on the right path.

When I stand, I make my way to the shower where I keep the water fairly cold, and tell myself I will never see Javier again. There's no need to.

✝

EACH DAY that I have confessional hours, I hold my breath praying he doesn't come in, and by the time the hours are up, I exhale in defeat, having held onto a small amount of hope that he would've.

I bury myself in work, grateful for the extra duties I have: baptisms, a marriage, and two funerals. I shouldn't feel grateful for presiding over funeral arrangements, but it's kept me focused on other things.

One evening, as I'm just getting home, Johnny calls.

"Hello?"

"Hey, kid."

"Hey. How's everything?"

Johnny releases a long sigh. "Think you can come by?"

My pulse spikes a bit. "Sure. Did something happen?"

"Just swing by. I'll see you soon."

He ends the call before I can say anything. I grab my

keys from the hook I just hung them on and walk right back out.

I drive in silence, not bothering to turn up any music. I'm in my head the entire time, wondering what conversation he needs to have in person. I hadn't been worried about my father since he told me he had talked to him.

This time, when I walk inside, the usual man who's there checking I.D.'s gives me a nod to go ahead. I walk down the hall and to the office door, taking a deep breath to prepare myself for any news.

I rap on the wood with my knuckles a couple of times, and a few seconds later Johnny opens it up.

I'm instantly studying his face, looking for a hint at what we're about to discuss, but it gives nothing away. When he takes a few steps back and allows me space to walk in, I freeze in my tracks when I look behind the desk.

"Dad." The words leave my lips on a breath.

His eyes take me in, and the tiniest of smiles tugs at his mouth. I notice his eyes linger around my neck, and I realize I never changed out of my collar.

"How you doin', huh?" he asks.

"I'm fine. How are *you*?"

I take a seat in front of his desk and scrutinize his appearance. He looks fine, untouched. No visible injuries, no bags under his eyes.

It's been about nine months since I've seen him in person, but he looks just as he did then. I would have never guessed he's got a target on his back, but then again, my dad has never shown a lot of emotion one way or another. I've never seen him frightened. I've never seen him cry. He's a stoic man unless he's angry.

His hair has a little more salt than pepper these days, and it's thinning a bit on the top. And though he has some deep wrinkles in his forehead and a few more around his eyes, he still has the aura of a man you don't want to cross.

He gives me a slight shrug. "I'm fine. Johnny tells me you've been in here a few times, concerned."

The way he says it makes me wonder if he's teasing me, like the idea of me being worried is funny and ridiculous.

"That's right," I tell him.

"Huh. Well..." He doesn't finish his thought, instead just leaving it to hang between us.

"What waves have you been making?" I question.

He grins. "Big ones, I guess. Not everyone likes the fierceness of the ocean."

"Is it over?"

"What? The waves?"

"The repercussions."

He tilts his head from side to side which lets me know probably not.

"In this business, there's always a bit of both," he says. "Someone wants to do something others don't agree with."

"I'm familiar with that."

His eyes narrow slightly but he doesn't reply directly to the barb.

Dad leans back in his chair. "Well, I think your involvement in this," he says, gesturing between us, "can be over now. If I could've met you somewhere else I would've, but I already have someone on the way to pick me up. I don't want you around here, you hear me?"

"What is this?" I ask, getting angry. "Did we go back in time? Am I a teenager again?"

"Carlo," he growls.

"I came here because you asked me to pick up a box."

"I asked Johnny to give you the box. I didn't tell him to

invite you here," he says, flashing a glare in Johnny's direction in the corner.

"I kept coming back because I was worried something happened to you, and now I'm wondering why I even cared. If I thought you could change, or if I thought your little box of memories was a sign that you had some sort of heart, you quickly remind me why we aren't close."

He inhales deeply through his nose, eyes pinned on me. "You're not as smart as you think you are."

I snort. "Nice. Any other insults you'd like to throw my way, Dad? I'm sure there's a select few you have cocked in the chamber."

I stare him down, waiting for his reply.

"How's the church?" he asks, keeping eye contact with me.

"Fine. You should come out. I bet you have some things to learn, or forgiveness to beg for."

"Ah. I don't ask forgiveness for anything. Everything I do is for a reason, whether it's something others like or not."

"I'm aware."

"You act like you can't get out of it," he says.

"Are you kidding? I went to school for seven years for this. I've devoted everything to being what you said I had no choice but to be. I've only been making a decent salary for two years, and you act—"

"Right. You're sounding ungrateful as you talk to the man who has paid for everything you need."

"It's only because you didn't allow me to do what I wanted to do."

"What? Paint pictures?" He huffs out a laugh. "Yes, I'm sure you'd be making millions off of that."

"Until I was seventeen, I assumed I'd be following in

your footsteps. You never acted like that *wasn't* the plan until—"

"Johnny," my dad says, jerking his head toward the door, dismissing him.

We stare at each other until we're alone.

"You think you can be what you are and be in this business?" he asks, his teeth grit.

"What I am," I murmur, shaking my head. "Can you even say it?"

"The answer is, you can't. You don't know these guys—how they act, how they talk. You don't know hatred and violence for being—"

"I'm pretty sure I do know hatred. I'm pretty sure I'll know it my whole life."

"Do you wanna be killed? Assaulted? Terrorized? Do you wanna live your life having to look over your shoulder all the time? This business has no place for you. There are rules that've been around since before my time."

"Queer people have been killed, assaulted, and terrorized."

He puts a hand up to stop me. "You know what I do. You saw and heard more than most people do before you had even hit adulthood. That doesn't mean you have what it takes to do what I do."

I huff out an annoyed sigh. "Why am I even here?"

"After what Johnny told me, I thought you'd be happy to see that I'm alive and well." He pauses. "Also." He leans in, his voice lowering. "I have a phone number to give you. Not many people have this number, but if you happen to need to get in touch, this is how." He pushes over a piece of paper. "Program it and then rip it up and throw it away."

"You leaving again?" I ask, reaching for it as I pull my phone out of my pocket.

"You never know."

I incline my head slightly as I type in the numbers in my phone. I'm too annoyed to care right now. I put the paper back on his desk, and he reaches for it and rips it to shreds.

Standing up, I pocket my phone. "Well, I guess I won't worry when you go missing again, that way you don't need to be concerned about me coming around here. I trust Johnny will let me know if you die." I cut my eyes to him.

He stands and rounds the desk. We stare at each other for a few seconds before he brings me in for a hug. His arms feel foreign around me. It's tight and awkward, and then his mouth is near my ear.

"Remember, my blood runs in your veins. Regardless of anything, you are a Gallo. Trust no one but yourself."

He pulls away and stares deeply in my eyes, like he's trying to communicate something else. My brows furrow, and as I'm about to open my mouth, there's a quick knock on the door before it opens.

"Car's here," Johnny says.

Dad nods once and goes to his desk. He looks at me and dips his head. "Take care of yourself."

A few seconds pass before I speak. "Okay. You too."

I walk out of the building, a cocktail of emotions and feelings swirling inside me. My whole life, my relationship with my father has felt like a rollercoaster. Some days we got along, other days we'd be fighting. One minute, I care about his well-being, just to finally talk to him and wonder why I cared at all. He's an asshole. He always has been. But he also has moments where I feel like there's hope for us.

I'm always left feeling confused, warring with two thoughts: Should I cut him off indefinitely or subject myself to his cruel personality in the hopes of getting a drop of approval?

And the one thing that always sticks with me is the thought that maybe we butt heads because we're too similar.

On the outside, it wouldn't seem like that's the case, but it's the outside we want people to see. We hide the truth that's deep inside us.

CHAPTER 15

Three days after I leave my father's office, immediately upon returning home from work, there's a knock on my door.

In my exhaustion, I don't bother to look through the peephole, instead pulling the door open to be met with the face of Javier.

Javier who has never been to my house. Who shouldn't know where I live.

"Hello," he says before walking past me and into my living room.

I close the door and turn around. "Uh."

"How'd I know where you live?" he questions, a smirk on his lips. "Easy. I followed you."

"Why?"

He gazes around the room before sitting on the plush gray couch. "So I would know where you live."

"Okay," I say, drawing out the word. "But why is that information necessary?"

"So I can come see you. Obviously," he says, stretching his arms along the back of the couch.

"Normally, people ask for an invitation."

He shrugs, his eyes scanning the room again before they land on me, giving me a slow onceover.

"Nice clothes."

"I just got home."

"I know. Something about this priestly getup really does it for me."

His gaze turns lascivious, and warmth spreads throughout my body.

I tug at my collar and his eyes track the movement, his tongue wetting his bottom lip.

"Taking it all off will really do something for me," he says with a grin.

I stop fidgeting with my clothes and walk to the kitchen simply to get away from him. "Did you need something?"

"Not really."

I look up at the ceiling as I'm tucked in the corner of the kitchen he can't see, wondering if he's here to continue the torture of our last get-together. With a deep breath, I open the fridge and pull out a pitcher of water.

"What have you been up to lately?" he asks, coming to the breakfast bar that separates my small dining area and the kitchen.

"Not much. Just working."

"All work and no play, huh? You know what they say?"

"Are you saying I'm dull?" I question, pouring the water into a glass.

"Definitely duller than I am."

I offer him the glass but he declines with a shake of his head. I wish I could argue that I know how to have fun, but I really don't do much outside of work.

"Well, we can't all be criminals, can we?" I say, putting

the pitcher back in the fridge. I pause, wondering if I should've said that.

When I turn around, he's watching me with a serious expression that soon melts into a half-hearted grin. "I suppose not."

I take a long drink of water before putting it down on the counter. He watches me from the other side of the bar with a look on his face that I can't pinpoint.

Slipping my hand in my pocket, I break eye contact to look out the window, but he doesn't say anything. When I flicker my eyes toward him, he's still staring at me.

"You look uncomfortable," he finally says.

I meet his gaze. "I am."

A hint of amusement touches his features. "Why?"

"You know why."

"Could be a couple reasons. The fact that you're a priest and I frequently violate the commandments. Or the fact that you and I are both into guys and we want each other."

I ignore the flood of emotions that pour over me, choosing to remain as stoic as possible.

"Oh, do we?" I take another sip of water.

He rests his arms on the bar and leans closer. "I want *you*." His eyes trail up and down my body. "I want you when I know I shouldn't. And you want me but you won't admit it. Doesn't mean I don't see the truth, as hidden as you may think it is." He sighs, still watching me. "I think it's because it's wrong. Forbidden. You can't have sex, and I want to be the one to fuck you. To make a priest break his vow," he bites down on his bottom lip, letting out a slight moan, "Well, that would be good for my ego."

I swallow, glad we have this breakfast bar between us. "I won't break."

His lips curl up on one side. "Oh, but I'd love to see you bend."

CHAPTER 16

"What are the church's thoughts on masturbation?" Javier asks.

"Stop," I tell him, walking out of the kitchen and through the living room. "We are not talking about this."

"I'm guessing it's against the rules. So, you can't have sex but you also can't masturbate. Honestly, it sounds sadistic."

"I'll be back," I say as I make my way through the hall and into my bedroom.

I hear him chuckle as I close the door, needing to get out of these clothes. Not that it makes much of a difference, but the collar was starting to feel really tight around my throat. The long sleeves of the shirt felt like they were trapping the heat of my body.

As quickly as I can, I remove my clothing and change into a pair of black joggers and a gray T-shirt. In the connected bathroom, I remove my glasses and splash cold water on my face, hoping the flushed feeling gets washed away.

Back in my bedroom, I stop near the bed, thinking about the scourge hidden under the mattress. I decide not to use it only because the sound of hitting my back will incite questions I'm not ready to answer.

When I return to the living room, Javier is standing in front of the fireplace, looking at the decorations on the mantel.

He does a double take when he sees me, giving me a small grin. "You don't have any personal photos anywhere."

"Nope."

I go to the kitchen and grab a bottle of wine, pouring myself a glass.

"Now *that* I'll have some of," he says, coming up behind me.

I hand him the one I just poured and grab another glass. After I've poured a significant amount of red liquid in it, I take a drink that cuts it in half.

"What are you thinking?" he questions, bringing the glass slowly to his lips.

"I'm thinking God is using you as a way to test me, because I have no idea why you keep showing up, or why I allow you to stick around when all you do is make me uncomfortable."

I didn't mean to be that honest, but the words were already on the tip of my tongue.

He gives me a slow grin, amused by my response.

"I think we're drawn to each other for the same reasons."

With the glass at my lips again, I murmur, "Hmm."

"We're opposites. Good and evil. Light and dark. Order and chaos." He puts the glass down on the counter next to him. "You're curious about my life because it's so different from yours. I don't want to be you. I don't want your job, but I find myself intrigued by the life you live." He steps closer. "I wonder if..." He pauses, his eyes roaming down my neck and chest. His finger touches the inside of my elbow and traces a path to my wrist. "I wonder if I were to taste you if you'd be as sweet and good as I imagine."

Several seconds pass between us as my heart thumps quickly in my chest. "I may not be as sweet and good as you think."

His eyebrow raises slightly. "Oh really?"

I finish the wine in my glass before turning my back on him to refill it. "Anyway, it doesn't matter. Any intrigue, on either end, won't lead to anything more. I'm dedicated to—"

Javier's body is against mine in a second, the warmth of him instantly heating my back. He traps me between himself and the counter, his crotch pressed against my ass as his breath hits the back of my neck.

"To a life of celibacy. To priesthood. Yes, I know. Tell me what the Bible says about sex, Father."

I swallow, trying to focus on anything but his body against mine. I shakily put the wine bottle and glass down, gripping the edge of the sink.

"To flee from sexual immorality."

"Mm. What else?"

"Whoever sins sexually, sins against their own body."

His body rubs against mine. "And?"

"Sex is a sacred act in a marriage."

"Between who, Father?" Javier's soft breath touches the skin below my ear.

"A man and a woman."

"But you don't want a woman."

"No." The word is barely above a whisper.

"And you can't get married."

I shake my head slightly.

"Tell me." His left arm moves, his hand coming to a rest on my hip, making me jolt. "Who would know? God?"

"Y-yes."

"And you think you'd go to Hell? He'd punish you to an eternity of fire and brimstone for simply having sexual pleasure? It's hardly the worst thing you could do."

"You don't fear the afterlife? You don't think about where you'll go?"

"No. I think I'll die and that'll be the end of it."

I envy his way of thinking, but I don't admit that.

"I can't," I say softly, refusing to turn around to look him in the eye. "It'll feel like everything I've done and gone through will have been for nothing. I'll be throwing it all away, and for what? A brief amount of pleasure that I'll regret the moment it's over?"

He shifts, moving to my side and facing me. "I don't know about brief, and regret isn't something I believe in. Which you know. It's why I'll never be absolved. I do everything with intention."

My eyes move in his direction. "I don't intend on doing anything with you. I hardly know you."

"I suppose everyone knows everything about every person they hook up with, huh? I know you're not in the dating game, but one-night stands with strangers do exist."

"You're dangerous."

"Have I threatened you?"

"I don't trust you."

"You probably shouldn't."

"I'm not doing this." I finally spin around and put space between us. "You shouldn't come around anymore. It's not right."

"I'm not sure what about me has given you the idea that I care about doing what's right."

I turn around and pour another glass of wine before marching to my living room where I sit on the couch with a huff. "You can see yourself out."

Unperturbed, he saunters into the living room. "Or I can show you something. It wouldn't even be you doing anything. No sacred bonds or vows would be broken."

He sits on the loveseat across from me, only separated by a rectangular coffee table. He runs his hand over his crotch, gripping the growing erection in his pants.

My eyes widen, frozen on the length and size of it against his thigh. Now that he's brought my attention to it, I can't not see it. He's turned on. By what? The thought of breaking me? Torturing me?

"You're not saying anything," he says.

He's right. I haven't told him to stop. I haven't angrily shoved him out the front door, offended by his actions. Instead, I find myself glued to the couch while all these conflicting thoughts bounce around in my head.

My brain tells me this is an easy decision. Tell him I'm not interested, even in watching, and he needs to leave. My suppressed libido tells me there's nothing wrong with watching. It would be more than I've experienced in a long time. Maybe enough to keep me going even longer. I'm not having sex. I'm not masturbating. I'm simply a viewer.

It's a slippery slope. A gateway drug, so to speak. If I see him, in the flesh. If I hear the noises he'll make and see the aftermath of his pleasure, would I want more? Would I want to touch, to feel, to taste?

"Please leave," I say, putting my wine on the table between us. "Because I'm not sure how much longer I'll be able to say that."

Javier doesn't move right away, but eventually, he stands, peering down at me with a grin tugging at his lips. I anticipate him making a move, even if that move is on himself, and I resign myself to let it happen.

Instead, he walks to the front door and leaves.

I sink into the couch, the tension leaving my body now that he's gone. I take a few deep breaths before I go to my room and remove my shirt, reaching under my mattress.

I'm not sure how much longer I'll be able to restrain myself.

Sure, in the privacy of my own home, I could touch myself and nobody would know. I've done it before, but I try to be good, and I've been on a six month streak.

But the truth is, I like the sting of the leather on my back. It gives me another kind of pleasure.

I swing the scourge and let the strips smack against my shoulder blade. I repeat the action, dropping my head with a moan, and then I hear the floor creak behind me.

"Well, well, well," Javier says.

CHAPTER 17

I spin my head around, heart in my throat as Javier steps inside.

I didn't lock the door when he left because I was too focused on coming here to do this, and of course I didn't think he'd come back in.

"I knew you were a liar," he says, his tone making it clear he's enjoying my humiliation. "I asked you about this." He walks over to me and plucks the scourge from my hand. "You said you didn't practice self-flagellation."

I'm too stunned and embarrassed to say anything. I simply watch him as he plays with the leather strips.

"Are you doing this to keep from touching yourself?" he asks, gently dragging the tails across my shoulders.

My body shivers, and I go to stand up.

"No, no," he says, pushing me back down. "You need this. You need punishment for these sinful thoughts, don't you?"

"Please," I beg. "Don't."

"Hmm. Let's just stop at please. It sounds so much

better." He sits on the mattress in front of me and threads his fingers through my hair, pulling my head up so I can look at him. "Were you thinking about me?"

I don't answer. I just keep staring at him. His jaw is set tight, but his eyes showcase the lustful thoughts he's having. My gaze travels down to see the scourge gripped tightly in his hand and laid across his lap. I swallow, licking my lips before I close my eyes.

"You praying?" he questions, letting his fingers trail down my scalp before he removes his hand from my head. "Think he'll listen to you while you're here with me?"

My eyes fly open and I see him lean back on one hand, his jacket opening slightly and revealing a gun in a shoulder holster.

His dark eyes zone in on me and I can't read his expression.

"Lean forward," he commands.

"Wh-what?"

He sits up and taps the space between his legs. "Put your head here. You can pray if that helps."

I know I'm a grown man with my own autonomy. I know I could get up and go to the bathroom. I could put my foot down and demand he leave. I'm not as meek as he might think, but for some reason, I want to listen to him.

Perhaps it's the years of drought. The pent-up desire.

I tell myself he has a gun. He's dangerous. He could kill me, and that's why I'll do what he wants. But there's a part of me, and it may be wrong, but there is a small part of my brain that doesn't think he'll actually do anything to me.

I meet his eyes again and he gives a single nod. "It's okay."

Slowly, I bend my neck until my forehead touches the

mattress. He shifts and I can feel his thighs on either side of my head.

"Ready?" he asks.

I take a breath and then feel the leather strips strike my back.

I suck in a breath, squeezing my eyes closed even tighter. He does it again without warning, and I hiss, my body jolting.

His fingers run through my hair and I almost nuzzle into the touch. Then he hits me again.

My hands move to his calves, squeezing the muscles.

"You still turned on?" he questions. I lift my head and peer up at him, ready to say I'm okay now, but his lips quirk on one side, and I guess he sees the answer in my eyes. "Oh, you definitely are," he says, pushing my head to the mattress.

He spreads the licks across my back, hitting each shoulder blade, my spine, and even catching part of my ribs. When he moves, his next strike hits even lower, the tips of the leather reaching for the top off my ass.

I make a noise in my throat as I move upward, my head touching his crotch.

Once again, he shifts, and this time I feel his leg slip between mine. I suck in a breath as his shin brushes against my balls.

He doesn't say anything about the change in position, but when the leather hits my skin again, I move upward and realize what he's done. He's given me friction. My cock rubs against his leg every time I jolt forward.

He hits me again, and the sting of the whip is the last thing on my mind. My erection is not going to go away now. The pain of the lashings is now being overridden when I grind against him.

A tiny voice in the back of my head tells me to get up and run, but that voice fades when his hand strokes the side of my face before cradling my cheek. His fingers find my chin and guide me up a little higher, placing my head on his thigh.

Now I'm staring at the wall to my right, my face pressed against him, and extremely close to his most intimate area.

"Have you had thoughts about this?" he asks, gently stroking my hair.

I nod.

"About me doing this to you?"

"Just once."

"I don't think it's punishment then. Maybe I shouldn't continue if I'm only giving into your fantasies."

"No." My body moves of its own accord, grinding against his leg, but I manage to stop myself. "It is a punishment."

"I think it's a kink," he says, running his fingers across the welts on my shoulder.

My body breaks into a shiver and even just that movement gives me a tiny bit of pleasure as I'm pressed so tightly against him.

"Pray."

"What?" I'm not thinking about praying at a time like this, though it's probably what I should be doing instead.

"If you need punishment for your filthy thoughts and fantasies, shouldn't you be praying to your god for strength? Pray."

"Will you...continue?" I ask.

He waits a few seconds. "We'll see."

I lower my head. "Heavenly Father. I ask for your strength to face today's challenges."

Javier strikes my back and I moan.

"I know that in my weakness—"

He hits me again and my cock grinds against his shin once more.

"Uh...in my weakness, You are my strength."

Another hit has me gripping his leg in my hands, forcing him as close to me as possible.

"Help me to rely on You. Ahh!" I cry out when the leather meets my skin and I jolt forward. "And...ah, trust that You will...oh God." I swallow, my hips moving faster than Javier's strikes are coming.

"Keep going," he says.

I don't pause to acknowledge that I'm humping his leg like a feral animal, I just keep going.

He hits me again, the sting getting stronger and stronger on my tender flesh. "I meant to keep praying."

"Oh God."

"Something like that," he says, humor in his tone.

"Uh. Trust that You will provide...oh God, oh, oh... provide everything. Oh please," I moan. "Provide everything I need. Yes. Oh. Yes."

I turn my head and sink my teeth into his thigh as my body shakes with my release. I'm left panting and grunting as the warm, thick liquid drips down the inside of my pants.

As I suck in shuddering breaths, he gently strokes my head, and clarity starts to seep in.

What did I just do?

How can I face him?

I keep my face buried in his lap as he continues to brush through my hair with his fingers. After a minute, he moves to the side and puts my head on the mattress. I make sure to face the other way and keep my eyes closed.

He crouches down next to me, his hand gently caressing my back while his breath ghosts over my neck.

"Looks like I provided you with everything you need. What does that make me?"

I don't bother answering, but a few seconds later, I hear his footsteps retreat and eventually the front door closes.

CHAPTER 18

I've been on sabbatical for almost two months now. I spoke to the bishop about wanting to leave the church, but after many talks and counsel, he offered to let me take sabbatical for personal renewal and study.

New priests don't typically get that offer, but Bishop Charles is a kind man who says he sees something in me. He'd probably think differently if I told him the real reason behind wanting to leave.

Instead of telling him I let a criminal flog me until I came in my pants, I told him I was questioning my place in the priesthood. Which is still true.

The shame and embarrassment still cling to me, and every day I attempt to wash it away with prayer, but until I can bring myself to confess to another priest, I'm afraid I'll never rest easy.

What's worse is that when I'm not drowning in shame, I'm swimming through lustful thoughts and wanton desires. Sometimes, alone in bed with nothing but darkness around me, I imagine what it would be like to do more. And now that I'm not actively working in the church, I find myself excusing it. Yes, I'm still ordained, but I'm not donning the clothes and spreading the word of God as a hypocrite.

Isn't this the time for me to actually see what it is I want to do for the rest of my life? How would I know if I didn't experiment?

The problem with that is that Javier has gone MIA. I haven't seen him since that night. And while it was appreciated at first, I'm starting to wonder why he disappeared on me. He did say he wanted to see if he could get a priest to break, so maybe he got the ego stroke he desired and now he's no longer interested.

My phone rings from my nightstand, jolting me upright. I look at the time before answering. It's nearly midnight.

A quick glance at the screen tells me it's my dad.

It's been a while since I've heard from him. After our conversation in his office that ended in an awkward hug, I talked to him once on the phone, but it wasn't about anything of importance. I've gone years actively avoiding news about the crime families and what's going on between them, but sometimes, if the story is big enough, something comes on TV.

Last I heard, the Mancini family's hitman was arrested. They say they could convict him of one murder that happened twelve years ago, which is surprising, since I'm sure he's done a hell of a lot more.

There has to be fear he'll turn and start working with the cops.

The Esposito family would not be happy if that happened, because they've worked with the Mancini family to bring down members of the Bonetti family.

I bring the phone to my ear. "Hello?" I'm met with a dial tone.

I think to call him back, but figure he'll call again. Someone probably interrupted him.

When I lay back down and close my eyes, I try my best to keep from thinking about Javier. Just when I think I'm successful, he meets me in my dreams.

✝

I'm jolted awake with the blaring of my phone. With my eyes still closed, I reach over and grab it, squinting just enough to see the green button.

"Hello?" My voice is scratchy and rough with sleep.

"Hello, this is a prepaid call from an inmate at South Bay Correctional Institute. To accept the call and charges, press one. If you don't wish to accept, hang up now."

I sit up straight, my eyes cutting to the clock on my nightstand. It's five past eight in the morning. It could be my dad. What was he calling me for last night? I quickly press one and wait.

"Hello?" the voice says.

My brows knit in confusion when it's not my dad's voice. "Hello?"

"Hello, Father."

The familiar tone of Javier's voice hits my ears. I forget to breathe for a second while I try to wrap my head around who is calling and from where.

"What's going on?"

"Ah, you know. The usual." His tone is light and unbothered, which is strange since he's in prison.

"Yeah? Is this your typical weekend getaway?"

He snorts. "I'm allowed a visit by a priest, you know."

My pulse spikes. "You want me to visit you?"

"Well, only if you want to."

"How long will you be there?"

"Mmm. Not too sure."

"*Why* are you there?" I question.

"Just a little scuffle."

"Hmm."

"I might have some confessing to do."

"I'm on sabbatical."

"Why?"

"You know why."

He chuckles, and the deep sound gives me goosebumps. "Have I made you turn your back on Jesus? You want to worship me now, is that it? I haven't even given you the good stuff yet."

I feel my face flush, and I'm glad he can't see me, but my mind remains focused on one word. *Yet*. "It's just a small break. To reassess and—"

"Come visit me," he says, cutting me off. "Wear your collar. Priests can visit us in our cell, or in a designated room. We don't have to be separated by glass."

"When?" I ask, and I wonder if he heard how breathy my voice was.

"Today. Tomorrow. Whenever."

"You have one minute remaining," an automated voice says.

"How'd you get my number?" I question, realizing I never gave it to him.

"I have ways. I'll see you soon."

The call ends, and instead of feeling too much conflict over what I'm planning on doing, I find myself more excited than anything. This trip feels...thrilling. I know it's something I shouldn't do, but I know I'm going to do it anyway.

CHAPTER 19

Only a few days go by before I'm traveling to the prison. Javier put my name on the approved list, and my credentials have been verified. The fact that I'm on sabbatical remains unknown to them, though it wouldn't matter, as I'm still ordained.

With my collar around my neck, I follow procedure and listen to the rules and regulations before I'm being escorted to a nearby room dedicated for clergy members to meet with prisoners.

The room is small, the walls stark white. A rounded table sits in the middle, with four round stools each connected by a curved, stainless steel pipe. Everything is bolted to the concrete floor, and the room is stripped of anything that could be used as a weapon.

"I'll be right back," the guard tells me.

I nod and take a seat on one of the stools that faces the heavy door with a window in it. I put the Bible down on the table and wait nearly ten minutes before I hear the crank of the lock unlatching.

Lifting my head, I watch as the guard brings in Javier.

He's wearing a navy blue shirt with buttons down the middle, and matching pants. His socked feet are in a pair of rubber-looking sandals, and his wrists are cuffed in front of him.

His lips quirk at the sight of me, but his eyes drink me in in a way that makes me want to squirm.

The guard moves in front of Javier and uncuffs him. "I'll be outside the door. You have thirty minutes."

"Thanks, Geno."

Javier slowly makes his way to the stool next to me, sitting down just as the door closes. He watches me for several uncomfortable seconds before I nervously reach for the Bible.

"They must trust you," I say.

"Why do you say that?"

"You're uncuffed."

"Do you think I'd hurt you?" When my eyes flicker up to his, he grins. "Outside of how you want to be, I mean."

Flustered, I sit up straight and gaze around the room.

"No cameras in here. This is confidential. Just a sinner looking for guidance from his priest."

"I see." I catch a glimpse of the guard at the window in the door, so I open the Bible to at least appear like I'm doing my job. "Why are you here?"

"I told you. A scuffle."

"You got thrown in jail for a little fight?"

"There may have been a weapon involved."

I shake my head. "And I'm here...why?"

"You tell me," he says with a smirk.

"Maybe you actually do need guidance."

He scoffs, but after a few seconds he says, "I didn't want you to think I just up and disappeared after our night together." The smile he sends me is wicked. "But I didn't have privileges right away because I got in a little trouble as soon as I got here."

I shake my head. "I wasn't necessarily looking forward to seeing you again."

"I think that's what you want me to believe. What you want yourself to believe." He shifts slightly, his foot sliding across the floor as his leg brushes against mine.

"It was true...at first. I had started to wonder why you hadn't popped up again."

"Are you ashamed? Is that why you're taking leave from the church? You don't think you can do your job if you get pleasure from another man?"

"I know I could, but it's the rules."

He makes a clicking sound with his tongue. "Rules make everything a little less fun, don't you think? Breaking rules, however, now that's fun."

"Says the man in jail."

He shrugs. "It's not too bad."

I let the silence stretch between us before I ask again, "Why am I here?"

"You want to see me," he says plainly.

I don't bother disagreeing. "Yes, but why did you invite me? You could've told me over the phone that you got arrested shortly after..."

"Our night," he finishes.

"But you wanted me to come out here."

He sighs. "Carlo, most people don't know why I do the things I do, and sometimes I'm one of them."

"I also think you could be a liar."

He smiles. "I am. But so are you. So are a lot of people."

With an exhale, I say, "Yeah, well."

"How long are you on this sabbatical?"

"I've got several months."

He nods. "I'd like for you to come back."

"When?"

"I can get daily visits from a priest. They don't count toward my two per week limit."

"And what am I coming back for?"

Javier grins. "To get to know me."

"I think I know enough to know I shouldn't come back."

"Yeah, but regardless, you will."

"How'd you get my number?" I question, hoping for a real answer.

"I've had it for a while. I called the church, gave someone there some made-up story about needing your number for counsel. Claimed it was an emergency."

"And they just gave it to you?"

"I'm pretty charming."

He sends me a smile that warms my cheeks.

"And you memorized it?"

He shrugs. "I have a good memory."

The door opens with a loud clank. "All right, time's up."

Javier stands, and I follow suit. "Thank you, Father," he says, opening his arms.

I glance at the guard who doesn't move to put a stop to this goodbye hug, and stiffly wrap my arms around him.

Javier whispers in my ear, "I can't stop thinking about the way you sound when you come." He backs away quickly, giving me a wink. "Same time tomorrow?"

I barely nod before the guard is turning him and cuffing his wrists together.

CHAPTER 20

"**D**o you have plans next weekend?" Javier asks about halfway into our second visit.

"Don't think so. Why? You gonna be free?"

He gives me a one shoulder shrug. "Could be."

"Well, you know where to find me."

He grins. "I do. I'm just hoping I don't find you in the company of anyone else."

I tilt my head, flirtation coming a little easier now. "Would you be jealous?" I ask with a small smile knowing damn well I won't be with anyone.

Javier leans forward slightly, his eyes staring deep into mine. "You don't want to see me jealous, *cariño*."

The timber in his voice makes goosebumps travel down my arms. I make a mental note to look up what cariño means later, but I'm too caught up in his gaze. Too caught up in a feeling I definitely shouldn't be experiencing.

My teeth dig into my bottom lip briefly. "Maybe I do."

His brow lifts slightly. "I feel like you're still wrapped in all these layers. I need to peel them away one by one to find out who you really are."

The way he looks me up and down makes me feel naked. I want him to peel away the layers and get to the core of me. Hell, I want to get to the core of me. He noticed it immediately, even through a lattice. He told me I wasn't being authentic. I was too practiced. He's right.

"Are you going to have an issue with," he hesitates, licking his lips as he stares at mine, "me fucking you?"

I don't know why in that pause I expected him to say something like *intimacy* or *physical touch*. He's never been one to mince words or be indirect, but the vulgar and blunt way he just propositioned me has my eyes widening slightly.

"Oh."

"Figured I need to jump on the opportunity while you're on sabbatical. Before you change your mind and run back to Jesus."

I get lost in my head, tons of erotic and sinful thoughts tangling with the ones that know better—the ones that tell me I still need to obey the oath I took.

"You do want that, yes?" He glances over his shoulder at the door where the guard stands on the other side. "You want me to flog you until you're a writhing, needy boy begging for my cock, don't you?"

My face heats up, and I know he can see the flush under my skin. I swallow, imagining the exact scene he just painted. Before I can reply, he continues.

"Or." He pauses, his hand reaching for mine under the table. "Do you want me to be sweet to you? Soft and gentle." His fingertips trace the top of my hand, going up my forearm. "I could tease you with touches until you beg for more." He pulls his hand away, sitting back in his chair to watch me. "Which one do you want?"

I lick my lips, stuck in my own head as these fantasies play out. "Both," I say on a breath, my voice barely audible.

He grins a wicked grin and a thrill runs up my spine at the promise behind his eyes. The door opens, and the guard enters, putting a stop to our visit.

When he hugs me this time, his fingers move gently up my back. "Will I see you again tomorrow?" he asks quietly.

"Yes," comes out from between my lips like there wasn't even another possible answer.

†

WHEN I WAKE up in the morning, it doesn't go unnoticed that I'm looking forward to a prison trip way more than anyone should be. I went for a run to try to gain clarity on what I'm doing, but all I could think about was him and the images he put in my head.

In the shower, I thought of him again, wanting so badly to touch myself, but convincing my hand to stay away, because Javier's would feel better.

I'm putting way too much care into my appearance and what cologne I use. I'm acting like this is a date when it's not, but I make sure I smell good, and that my hair is perfectly in place. I choose to not wear my glasses today, instead going with contacts.

With a sigh, I kneel at my bed and say a prayer. I ask for guidance in my life choices, and then I get up and go to my car.

The whole drive there, I look for signs to tell me I should turn around. There's no traffic, no accidents or road closures. Everything seems to be clear and fine to get me to the prison. In fact, this has been the quickest and least stressful drive to the prison I've had.

Is this a sign that it's okay?

Or am I a crazy person seeing only what I want to see?

At the prison, after waiting in line, I'm finally at the front to sign-in.

"I'm here to see Javier Perez."

The woman begins typing into her computer, and I watch as her brows furrow. "Oh. He isn't able to get visitors today."

"Oh. May I ask why?"

"Disciplinary measures."

Of course.

"When might he be able to have visitors again?"

She huffs, annoyed with me already. "I don't know, sir. That depends on him, doesn't it? You can call next time before driving all the way out here."

I nod. "Okay. Thank you."

On my slow walk back to the car I wonder...is *this* the sign I was waiting for?

CHAPTER 21

I don't go back to the prison. I don't even call. For a week after my last drive out there, I mostly stayed home, except to go to the grocery store. I've spent my time praying and meditating, and I almost called another priest from St. Joseph, thinking I was ready to confess, but after two rings, I hung up.

After a shower, I make myself some dinner, and turn on the TV, ready to settle in on the couch. Before I can take a bite, three slow knocks hit my door.

On my way across the living room, my stomach tightens and my pulse begins to race. I already know who it is before I open it.

Javier's leaning against the door jamb, a lopsided grin on his lips. "I believe we have plans."

My stomach does a somersault, but I remain impassive. "Do we?"

His grin widens as he looks me up and down while strutting in.

I close the door and take a deep breath before turning around.

"This is your idea of fun on a Saturday night? A pasta salad on a TV tray while watching the news?"

I purse my lips and tilt my head. "I'm sorry, should I be getting into fights and thrown into prison instead?"

He chuckles. "Touché. But as you can see, I'm out, and I remember a conversation we had while I was locked up."

"I don't recall," I lie, shifting my feet.

The smile he sends my way has a jolt of electricity running up my spine, but then he begins taking steps toward me, the smile falling. He grabs my chin in his hand, running his thumb over the seam of my mouth.

"I don't like when lies fall from these pretty lips." I almost forget to breathe as he stares into my eyes, his grip still on my face. "You remember our conversation, don't you?"

I nod once and he loosens his hold on me, his hand cradling my jaw. "Yes," I say quietly.

"And you want what I want."

It isn't a question, but I reply as if it was.

"Yes."

With his other hand, he touches my stomach and slowly slides his hand down my body until he reaches my growing erection.

"Yes," he purrs. "Good."

I swallow and lick my lips, trying to ignore the voice in my head that's telling me this is wrong. I'm violating an oath. I'm about to sin.

"You're thinking too much," he tells me, massaging my cock through my pants.

"I'm sorry."

"Don't apologize to me. I'm not going to apologize for making you break your oath. We're doing what we want. Simple as that."

119

When I don't relax, he continues.

"Do you need to feel like you don't have a choice?" he asks, hand sliding to my throat. "Do you need to feel like something is being done to you versus taking part in it?"

A thrill runs through me at the thought and I hate myself for enjoying the idea, but he saw something in my eyes when the words left his lips. He grins before walking me backwards until I hit the front door.

His body presses against mine as his mouth moves to my neck. He speaks against the skin under my ear.

"I've been waiting for this for a long time. You're not gonna make me wait any longer."

Molten hot lust explodes in my chest and rushes through my veins as his tongue dances along my flesh before he bites down just hard enough to make me gasp.

He's hard and rough as he takes my wrists and slams my hands above my head, holding me in place. His lips kiss along my jaw and his teeth bite into my chin before his tongue licks a trail down my throat.

Releasing his hold on me, he reaches for the hem of my shirt and lifts it over my head, throwing the material to the floor.

His eyes drink me in before he's lowering himself to his knees. Once again, my breath catches in my throat as I press one hand against the door and squeeze the doorknob in the other.

I watch as his fingers dip into the waistband of my pajama pants and tug them down. My erection strains against my navy blue briefs, harder than I've been in a while.

Javier teases me with kisses around the edges of my underwear. His tongue traces the outside of the material, slightly dipping underneath and robbing me of air. A noise escapes my throat as I long for him to do more, but I don't beg for it.

His hands reach around and squeeze my ass, his nose nuzzling into my cock as he breathes in.

"Fuck," I mutter quietly, lifting my head toward the ceiling.

I tell myself there's still time to stop. I can shove him away and step aside. I can and should put an end to this. Nothing's really happened yet.

Then I feel my underwear being pulled down. I drop my head and gaze down at him only to find him staring right back at me.

When my underwear get to mid-thigh, my cock is pointing right at him, hard as a rock—the veins full of blood.

"You got me on my knees, Father. Should I make a confession?" I nod once. "I'm about to ruin your life."

Then he opens his mouth and takes me across his tongue.

"Oh, God," I gasp, gripping the doorknob tighter.

Javier devours me.

I've always thought I was just a little above average in the size department. Maybe seven inches and fairly thick. But the way he takes me all the way into his mouth, you'd think I was small. He doesn't struggle to suck me deep. He moans as his saliva coats my length, his tongue swirling along the bottom of my shaft.

Javier's experienced—more than I am, and I feel a surge of jealousy and inadequacy. I won't be able to please him as well. But damn him for being able to give so many blow jobs to men to know how to be so good. I'm both thankful and resentful.

It doesn't take long for me to feel an orgasm building. I haven't had one since I came in my pants when he was here before. But the last one I had with physical touch was so long ago, I couldn't even put a timestamp on it.

"Please," I pant, reaching down to touch his head. "Stop."

He slows down but doesn't stop immediately. His tongue flickers against the underside of my head before he lets me fall from his mouth.

"I'm not done with you yet."

My tongue touches the corner of my mouth as I attempt to catch my breath.

He stands and quickly turns me around, my face pressed against the door as he runs his hands down my sides, squeezing my hips before gripping each cheek.

"God," he breathes. "Your ass is so soft and round. It's made for sin, *cariño*."

I exhale, a small whimper coming out as well.

"I need to bury myself in it," he says, still kneading the flesh. "First my tongue. Then my dick."

My back arches just slightly and he runs a finger through the crack. "Not here."

He quickly shoves my underwear down and I step out of them. Taking my hand, he leads me to my bedroom like this is his place.

"Get on the bed," he says, removing his jacket.

I sit on the edge, almost tempted to stroke myself as I watch him undress.

Javier removes something from his pocket and tosses it next to me. A small bottle of lube.

He places his jacket on the chair in my room, removes his shoes, and begins undoing his pants.

His shoulder holster is on over his T-shirt, and I can see

both guns sheathed in the leather. The sight of him makes my cock jump.

Javier doesn't finish undressing. Instead he drags the chair over to the side of the bed.

"Hands and knees," he says. "Right in front of me."

I look at him and to the chair, then I get in position in front of his seat. Right as I'm about to start feeling vulnerable and embarrassed, he sits and caresses my ass with a moan deep in his throat.

I lift my head and see the crucifix on my wall.

Lord, forgive me.

Javier's arms hook under my thighs, lifting me up slightly while also pulling me closer, and then his tongue slides between my cheeks.

"Oh, God," I whimper.

"Mmm," is his response.

Once again, I'm consumed. He doesn't let a single part of me go untouched. His tongue slides up and down the crease. His fingers dig into my flesh and the tip of his tongue prods at my entrance.

When he backs away, it's only to show attention to my balls, drawing them into his mouth one by one.

My fists gather the comforter in their tight grip as he continues his delicious assault.

He brings his arms back and uses his hands to spread me apart, moaning and grunting his delight at seeing my hole. He fucks me with his tongue, and my arms buckle.

The chair slides across the floor as he stands, and I watch through my spread legs as he pushes his pants down and removes his erection from his underwear.

My tongue darts across my lips as he begins stroking himself. He leans down to keep licking me, moaning as he brings us both pleasure.

He pulls away and snatches the lube from the bed, popping open the cap.

"I don't want to hurt you," he says, "But I absolutely want to ruin you."

A chill runs over me, but I'm not afraid. Not of him. Not of the pain. I'm afraid I'm about to be irrevocably changed after this, and I don't know if there will be any coming back.

Cold liquid hits my ass, and he begins spreading it around before gently inserting a finger.

Javier takes his time trying to get me prepped, and I imagine it's taking a lot of patience on his end. For a man like him—violent and brazen, he's not going about things as I thought he would. I am both appreciative and yet somewhat disappointed.

I almost wanted it to feel like a punishment. If it was hard and rough and done with little thought about my pleasure, I'd be able to say I didn't enjoy it. That it wasn't what I wanted. I'd probably not want it to happen again.

My cock begins to leak as he puts another finger inside me, and tears burn the backs of my eyes at how good it feels.

While his fingers work inside me, his other hand grabs ahold of my erection and begins to move.

"Ohh," I moan, voice shaky.

He smears the precum over my head and continues to stroke. This lasts another few minutes before he's easing away.

The sound of a condom wrapper hits my ears as he rips it open. The undone belt on his pants jingles as he pushes them down, and then the wet slithery noise of the condom being unrolled onto his length is the final thing I hear before he says, "Roll over."

I get on my back and see that he's still mostly dressed.

The shirt and holster remain on and his pants and under-wear are pushed down his legs. But all of that takes a back-seat to his cock which is covered in latex, and yet, still mouthwatering.

He's long, slightly curved, and thick enough to know I'll feel entirely full without being afraid I'll be ripped apart.

With another squirt of lube, he coats himself, then his fingers, and slides them inside me once more.

When he disengages, he grips himself in his hand and positions his cock at my entrance. Leaning over, he holds himself up with one hand, and while staring into my eyes, slowly begins to sink into me.

My eyes slam closed as my fists grip the blankets beneath me.

"That's it. Try to relax for me," he says, his voice low and raspy. "You can take it."

A moan escapes my lips as he continues to slide in deeper.

"Breathe," he says softly. "Look at me."

I open my eyes and stare into his lust-filled gaze. His tongue appears briefly between his lips as he wets them, and his dark eyes are completely blissed out as he watches me. He pushes in a little deeper, his teeth sinking into his lip as his eyes flutter closed and a moan vibrates in his throat.

My mouth falls open with an inhale. He's breathtaking.

I become hyper-focused on him. I watch the way his body moves and muscles flex. The veins in his arms, specifi-cally the thick one in his right bicep, grab my attention. His teeth still dig into his bottom lip, and I fight the urge to reach for him to kiss it and make it feel better.

The sinful and sexy noises that climb up his throat and float over his tongue make my body heat up even more.

"Fuck, you feel so good," he groans, hooking his arms under my legs. "You taste so good, too." His hips piston back and forth slowly. "God, everything about you...so good."

He reaches for my cock with one hand, and I can no longer control the sounds that leave me. Javier has a steady rhythm as he pumps in and out, but now his hand is sliding up and down my shaft, and the sensation is almost too much to bear.

"Oh, God," I moan, watching his large, tattooed hand stroke my cock.

"You like the way I touch you?" he asks.

I nod my head, scraping my lip with my teeth.

"Tell me you like it," he commands.

"I like it." The words come out on an exhale. "Ah. Feels so good."

I watch as a perfectly placed stream of saliva falls from his mouth and onto the tip of my cock. He smears the liquid, giving us some lubrication as he continues to stroke.

"Oh my God," I say again.

His thumb rubs the underside of my head and my back arches off the bed.

"You praying?" he questions. "Or worshipping?"

My eyes meet his and I see a slight smirk on his lips. Before I can think to say anything, he takes a hold of my legs and pushes them farther back and begins to drill into me. He doesn't move fast and shallow. He's giving me measured, long strokes that hit deep, making sure I feel every inch of him as he moves.

"Oh God. Oh fuck," I moan through grunts and pants.

He stops, and the whine that leaves my mouth is almost embarrassing, but then I see the frenzy he's in.

Javier removes the shoulder holster and drops it to the

floor, followed by his T-shirt. He pulls out of me just long enough to step out of his pants, and then he's leaning over me, and hooking an arm under my back to push me higher up the bed.

Before he slides back into me, he drops lower and sucks my cock into his mouth.

"Oh fuck," I gasp, my hand going for his head. He moans his delight at my touch, so I thread my fingers through the dark strands of his hair. "Yes," I hiss, drawing out the word.

He takes me to the edge of ecstasy, then pulls away. This time, he pushes inside of me with less gentleness.

He lays over my body, my legs now resting on his shoulders.

"Fuck!" he exclaims moving faster, his thrusts hard and deep. "So fucking good, Carlo."

My eyes roll to the back of my head as he says my name, and my hands find placement on his sides, squeezing and caressing as much as I can.

His stomach is rubbing against my shaft, bringing me some friction, but not enough to make me come. And I'm desperate for the release.

"Touch me," I pant.

"What's that?" he asks, his face in my neck, giving me a whisker burn I'm sure I'll feel for days.

"Touch me," I say again.

He only moves slightly, his lips pressing kisses across my jawline until he gets to my chin. Javier lifts his head until we're staring at each other. He's buried all the way in, rotating his hips just enough to drive me crazy.

"You ready to come for me?"

I nod, then I say, "Yes."

"Mmm," he moans.

So quickly I can barely register it, he plants a kiss on my lips and then he's moving away. I'm still thinking about how I didn't even get a chance to return it when he begins pumping into me while simultaneously stroking my shaft.

"Oh yes," I moan, closing my eyes. "Yes, God, yes."

"That's it," he breathes. "Make a mess for me, Carlo," he says. "I want it all over my hand."

"Oh God," I cry out, my muscles flexing. I open my eyes to watch his hand move up and down my shaft. To see him thrust in and out of me.

He's completely focused on watching my cock in his grip. His skin is flushed, and sweat shines across his forehead. His hips continue to move, and his brow furrows as he groans. He's getting close too.

"Fuck," he grunts. "Give it to me."

"Oh God!" I yell as my orgasm explodes out of me.

Animalistic grunts and groans leave my mouth after that. I'm reduced to deep breaths and chants of *Oh God*, but it's not God I'm talking to. Not now. Not this time. Javier is the sole recipient of my worship.

"So good. Yes. Oh God."

Thick streams of cum run over his hand and down my shaft. Drops are pooling on my stomach, and the sheer amount would make you believe I've never orgasmed in my life.

"I'm about to come," he says quickly.

Javier pulls out, rips the condom off, and uses the same hand that was just on me to stroke himself to release.

"Fuck," he grunts before a guttural roar fills the room as he empties his load onto my cock and stomach.

The tip of his dick slides across my shaft, and his cum mixes with mine in a pool on my abdomen.

"Oh fuck," I say through shaky breaths.

Javier brings our shafts together—his a little longer and mine a little thicker, and using our combined release, he begins to stroke.

My body twitches and spasms as my sensitive head rubs against his. It's almost too much to take.

"Javi..." I swallow. "Javier, please." I run my hands through my hair, tugging hard on the strands. "Ohh shh..." I don't even finish the curse as my body breaks out into a full blown shiver.

He releases us and then flops onto his back next to me with an exhale. "Oh yeah. That was..." He sighs. "I needed that."

I let out a little snort.

"Oh, I'm sure you needed it more, huh?"

I fight a grin and then look down at the mess on my body. "I need to shower."

"Me too," he says, standing up. "I'll get it started."

He saunters off, stark naked. When I look to the wall, I'm met with the crucifix—Jesus looking down at me, covered in both mine and another man's cum. I await the guilt and shame to wash over me, but it doesn't hit like a tidal wave. Instead, there's only a splash. The thought that, yeah, maybe this was wrong because I'm ordained, not wrong because we're both men. I broke a rule, but I've never thought I was a sinner simply for my sexual identity. That may be how the church views it, but not me.

"You coming?" Javier asks from the doorway, his naked body on display as he gives me a grin.

With a small smile, I get out of bed and walk toward him.

CHAPTER 22

Grateful for the large walk-in shower, I spin around under the shower head without having to worry about bumping into Javier as he lathers his body up.

"How you feeling?" he asks without looking at me.

"Fine."

He barks out a laugh. "Ouch. I was hoping for *incredible, mindblown, changed forever.*"

I chuckle as I turn to rinse out my hair. "Oh, well, sure. All those things, too."

Javier snorts, and then I feel him at my back, his face burrowing into my neck as his hands slide around my stomach.

I break out into goosebumps, even under warm water.

"But really, I was asking about this," he says, moving his hand to the crease between my ass cheeks. "Is this okay? Or do I need to kiss it better?"

My body shivers. "I...I'm okay."

He spins me around until my back hits the shower wall.

"And this," he says, taking his finger and tapping my temple.

My eyes fall to his lips where water drops from his hair and lands on them. I want to wipe the wetness away with my tongue. I want our bodies to collide and smack against each other in this shower. I want—

Javier snickers, cutting off my thoughts. "Oh, I think you *are* changed forever."

I try to remain nonchalant, because the truth is, I don't know what this means. I always knew I was gay, so that's not a revelation. That I had sex with a man known for violence and worse, couldn't possibly be where my future leads. This was a thrill. This was doing what I've been craving for years. And for him? Just another romp in the sack, probably. There's no use getting excited about this when I don't know what it is.

"I really enjoyed myself," I tell him, reaching out to touch his hip. "A lot." I give him a smirk. "Mentally, I'm okay," I say with a shrug. "Maybe the guilt will hit later. I don't know. Right now, I'm happy."

His fingers graze the front of my thigh. "But?"

"I'm not going to fool myself into thinking this is anything serious." I laugh, and it comes out a little more derisive than I intended. "It can't be. This was a one and done."

His brows furrow slightly as he studies me. "Not sure why you'd think that."

"Come on," I say with a chuckle. "I'm not someone you want to be with all the time. We come from different worlds. I could go back to work soon, and then what?"

He steps away. "I see. You're projecting. You say I don't wanna be with someone like you, when really, you don't wanna be with someone like me. I get it, Carlo. You could've just said that. It's not like I thought we'd be anything more than fuck buddies anyway. You're too boring, but you have a nice ass, and I was hoping to find out how soft your mouth is."

"Javier."

He forces me out of my space so he can rinse off. "No, really. I'm all good. I did what I wanted to do anyway."

His phone starts ringing from the bedroom and he quickly steps out of the shower, yanking a towel off a nearby hook.

"Javier," I say again.

I sigh, realizing I probably should've kept my mouth closed. Why couldn't we have messed around a couple more times? I'm sure it would've slowly faded into nothing anyway.

Taking my time, I finish cleaning up before I step out and grab a towel. I get dried off and then put lotion on before heading into my room where I look for my clothes.

Javier isn't in the house, but his things are still on my floor, so I guess he took his call outside.

When I find the remote, I turn on the TV that's hoisted up on my wall opposite my bed, and start to get dressed.

The news is already on, talking about the weather forecast, and just as I pull my shirt over my head, it cuts to two people behind the news station desk.

"We have some news out of South Bay Correctional Institute. Antonio Caruso, suspected hitman for the Mancini Crime Family, was found dead in his cell last week. They are currently calling this a suicide."

I slowly lower myself to the mattress and stare at the TV as the newscasters begin talking about something else.

A myriad of thoughts bounce around in my head as I try to snap myself out of this daze. I quickly get up and go to my bedroom window which faces the front yard. I spot Javier leaning against his car that's parked in front of the house next door. He's only wearing his pants, but he's no longer on the phone. He appears to be zoned out with his gaze frozen down the street.

I glance over to where he's looking to see if I can spot anything unusual, but the street is quiet.

My phone blares from the living room, making me jolt up straight. I speed walk down the hall until I find it next to my forgotten plate of food. Gazing down at the screen, I see a number I don't recognize.

"Hello?"

"Kid, I'm sending someone to get you. He's about an hour away."

"Johnny? What's going on?"

"Pack a small bag."

"Johnny, what the hell is happening? Where's my dad?"

"Listen. This guy will be there in a little while."

"What the...tell me what's happening? Am I in danger?"

There's silence on the phone, and then it goes dead.

The door opens and Javier strolls in. Considering how things took a turn in the shower, I doubt he'll be willing to stay much longer, which right now, is a good thing. I don't want to explain to him that some man is coming to pick me up.

"I didn't mean to be rude earlier. I really did have a good time," I say, walking back to the bedroom with the hope that he'll follow and grab his things.

"I know you did," he says. "Your body doesn't lie as easily as your mouth does."

I chuckle nervously. "Uhh, yeah."

Javier moves without a care, taking his time to pick up his shirt and slide it over his head. He grabs his socks and shoes and takes them to the chair where he casually puts them on.

I find myself fidgeting with my phone, checking the time, and wondering when he'll leave, and if I'll have enough time to pack before my ride gets here.

Javier notices. "What's going on with you?"

"Nothing," I say, but even I could hear the slight pitch in my tone.

"Sure."

He walks over to his discarded guns and shoulder holster, picks them up and puts them back on.

"As we reported earlier, Antonio Caruso was found dead in his cell, an apparent suicide. However, reports are coming in that he was in protective custody, and the cameras outside his cell weren't working. His attorney is questioning the ruling of a suicide, claiming Mr. Caruso was not at all suicidal. We'll bring you more news as we know it."

The broadcaster's voice is replaced by an insurance commercial, but Javier and I slowly make eye contact from across the room.

Something in his expression has my curiosity spiking. Then a light bulb goes off. "Did you..."

He shifts, putting his hands in his pockets. "Did I...what?"

"I didn't realize you were in the same prison," I say, gesturing toward the TV.

"And?"

"Did you kill him?"

I whisper the words like it'll make a difference.

"Why do you think I was there in the first place?"

"You said you got into a fight."

"I did what needed to be done to get put in there. I have a job to do, Carlo."

My brain starts short circuiting. Theories and questions begin forming. If he killed Antonio, he works for a family. He has to.

"Who do you work for?"

He watches me for a few seconds before he speaks. "I have a confession."

I roll my eyes. "Now's not the time."

His lips quirk slightly. "I'm here for you."

"What are you talking about?"

"I'm your ride."

My brows furrow and my head tilts to the side as I take a step back. "No. What—what are you talking about? I don't have a ride," I say.

He makes a tsk tsk sound with his tongue. "Lie after lie after lie."

"I'm not lying."

"You're telling me you didn't get a call when I was outside? Before you answer, I heard the ring. You got the damn volume up as loud as possible."

"You know Johnny?" I ask.

He nods once. "Johnny Sabatino? Yes, I know him. Now let's pack that bag. I think we have a few things to go over."

CHAPTER 23

J avier lingers in my room as I pack, watching my every move.

"You work for the Esposito Family?" I question as I fold clothes and place them in a small suitcase.

"What do *you* do with the Esposito Family?"

"Nothing. I'm not a part of that life."

It's not a lie, but I am omitting a large truth.

"You questioned me about another family before," he says. "You were in a bar that's affiliated with the Espositos. You spin lies like spiders spin webs. So, tell me something that's true."

"If you work for them and you don't know who I am, then maybe you shouldn't."

His eyes narrow on me but I spin around and head for my bathroom.

"I knew you were keeping things from me. I told you we were both liars, but I've been more honest than you, it seems. You're a priest, I know that much is true, but you're clearly important to a family I've worked with for years, and yet, I've never heard about you."

"That's not my problem," I say, coming into the bedroom to deposit more things in the suitcase. "So, you killed Antonio for the Esposito Family?"

"Yes."

"Who do you work for specifically?"

"Why does it matter?"

"You're not made. I know that."

"Clearly. The Esposito Family is Italian. I'm not."

"But they trust you."

"At least one of them does."

"Where are we going and why? Can you tell me that?" I ask, spinning around to face him.

"No."

I turn around and finish packing before swiping my phone from the bed and going to the bathroom.

I turn on the faucets and call my dad. He picks up after two rings.

"What's wrong?"

"What's going on?" I ask in a quiet tone.

"You safe?"

"I'm at home. Someone is here."

"Javier?"

"Yes."

Hearing my dad say his name feels weird, but at least I know Javier is telling the truth about this.

"You can trust him. I was going to tell you about him a little while back, but someone walked in."

That explains the random call.

"Where am I going?"

"I'm going to call him."

"Does he know who I am?"

"No."

"Well, he will soon, won't he?"

"Probably." Dad muffles the phone and starts talking to someone on his end. "Look. Something is happening. I'll explain in person."

"Okay."

Before I can even finish the word, he's ended the call.

I take a few seconds to collect myself and then shut off the water and walk back into my bedroom.

Javier has my suitcase closed up and is holding it by the handle. "Ready?"

"I guess."

His phone rings and I know it's my dad.

He glances at the screen, then at me, and walks into the living room.

"Hello?"

I linger in my doorway, listening.

"That's not what he said. No. Okay. So what's he doing? Oh. Is that something I need to take care of? Right, of course. Well, let me know. I will. Okay."

Stepping into the hall, I make my way to the living room. "Who was that?"

"Nobody," he says. "Ready?"

"I don't think I have a choice."

"You're right about that."

Outside, I climb into a black Audi and settle into the leather seats as he puts my suitcase in the trunk. He gets into the driver's seat and starts up the car, starting our journey to a location I don't know anything about.

Neither one of us speaks for a while, both caught in our own thoughts.

After about fifteen minutes, he breaks the silence.

"Carlo. Carlo."

"What?"

"Is that your full name?"

"Why?"

"Carlo sounds Italian. If it's Carlos it could be Spanish."

I see where he's going with this, so I don't answer. Instead, I pivot with my own question. "How did you get work with an Italian mob family? You're not Italian, you're covered in tattoos, and you're bisexual. You check all the boxes of things they don't normally put up with."

"I'm not in the mafia," he says simply. "And certain things are kept private." He shoots me a look as if to warn me about his sexuality being a secret.

"Ah, so I'm not the only one keeping things to myself."

"I'm not dumb, *Carlo*." He says my name like he's no longer sure it actually is.

We fall into another several minutes of silence as he takes a few turns and I begin to realize we're heading out of the city's limits.

My brain starts replaying all of our moments together, from the time he showed up in my confessional booth, to the time he was hurt and needed my help, and to his request for me to visit him in prison. None of it makes sense to me. Why? Why me? I decide to ask.

"Why did you come into St. Joseph's that day? And don't give me some bullshit answer about existential crisis."

"Well, it's not a bullshit answer. I was mostly honest. I was struggling with something that I knew could be coming. I don't have friends like most people. I don't talk about my work with anyone, because as I'm sure you can understand, it's not possible. I don't struggle with the work itself, because it's what I know. I'm not cut out to be a normal man with a normal job, but I also have been aware that I've been hiding and lying for years. Could I keep up with that? I don't know."

"What's coming?" I question.

"Something work related."

"Okay, so, I was right before. You just needed someone to talk to who couldn't repeat what you said."

"I was walking by. I saw the church and didn't think much about it. I went in, met you, and was immediately intrigued, so I kept going back."

"Intrigued by what?"

"I could sense your lies. Your falseness radiated off of you and I wanted to know more. I, too, have been lying. I thought, maybe I'm not so bad if a priest is doing the same thing as me." He glances in my direction. "We're different, but we're also a lot alike. You became a priest at the behest of your father. I do what I do because of my father. You're not straight, and neither am I, and we're both in fields where that's not okay. You helped me, knowing I wasn't a good man. You didn't seem affronted by my actions. Not the way any normal person would be. I told you what I've done, and yet, you wanted me. Tell me how I'm not supposed to be intrigued by that."

"I'm not supposed to judge others—"

"Don't. It wasn't some priestly *judge not, lest ye be judged* BS. It's because it wasn't foreign to you." He stops at an intersection and stares at me, hoping for some information. When I don't say anything, he sighs and continues driving. "You know I'm going to find out, right? You do know where we're headed, even if you don't know the location."

I look out the window and exhale. "Oh yeah. I know, but I don't think you're ready for what you're about to find out."

CHAPTER 24

I was staring out the window as we passed the sign that alerted me we'd crossed the Massachusetts border and into New Hampshire. That was an hour ago. We're now seemingly driving into the White Mountain National Forest. I'm assuming this is where one of my dad's safe houses is, so I don't bother questioning Javier. Especially when I doubt he'd tell me anyway.

I close my eyes, intending to sleep for a while, but before I know it, Javier is nudging my arm to wake me up. When I glance at the clock, it reads twelve forty-seven. We've been driving for just over two hours.

"Come on," he says gruffly, turning off the car and opening the door.

I take a second to look at my phone to see if my dad has tried calling or sending a message, but there are no new notifications. With a deep breath, I step out into the night air and meet Javier at the trunk.

He's already put my suitcase on the ground, and now he's reaching for another bag.

"You're already packed?" I question.

"I always have a bag in the car."

After shutting the trunk, I realize we're parked underneath a second story deck with room for a few more cars. We walk around to the side of the house where a staircase leads us to a door to the house. To my left, I can see a table and several chairs, but it's too dark to make out any details.

Once inside, Javier turns off the security alarm, closes and locks the door, types in a code, and then flips on a light switch.

It's a nice cabin, which isn't surprising if this is where my dad spends any amount of time. The living room is cozy, with two leather loveseats and an accent chair positioned around a small rectangular coffee table, all facing a fireplace with a TV mounted above it.

A black dining room table sits in on the other side of the room, past doors that I suspect lead out to the deck.

Javier disappears through a doorway and another light filters in. The sound of water hits my ears, and I assume he's in the kitchen.

It's clear he's been here before with how familiar he is with everything, and I begin to wonder just how close he is to my dad.

I wander around and find a bedroom that houses a king sized bed. When I find the stairs, I walk up and come across a loft space that looks down on the living room. A couch and table sit on top of a nice rug, and a hall leads to what has to be the rest of the bedrooms.

"Carlo," Javier yells.

"What?"

"Come here."

I sigh and head back down the stairs. "What?" I ask, not bothering to hide my annoyance.

"He's about to be here, and I shouldn't have to tell you,

but I'm going to anyway. Do not say anything stupid. Don't say anything that doesn't need to be said. We will get our orders and we will abide by them."

I fight the grin my mouth wants to form, because I know he isn't aware of my relationship with who he seems to hold in such high regard. He probably respects my father, and well, I hold him in disdain most times.

I lift my brows. "Sure."

"I'm serious."

"Okay," I say, holding up my hands and going to the couch where I flop unceremoniously.

The sound of doors closing are followed closely by muffled voices as they hit the stairs. Javier rushes to the door to turn off the alarm, and then the door opens. I don't bother turning around to watch him enter. He knows I'm here. I was instructed to be, after all.

"How was the drive?" my dad asks.

"Good. Nobody in sight."

"All right, well." He stops talking and his footsteps bring him closer to me.

I angle my head over my shoulder as he rounds the couch.

"Carlo," he greets.

I dip my head in response then look behind me, expecting to see Dad's right hand man.

"Where's Johnny?" I ask, brows furrowed as I spot someone I've never seen before.

"Somewhere else." Dad waves his hand at the man lingering in front of the door, and he goes to stand outside.

"Do I get to know why I've been driven to the mountains now?"

Javier walks over and stands near my dad, trying to send me a message with his eyes.

Dad walks over to the accent chair that sits caddy corner to me. Hiking up his slacks, he sits down and gestures for Javier to sit on the other couch.

"We need to lay low for a little while."

"Still making waves?" I ask.

"The waves have never waned."

"What does this have to do with me? This is your problem, is it not?"

Javier shifts, uncomfortable with how I'm speaking to him.

"Well, unfortunately for you, it's become your problem."

"How? Why?"

Dad leans back in the chair, crossing his ankle over his knee. "Because you've been found out."

My eyes slide over to Javier whose own gaze is bouncing between the two of us as he tries to figure out what's going on.

"How did that happen?"

"We have a rat."

I sit up, leaning my elbows on my knees. "Who?"

"I have theories."

"And this is separate from your other problem?"

"Yes, but because of my other problem, and the fact that people are now aware of your proximity to me, you are in danger."

I inhale slowly through my nose. "So, we're all staying here?"

Dad shakes his head. "No. Javier will watch over you. Marco and I will be heading to another location. You and I shouldn't be around each other."

"How long is this going to go on for? I have work. I have—"

"No you don't," he says, cutting me off. "You're on sabbatical."

I send Javier an accusatory look but he just deepens his furrow.

"I don't know why you're on sabbatical," Dad continues, "But I know it's true."

"Are you spying on me?"

"I don't have time to spy on you, Carlo. I know what I need to know, and I know you don't have a job to get back to anytime soon. So, you will be here with Javier, and he is the only person you should trust."

I snort, leaning back into the couch. "Great."

"Listen to me. I trust Javier with my life. He's the only person I can say that about, so you—"

"Nice," I say derisively, cutting him off.

"Don't act like a petulant child now. You said you wanted this life, and I've tried protecting you from it, well it looks like you're finally getting your way. You're in it, whether you like it or not."

"Protecting me?" I bite. "Or excluding me?"

Dad's nostrils flare as he stares at me. "Protecting you. I always mean what I say."

"Good to know, because you've said a lot over the years."

"I don't sugarcoat the truth. You've heard exactly what you needed to hear, and for thirty years you've been safe from any fallout because I kept you away. Just because you don't like the way it happened, doesn't mean it wasn't done without your best interest in mind."

I cock my head, trying to hear what he's saying in the omissions. "So, I'm here because you think someone will kill me."

"Yes."

"But they're also trying to kill you."

"Yes."

"And that's why we shouldn't be together. Because we could both be killed at the same time."

"Because they're coming after me, and if they get me, you need to stay alive."

"Why?"

Dad sighs. "You're my son. Why do you think?"

Javier sucks in a breath, and both Dad and I turn to look at him. Before he can say anything, Dad speaks up again.

"There's something I need to tell you about Javier."

CHAPTER 25

"I'm sorry. Did you say *son*?" Javier asks, his eyes wide.

Dad holds up a hand to quiet him.

"What do I need to know about Javier?" I question.

"The waves I've been making? Javier's the earthquake that kick-started them."

I shake my head in confusion. "Meaning?"

"I knew Javier's father. He was a contract killer and the best one I knew. He had no allegiances to anyone, and for a long time, he worked with any of the families. Everyone used him, but I was the one who got close to him. We were friends for several years, and I knew his son was following in his footsteps.

"When Diego died, I took Javier under my wing. He was already grown and already working, but we had a connection. We grieved together. We exacted revenge together.

"Hiring contract killers isn't new for any mafia family, but they're always Italian, and they can work with whoever they want. Since it was a member of another family that killed Diego, both Javier and I wanted to keep our work exclusive. He is *my* killer. And well, people don't like that. Now they're talking about how I'm making changes they don't like. He's not one of us. He shouldn't work for just me, because it looks like he's been made and brought into the family." Dad waves his hand in the air like it's all nonsense.

Different thoughts and emotions swirl through me, but I filter them down to get to what's important.

"When you were hiding before, he was the one who knew where you were?"

Dad nods. "Yes."

"And when you were able to come back it was because..."

"Javier killed the man who was after me."

"But there's someone else?"

"There's always someone else."

"So when does this end?"

"When I kill them all," Javier chimes in.

I turn and look at him. "I doubt that's possible."

His small grin is wicked. "You don't know me very well."

"Clearly," I say after a few seconds.

"The other families don't want the chance to work with Javier. Not anymore. They want him dead."

I run my hands through my hair, completely overwhelmed with all this information.

"And I'm in the crosshairs because someone in some family now knows you have a son."

"Yes. I was sent a picture of you in front of your house. On it was your full name. Not the name you've been going by, but Giancarlo Gallo. It was a threat."

I massage my temple, feeling a headache coming on. "So all three of us have a target on our backs, and we hide

148

out until when? Forever? Someone has to do something, otherwise we'll never go back to our lives."

"We're going to take care of it," Dad says. "But we're laying low for now until we can execute our plan."

"And that's to kill the entirety of every mob family? Seems highly unlikely."

"I have allies, Carlo. Not everyone, even in other families, wants me dead. Not when I have things to offer. Money and power always trump morality. We get rid of the troublemakers and incentivize others. It's just taking some time."

"And if you die in the process?"

"He won't die," Javier states.

"You said *we get rid of the troublemakers*. Who is *we*? I'm assuming that doesn't include me."

"No, you stay here."

I shake my head. "Of course. But what happens if you die before this plan of yours can be seen through to the end?"

He hesitates, his eyes flashing to Javier briefly before looking back at me.

"Well, I don't think it's time to get into that just yet. The plan is for me to stay alive, so let's focus on that."

"You can't possibly mean to have Javier take your place."

"I'm going to try not to take offense to that," Javier says.

"I just mean, you're young. You're..."

"Latino?" Javier offers, eyebrows up.

"That's not what I was going to say."

But we both know I can't say what I was actually thinking, so I come up with something else. "You're already a target."

"Javier doesn't want the job," Dad says.

What bothers me about his tone is that it seems like he's already asked him and was turned down.

"So, Johnny would take over?"

Dad and Javier share a look, and I start to get really irritated over feeling like an outsider.

"Probably not," Dad says. "We think Johnny's the rat that gave you up."

"There's no way," I exclaim. "I was with him when you were gone. He seemed stressed and worried. You've been friends for decades. He wouldn't do that."

Dad doesn't give me anything else. Just a shrug. "We're looking into it."

"Okay, so again, what happens if you die? Do I have to move away? Change my name?"

Dad's eyes narrow, his jaw clenching. "No. We do not back down and cower."

"So, what?"

He dusts some invisible dirt off his pants, shifting his position in the chair. "I want you to take over."

I turn my head slightly, giving him my ear. I couldn't have possibly heard him correctly. "I'm sorry. What?"

"You are a Gallo," he says with a bite. "You finish what I started."

My eyes nearly fall out of my head as I stare at him. "I can't. I'm also a target. I'd just be killed."

"Javier will be your right hand man. He will not let that happen."

I meet Javier's gaze and he looks almost as surprised as I feel, but he's doing a better job masking it.

"I'm not made. I haven't been involved in any of this."

Dad stands up, cutting his hand through the air as if to stop my train of thought. "It's not something to worry about now. I don't plan on dying, so this may never need to happen."

"Right, but there's also another issue with this backup plan *if* it does need to come to fruition. I'm Italian, and I'm your son, but I'm also gay. Talk about creating waves, unless of course you intend for me to continue being celibate. Not to mention the fucking story of a priest becoming a crime boss." I stand up and run a hand over my face. "Oh my God, I can't even believe I'm talking about this. I can't do this. I can't. I'm supposed to go back to St. Joseph's."

Dad sighs, and when I turn around I can see him and Javier having an unspoken conversation with their eyes. I guess he didn't want me to reveal that secret. Little does he know Javier isn't going to be surprised about my sexuality.

"I don't care about anyone's private life," Javier says, holding up his hands.

"Don't get worked up over it when we don't know if it'll even have to end up that way," Dad says. "But you were just in my office talking about this is the life you always thought you'd get. Well, be careful what you ask for."

"It's very different to be thrust into it after years of devoting your life to church and Jesus because your father gave you no choice, than to, I don't know, be taken under someone's wing and live it day in and day out."

"Don't get sensitive now," Dad says. "Javier was in the life way before I knew him. I simply stepped in when his dad died."

I move toward him, anger pulsing in my veins. "You had a son! I would've done anything for you. I idolized you! But you weren't there when I needed you, so I don't wanna hear that shit."

"Carlo, watch yourself," Dad warns. "I've supported—"

"No. You try to throw your money in my face as a way

that you were there for me, but you set me up for failure. You can't throw me in the ocean then expect me to thank you when you toss me a floatie. You took away what I thought I'd do and become. You forced me into a different life because you knew I couldn't afford to do anything else on my own. I was just barely an adult who still wanted his dad's approval and respect, and I was constantly met with rejection and criticism even when I followed your rules. So, no. You haven't supported me, and I'd appreciate it if you could take some responsibility for your failures."

Dad remains quiet for several seconds, his face hard and etched with fury. Nobody talks to him like this, and he's not used to it. If I were anyone else, I'd be on the floor right now.

He takes a deep breath. "You wouldn't have been accepted or respected. I was still working my way up and you were being reckless and selfish."

I step up to him, my foot hitting the tip of his fancy shoe. "Fuck you."

"Hey," Javier says, standing up and getting closer.

"You were young and dumb," Dad continues. "You only cared about yourself. You go on and on about *the life*, acting like you knew so much back then. If that was the case, why did you think you'd ever get in? You knew your preferences. You say you knew enough about the lifestyle. So, tell me, how would that have worked?"

I inhale through my nose, my jaw clenched. "I would've made it work."

"Oh? How would it have been different from what you're doing now? You're lying. You're hiding. Anything you do has to be done in secret. You blame me for making it to where you have to do those things, but the same things would be happening if you were in the *family*. You know the difference? Go on, if you're so smart. Tell me what the difference is."

I lean in even closer, my chest heaving with deep breaths as I try my best to stay under control. Javier remains close by, ready to push me away if need be.

"You were my dad."

"I still am," he bites back.

"I thought my dad would make sure his son was protected. I thought you'd threaten anyone who dared have anything to say about me. That's what you did for yourself. For Johnny. For the last boss. I assumed you'd be frightening enough that if anyone ever found out, they'd be too afraid to say anything about it because they'd have to answer to you. After all, that was the reputation you were getting." I shake my head. "No. You're the head of the *family*, and you might even be pretty good at it, but you were a shit father."

"Come on, man," Javier says, putting his hand on my shoulder and trying to move me away.

I shrug him off, pinning him with a glare before I look back at my father.

"The difference is, Carlo," Dad continues, "I made it to where you could hide and lie and sneak in the priesthood because doing those things in the *family* would get you killed. If you're caught, you're killed. What happens if you sneak around now? You lose your job? Boo fucking hoo. You're still alive."

"After years of indoctrination, I'd believe I'd go to hell!"

"Nobody said you had to buy into their beliefs."

"You could've just sent me away to a college on the other side of the country. You could've sent me to a whole new fucking country. I'd have been able to live my life the way I wanted and would've been far enough from you that nobody would have found out your terrible secret. That you had a gay son."

"Jesus Christ," Dad huffs. "I'm done with this conversation. We have more important things to worry about."

I snort, not backing away. "Typical."

"Keep it up," Dad spits, shoving his finger in my chest. "I only have so much patience."

"I'm not afraid of you."

"You never had to be, but that can change."

My lips curl up into a wicked grin, holding more malice than happiness. "You think I won't protect myself? Even against you?"

Dad's own lips quirk, and I see a hint of amusement in his eyes. "You may not think of me as your dad, but half of your DNA came from me. You're more like me than you want to be, and if you're not happy with how I went about things, then do them better." He smacks his palm on my chest twice. "Because I'm starting to think you just might be able to."

CHAPTER 26

As I pace around one of the bedrooms, I can hear Javier and my dad talking downstairs. I can't make out what they're saying, but at this point, I don't care.

I'm tired of every encounter with my dad turning into something hostile. Something about him always seems to get under my skin, and now I have new information to stew on.

He's basically been acting as a father figure to Javier for years. Sure, he didn't raise him or live with him, but he said he stepped in when Javier's dad died. It's hard to not find that insulting considering he was absent from my life.

My dad trusting Javier more than anyone...*anyone*, is almost beyond belief to me. I suppose I shouldn't think he'd trust me, but it doesn't lessen the sting.

However, the main thing is the way he's willing to make waves for Javier, but never thought to do the same for me.

A knock at the door yanks me out of my thoughts, and I march over to pull it open.

"He's gone."

"Good."

"So, that was a surprise."

I turn around and head to the bed where I sit on the edge. "Good ol' Dad," I say with a sigh.

Javier takes a few steps inside, leaning against a mahogany dresser. "He's trying to look out for you."

"You know, I really don't wanna hear it. Not from him, and definitely not from you."

"He doesn't show emotion. He's never vulnerable or open, but I've spent a lot of time with him, and trust me, he's different with you. You have to read between the lines."

"Regardless of your years with him, I had more. He likes you because you're like him."

"Oh no. Is that why you like me? Some sort of daddy issue where you're trying to resolve unresolved conflicts."

I look up at him and pin him with a glare. "I never said I liked you."

He grins. "Right."

"He also doesn't know your sexuality. That would probably change things."

Javier sighs. "He's not wrong about what could happen. Why do you think I hide that part of me? These guys take their rules seriously. On top of that, they're cruel, vicious, and prejudiced people. They think being gay strips you of masculinity, which means they don't think you're capable of being violent. It's a very antiquated way of thinking, but the older guys—the bosses, they won't tolerate it."

"My dad is the boss. He could change things. He could say something."

"And risk his life?"

"He's risking it for you, isn't he?"

Javier doesn't say anything for a while. "But I'm still not going to be in the family. It's the other families' reaction that is making this a big deal. You, being a made guy in the mafia and being openly gay is a much bigger issue than your dad wanting to exclusively work with a Latino."

I shake my head. "I really don't care to talk about it anymore."

"You didn't know I worked for him?"

"I assumed you did work for some family, but not his."

"Those questions you were asking. The ones about the Bonetti family."

"Johnny told me my dad was in hiding, and then he'd gone missing. He told me the family they thought was after him, so I wanted to know more because I was concerned, but then I got word that Dad was fine."

"I was tracking someone. He was getting close to your dad's location, so I told Cortez so he could leave, and then I killed the man who was going to kill him. I came to see you the next day."

He says it like he did a normal errand, and even though I'm aware of the things that go on in the criminal underground, I can't imagine I'll ever get to the point where I'll kill someone and mention it so casually. So unaffected.

"When you were hurt," I mention, curious now. "What was that from?"

"Ah. Just a foot soldier for another family that was causing issues. Your dad needed him gone, so." He shrugs.

"You do what my dad says," I say with a humorless laugh. "Guess that's two of us."

"He's my boss."

I sigh and lie back, my feet still on the floor. "Sorry about your dad," I say after a few seconds.

"It's fine," he replies quickly. "It's the nature of the game."

"You got justice?"

"Thanks to your dad."

I stay silent and then I feel the bed dip next to me as he sits.

"I know this is complicated. You don't get along with your dad, but I respect the hell out of Cortez. He's the closest person I have to family and I'd do anything for him. And now I'm fucking his son, which actually makes me feel weirder than fucking a priest."

I choke out a laugh. "You're ridiculous."

"I'm serious," he says, turning to look at me. "He can't find out. He'd kill me."

"You *fucked* me. You're not *fucking* me."

"Oh right," he says, eyes narrowing slightly. "A one and done situation."

I sit up, invading his space. "Or." His brow quirks slightly. "Maybe I can fuck you. Would that be better? If you felt like something was being done *to you*." I repeat his earlier words back to him.

"You're trying to turn the tables," he says.

"You think it's only because I want to be able to fuck the man my father respects and trusts so much?" My hand travels up his thigh. "The man he took under his wing to replace the son he shunned for being gay? You think that's why?"

Javier's gaze bounces between my eyes and my mouth. "I know you wanted to fuck me before being aware of all that, but now I think you want to use me as a get-back to your dad, even if he never finds out. You'll get off on it."

I brush my hand over his crotch as I move it to his other thigh, dragging my fingers down to his knee. "Just like you got off on making me break my vow as a priest."

"I wasn't afraid of God striking me down."

"You're more afraid of my father than God?"

"Yes."

I grin, my hand moving back up to feel his erection growing beneath his pants. Leaning forward, I nuzzle into his neck before placing my lips at his ear. "Does your dick know you're afraid? Because it doesn't feel like it."

He grabs my wrist, but he doesn't move it away. I smile against his jaw before pulling away and standing up.

"Well, I guess I'm gonna turn in for the night."

He watches me from the bed, his expression telling me he's not amused with my antics, but I don't care. It feels good to be the one with the power.

Once he stands up, he stops next to me, our shoulders touching. "I added something to your bag. You might need it."

My brows knit briefly, but then he walks out, and just like that he's taken the power back.

I try not to rush to my suitcase, but my curiosity gets the best of me. I lift it from its place near the window and lay it on the bed. After I unzip it, I pull it open and find the scourge splayed across the top of my clothes.

Goddamn him.

CHAPTER 27

At the breakfast table, Javier told me the plan was to stay here for a while. There's no definitive time-line. Dad's given Johnny false information about his whereabouts to see if he passes it on to anyone else.

Dad's also set to have meetings with a couple of the other bosses, and for those encounters, Javier is going with him.

I guess my dad is hoping to gain favor with a few important people using certain business deals, in the hope to get more information about what's going on behind his back.

In the meantime, I'm stuck in a house in the middle of the forest. We have TV and we have our phones, and even though I never went out much before, knowing that I *can't* leave is going to bother me.

As I'm cleaning my plate, I say, "I have food that's gonna go bad in my fridge."

"Then don't eat it when you get back."

I roll my eyes. "I can't go back to throw it out? Or my trash? I should've brought some books with me."

"I'm sure there's a bible in one of these rooms."

"I doubt it. It's not a hotel, and that's not what I meant. I don't have any form of entertainment here."

"You're not going back there," he says with finality. "We don't know what could be waiting for you."

"You think Johnny is trying to get me killed? Why would he do that? What would my death do for him?"

"It's probably less about you and more to do with your dad."

"It still doesn't make sense. I don't think he's the one who gave me up."

Javier looks at me from the kitchen table. "Johnny didn't send me to your house to pick you up."

"What do you mean? You said you were my ride."

"Which was true, but my orders came from Cortez. Johnny had someone else coming to pick you up. That call was overheard by someone your dad trusts, and the information was passed on. Your dad was already suspicious of Johnny, so he had me get you before the other guy got there.

"Johnny didn't have orders to get you picked up and taken anywhere. Those were his own orders. Now why would he do that? Why wouldn't he talk to Cortez?"

"So you're saying the guy Johnny was gonna have to pick me up was actually going to kill me?"

"The phone call that was overheard between Johnny and whoever he has working for him, also included the location where you were to be taken. It was one of the safehouses we have. He likely was going to use you as ransom to get Cortez over there."

I shake my head. "I still don't understand why."

Javier shrugs. "Doesn't matter. In this life, it could be anything and nothing at all. Maybe he wants to be boss.

Maybe he felt disrespected by your father. Maybe he's in debt to someone and the way to save his own life is to do a job someone else wants done."

We fall into silence while I lean against the counter, trying to make sense of my dad's best friend of thirty plus years turning on him and pulling me into the crossfire.

"You think you could do this?" Javier asks. His tone doesn't hold judgment. Just curiosity.

I meet his gaze. "No."

"That's probably the best answer. Overconfidence usually leads to mistakes, and mistakes are deadly."

"Inexperience could be deadly too."

He nods. "Would you rather go back to the church?"

I hesitate for several seconds. "I don't know."

"Probably something to think about."

I nod. "Yeah."

He stands from the table and makes his way upstairs while I stay in place, thinking about what I should do if I survive this ordeal.

I didn't want to become a priest, but it hasn't been bad, job wise. I don't believe in all the teachings of the church. I don't think I'm a sinner for being gay. I don't want to be celibate the rest of my life, but I know the job. I know the people, and I like them. I enjoy feeling like I'm helping others.

However, I do often feel hypocritical when I preach about asking for forgiveness and holding yourself accountable. I'm well aware of all the terrible things my dad has done, and there's probably plenty more I don't know about. Anyone who believes in heaven would know my father wouldn't be welcome. And yet, I'll never hold him accountable. I'll never tell anyone what he does. Am I capable of preaching the word of God if I can also be okay with murder at the hands of someone I love? Or someone I'm sleeping with?

I've had two different lives in the same lifetime. I grew up aware of my dad's doings and dealings. I knew he was involved in criminal activity, but it was normal to me. You grow up accustomed to the world you're brought up in. When Dad told me I'd be going to seminary school, I was devastated. I wanted to be just like him. I was already starting the journey before I got caught with another guy.

But in my adult life, I've stayed away from all of that. I've studied the Bible and God's word. I've been told that everything I've ever known and been was wrong and a sin. I'm aware that I have one foot in the light and one in the dark. I could go either direction and know enough to grow and thrive in each.

I just have to choose.

Snapping out of my thoughts, I walk toward the living room, ready to settle in for a day of TV watching, but Javier's footsteps get my attention. I look up toward the loft area where he struts across wearing only his boxer briefs.

He's the embodiment of sin. His body is carved into muscular perfection. Not body-builder massive in size, but very much in shape. To add to his physique are the eye-catching tattoos that cover his skin. And though I try not to stare, the front of his boxer briefs leave little to the imagination. Luckily, or perhaps, unluckily for me, I know what he's working with already. If I didn't know and was just catching a glimpse of him in his underwear, there would be no question that he's quite endowed.

When my eyes finally travel back upward, he sends me a wink, already watching me.

He keeps moving, heading toward the bathroom where I hear the shower turn on.

The temptation to sin and take another step into the dark is getting stronger. Sure, I already had sex once, but I could leave it at that and go back to St. Joseph's. I could re-dedicate my life to God and never do it again.

Memories of last night flash through my head. His body. His cock. His cum on my stomach, and his tongue in my ass. The grunts and moans he made, and the way he made me feel.

My dick twitches in my pants, waking up as I continue to relive that moment.

I *could* go back to abstaining.

Or I could have a little fun.

CHAPTER 28

Around nine-thirty, after we've had dinner, Javier brings a glass of whisky to the couch. He props his socked feet on the coffee table and tunes into the show that's on TV.

Out of my periphery, I see his head turn in my direction a couple of times, but he never says anything. He's just looking at me.

We've had normal conversations throughout the day, but it's been limited. We're both aware of the situation we're in. We're alone in a house far away from anyone else, and there are no longer any secrets between us.

I know he's into me, and he knows I'm into him. We've already had sex, but now my father sits figuratively between us.

He's my dad, but he's Javier's boss and maybe friend. Javier respects my father, and while his respect didn't extend to the cloth or even the vow I took, he clearly takes my dad more seriously.

The truth is, I don't know what my dad would do if he found out, but I definitely care less than Javier.

A few minutes later, Javier's phone rings. He picks it up from the table next to him and glances at the screen before answering.

"Hello?"

From my side of the couch I can hear my dad's voice on the other end.

"Yeah, everything is all good over here."

I put my phone down and scoot over. We're on a loveseat, so there's not a lot of space between us as is, but I get close enough to him that I can lean over his lap and reach for the remote on the table.

He eyes me as I do this and I give him a grin.

Javier clears his throat and stands up. "Have you talked to Johnny yet?"

I watch with amusement as he begins to walk toward the kitchen, trying to put space between us.

"Oh. Yeah, I thought that might be the case," he continues. "No, sir."

With a huff, I push myself up from the couch and follow him. He's facing the cabinets, his fingers drumming on the counter as he listens to my dad.

I walk up behind him and place my hand on his back as I lean in and reach for the knob to pull open the cabinet.

"Excuse me," I say quietly near his free ear.

He goes stiff, but I step to the side to reach into the fridge for a bottle of juice. After I pour it and return the bottle to its place, I lean against the opposite counter and take a drink.

Javier doesn't take his eyes off of me. I put down the glass on the counter and step toward him. His brows furrow as I invade his space completely.

"Yeah. I agree," he says into the phone. "No, he asked about that, but I said no."

I lift a brow, knowing he's talking about me. He shakes his head.

My hands go to the waistband of his pants, fingers dipping inside. "Are you saying no again?" I ask quietly.

"What was that?" he asks. "Oh. So nobody's heard yet?"

One hand slips into his pants, and my palm runs over the front of his boxer-briefs. He grabs my arm but holds me in place rather than pushing me away. His face is stern as he watches me, but he can't say anything right now.

"I'll let him know." He pauses, listening to my dad as he studies my face. "Yes. He seems a little stubborn."

My lips flatten into a thin line and I pull my hand back. Javier's quick though, and he steps around me, pushing me into the counter as he positions himself behind me, trapping me in place.

"Yeah, I'd hate for him to misread the situation."

The statement is for both me and my father.

"Okay, I'll talk to you tomorrow."

The phone clatters on the counter next to me, and Javier's hands go to my hips as he leans over my back.

"What do you think you're doing?"

"I thought it was obvious. Or were you misreading the situation?"

Javier spins me around, our bodies mashed together. "I told you it would feel weird to fuck my boss's son. I didn't say I wouldn't continue to do so."

I scrape my teeth along my bottom lip. "You said he'd kill you."

"If he found out, but you were the one who said it wasn't going to happen again, and now you're over here groping me while I'm on the phone with the man that would take my life for fucking you."

When I don't reply, he continues.

"You want the power. I can see that. You've always felt like everything was out of your control, so you want to pull the strings and get me to do what you think I don't want to do. You want to disrespect your dad even if he doesn't know what it is you're doing. But here's the thing you might not realize, Carlo. I'm all for playing games, and I'll be your puppet if you're wanting to use me, but you need to make a clear decision on whether this is truly what you want to get into. I don't want to deal with your Christian guilt. I know I'm a sinner, but I'm not trying to be saved, and I think you're still trying to decide if you can be."

He steps away, giving me space. "I'm leaving tomorrow to be with Cortez as he meets with another boss. You have to stay here."

As soon as I nod, he walks away, heading upstairs. Once again, the power I thought I'd have is stripped away from me, and I'm a little less than happy about it.

CHAPTER 29

J avier left fairly early in the day, because he had to drive two hours to where my father is staying. They had plans to talk to a few people and check into a few business deals before needing to drive another three hours to meet with the boss of the Mancini family.

It's already a quarter past nine at night, and I haven't heard anything. I don't know if any of these meetings went bad. I don't know if whoever is after us found them and they're both already dead, and the lack of communication is starting to wear on me.

However, having all day to myself has been nice. It's been a day full of reflection and thought. And now, as I'm worried that something might have happened to Javier or my father, the emotions swirling inside me add an additional layer to my thought process.

Because not only do I fear my dad dying, regardless of our tumultuous relationship, I now have to be concerned about where that puts me. And if Javier is also killed, I'm left with no one I can trust.

A sense of disappointment also floods my brain,

because as cliché as it is, life is short. We don't know when we can go, but in this life, your odds of dying early are greater. I've had one experience with Javier, and thinking that could be the only one is like a fire under my ass. I have to make a decision and stop pussyfooting around.

My parish is large, and considering the town is small, almost everyone knows who I am. I'll never find a guy willing to look past the priesthood in order to have a secret hookup with me.

But it's not even about knowing I'll never find a random guy to sleep with. I don't want a random guy. It's Javier. He's the one I'm interested in. He doesn't care about the fact that I'm a priest. He wouldn't care about my dad's profession, even if he didn't know him, and it's for the same reason I don't judge what he does. It's what we know.

Yes, we seem very different, but are we?

At nine-forty, my phone rings. I quickly go to snatch it up, but freeze when I see Johnny's name on the screen. I ignore it and decide to text my dad. I was trying to avoid reaching out due to the nature of their meetings today, but this is important.

> Johnny's calling me.

I DON'T HAVE to wait long for a reply. About two minutes later, my phone rings.

"Hello?"

"It's me," Javier says, calling from my dad's phone.

"Do I call him back?"

"Not yet."

"I've never not answered one of his calls. If anything, I've always had to wait for him to get back to me. He might get suspicious."

"We're getting in touch with someone who should be around him. We found the guy he sent to pick you up. Talked to him for a little while."

"*Talked* to him?"

"He's not saying much anymore."

That statement is loaded.

"So, it was Johnny."

"Yes, but there's a lot more information we have. I can't talk about it right now, but I'd say Johnny is reaching desperation at this point, and that's not good."

"I think I have an idea."

"We can talk about it later. Don't answer his calls and don't call him back. Wait until I'm there."

"When will that be?"

"A couple hours maybe."

"Okay."

He ends the call, and a text from Johnny immediately comes through.

> Hey, kid. You okay? My guy said you weren't home yesterday.
>
> I'm afraid you might be in danger.

I sigh as I read them over and over. I can't believe a man I thought of as an uncle when I was growing up is trying to get me killed. The betrayal sends fury through my veins. I can only imagine how my dad feels.

Javier and my dad don't want me making decisions without them, but I know going silent will only draw suspicion and I have to keep Johnny from suspecting that I know anything.

I think it over for almost two hours before I type out a response.

I'm okay for now, but I think you might be right.

I PUT the phone down just as Javier walks through the door. He looks exhausted as he makes his way to the kitchen sink.

"You okay?" I ask.

He nods, turning on the water.

When I come to a stop next to him, I can see the dried blood on his knuckles and around his fingernails.

My eyes flicker up to his face but he doesn't look in my direction. I grab a couple paper towels and hand them to him when he finishes scrubbing his hands.

"I'm glad you're alive," I say, actually feeling the relief in my chest.

He turns, his lips curving up on one side. "Oh yeah?"

I nod. "I was worried. Just for a second."

Javier chuckles. "You ever worry about me before? When I'd disappear on you for days or weeks?"

"No."

"Hmm."

I slide my hands under his jacket, pushing the material over his shoulders. He shrugs it off until it falls to the floor. I put my fingers under the leather straps of his holster, and I wonder which gun he used today, or if he used one at all.

Javier expertly removes the holster, laying it on the counter, his eyes never leaving my face.

My hands curve around his waist, but my fingers bump into something along the back of his belt.

"Knife," he says simply. "It's sheathed horizontally. You won't cut yourself."

I move past it and run my hands up the middle of his back. "I really hope my father doesn't kill you."

He grins, understanding what I'm saying. "Try to make it worth it then."

I look into his eyes and then move in closer, my lips hovering in front of his for a few seconds before they meet.

CHAPTER 30

His tongue parts my lips, slipping into my mouth and across my tongue. My fingers dig into his back as I return the kiss. Besides the quick peck on my lips he gave me the last time we had sex, this is the first *real* kiss I've had in about ten years.

Javier wraps one arm around my back, pushing me into him as a low, hungry growl rumbles in his throat. A moan leaves my lips, and he swallows the sound as he sucks my tongue into his mouth.

My knees go weak.

He crowds me, walking me into a corner. When my head hits the wall, he pulls away and begins kissing and licking my neck. I groan as my hands travel to his hair, tugging on the dark strands.

"I think we should go to my room," he says against my ear while his hand slips under my shirt.

"Okay." The word comes out breathy.

Javier pulls away enough to look me in the eye before cradling my jaw in his hand and planting another kiss on my lips. Hungrily, I slide my tongue into his mouth, one hand going to the back of his head, while the other rests on the small of his back.

Our kiss borders on rough, but I revel in it. I love the feel of his facial hair on my skin, and the deep, sensual noises he makes as he grinds into me. His teeth find my bottom lip and sink in.

"Fuck. Let's go," he says, taking my wrist and rushing to the stairs.

As soon as we cross the threshold of his room, he's kicking off his shoes and undoing his pants, so I remove my shirt and shove my sweats down my legs.

Our bodies crash together, hands exploring, tongues tasting. This is already very different from last time. Last time, I was hesitant. I was still trying to have self-control. Now, neither one of us seems to have any. We're frenzied and desperate.

We stumble toward his bed, and when the backs of my knees hit the mattress, I drop to my ass. He stands in front of me and pushes his boxer-briefs down.

His cock springs free, stealing my attention. I study the size of it, wanting to run my tongue along the shaft and wrap my lips around his engorged tip.

"I'm not sure how good I'll be," I admit, "But I want to try."

His eyes flash with excitement and he begins to slowly stroke himself. "I'll talk you through it," he says with a smirk.

When he steps forward, I lean closer, reaching for his shaft with my right hand. I give it a few languid tugs before swiping my bottom lip with my tongue and opening my mouth.

My lips encircle him, my tongue undulating underneath his tip before I swirl it around the entire head.

"Oh, yeah," he groans.

I start taking him farther across my tongue, his length filling my mouth before I can reach the base.

"That's it," he says, voice low and rough. "Take it as far as you can." He groans."Fuck, your mouth is so soft."

I begin to ease back and forth along the shaft, trying to get a little more with each venture forward. His hand runs through my hair, resting at the crown of my head.

"You can do it," he says. "A little more."

His confidence spurs me on, and I grab ahold of his thighs as I take him deeper.

"So fucking good," he moans.

I pull back when I'm afraid my gag reflex is going to get triggered, but I continue the blowjob with fervor. I stroke and suck simultaneously. I ease away entirely, just to run my tongue all the way to the base to get the whole thing wet.

Javier begins moving his hips, fucking my mouth as I grip his waist with one hand.

"Oh, you're doing so good. So good," he repeats with a groan.

After another minute, I pull away, my lips and chin wet.

He swipes at my face with his thumb, cleaning me up. "My turn. Lie down."

I scoot up the bed and watch as he climbs over me, looking like a predator about to pounce. His eyes are dark and narrow, raking over my body. His muscles flex as he moves, making the dark flames of his tattoo appear to flicker. Within the swirls and lines that look like lightning are skulls, flowers, and other objects, but I lose interest as soon as I feel the warmth of his mouth on my lower stomach.

His lips dance along the V lines before planting kisses

all the way down to my shaft until he gets to the tip. I watch as he opens his mouth and takes me in.

Javier glances up at my face as he devours me, which really elevates the moment. He bobs up and down with experience, his tongue moving in ways I'm not sure I can fathom. When he eases back to the tip, he flicks his tongue along the underside and it brings my back off the mattress.

"Oh God," I cry out, head back and fists grappling for the covers. His tongue travels down the shaft, reaching my balls. "Oh, oh," I say, my breath coming in staccato bursts.

I'm not sure how much time goes by, because my brain flies off into the clouds as he explores every part of me, but I come back to myself when he begins to climb over my body.

"I'm not opposed to switching," he says, taking a break to nibble at my neck. "But I really want to fuck you again."

I grab his hair in my hand, shoving him back into my neck where he sucks the flesh into his mouth.

With a wanton moan, I say, "Okay."

Javier moves, but he grabs my face in his hand, his fingers along my jaw as his thumb is on my chin. He kisses me like he knows how much I want him to. I nearly melt into the bed, but then he's up and moving.

He brings a condom and some lube from his end table.

"A little presumptuous to be so prepared."

His lips form a smug grin. "Hopeful."

In between my legs, he pours lube onto his fingers and begins rubbing it around my hole.

"Are you still sore?" he asks.

"Would it change things?"

He smiles. "I'd be a little gentler."

I bite into my lip. "No. I'm not sore."

Javier slides two fingers inside me, eliciting a gasp and moan from my throat.

"A naughty fucking priest," he says with amusement. "How'd I get so lucky?"

"Maybe God answered your prayers," I say with a smirk.

He laughs. "Did your god know this would happen then?"

"Everything happens according to His plan," I say, gasping as he goes deeper with his fingers.

"Fuck," Javier groans. "Keep saying shit like that. It turns me on."

"You want me to tell you how the body is meant for the Lord and not for sexual immorality?"

He removes his fingers and grabs the condom. "I think your body is meant for me." He covers his length and pours more lube into his hand. "I think I have a religious kink. Is that a thing?"

"Hierophilia maybe. Or blasphemy kink," I say as he takes my cock in his hand and strokes.

"Mm. Well, I'm about to be very, very sexually immoral with you."

I bite down on my lip as he begins to enter me. "I'll pray for you."

He groans. "God, I'm fucked up."

Javier slides in with less caution than last time, burying himself deep inside in just a few seconds.

"Oh fuck," I moan.

"Language, Father."

I drag my nails down his back as he moves, stretching me wider.

"You like having my cock in your ass, don't you?"

"Yes," I cry. "You feel so good."

Javier manipulates my body in ways that always seem to add to the pleasure. When he pushes my legs back, his cock goes impossibly deep. When he stops, fully inserted inside me, he rotates his hips and allows me to feel just how full I am. He licks his palm and strokes my cock while one of my legs is on his shoulder, and the combination nearly makes my brain explode.

"Turn over. I wanna see this ass."

On my hands and knees, he palms my cheeks, spreading me apart as he slows his movements.

The wet sound of the lube as he drives in and out combined with the slap of his body against my ass is like a beautiful symphony.

"Your hole is trying to hold me hostage," he says. "But you're gaping so beautifully for me."

Words I never thought I'd hear, let alone be affected by, now have me moaning and preening, happy that I'm pleasing him.

I reach down and grab my dick, giving myself the friction I need while he pumps in and out of me.

"Oh yeah, stroke that big cock of yours," he says.

With my ass in the air, I drop my face into the pillow, biting down on the material as my fist moves faster over my shaft.

"Fuck, Javi. Yes, deeper. Harder."

A growl rumbles behind me and his fingers dig into my hips as he obeys my instructions. "Look at you," he pants. "A needy slut now."

"Yes, yes."

My orgasm builds as he continues talking.

"You want me to use you every day, don't you?"

"Yes," I pant. "Oh god, I want it all the time."

"I'll give you anything you want any time you want it, *cariño*."

"Oh fuck," I grunt, my back bowing.

"That's it. Spray that cum all over my bed."

"Yes, yes. I'm about to come. I'm, I'm...I'm gonna com—come," I yell, body tensing as my orgasm shoots out of me.

"Fuck yeah," Javier says, smacking my ass. "That's what I like to hear."

Moans and grunts are ripped from my throat as Javier begins moving faster. I'm breathless, my bones turning to Jell-O, but I remain upright as he fucks me.

"Come," I tell him. "I wanna know how it feels when you come inside me."

"Oh, baby," he grunts.

"Please, please, please," I beg. "Give it to me."

A few seconds later, Javier gasps. "Oh fuck. I'm coming. I'm coming. I'm..." He cries out, his voice husky as he holds me tight, his cock twitching deep inside me as his release pours out of him.

He moves out then pushes back in, his dick still spasming with the aftershocks of his orgasm.

We both pant heavily, trying to catch our breath as we slowly break apart. When he pulls out of me, I collapse to my side, avoiding the mess I made earlier. Javier gets out of bed to discard the condom, then he's right next to me.

"Next time," he says, taking a few seconds to suck in some deep breaths. "Next time I fuck you, I don't want to use a condom.

I stare at him before nodding. "Okay."

"I want my cum to fill you up until it starts dripping out."

I squirm, teeth digging into my lip. "Okay."

"You like that idea?" he questions with a grin.

"Maybe."

He smiles. "While we're adding things to our to-do list, I really want to fuck you with your garments on."

I make a face. "Are you serious?"

"You thought I was teasing when I said your priestly garb did it for me. Hell, I thought I was teasing. But shit, I'm gonna get turned on again thinking about it."

I chuckle and shake my head. "You wanna be on your knees under my robe?"

His eyes flash with excitement. "Hell yeah. I wanna go back to the church and do blasphemous things in the confessional. I wanna spread you open on the altar and have my way with you."

I shift, reaching for his thigh. "You're obscene."

"Absolutely debauched."

"There's no heaven waiting for you."

He runs his hand up my stomach. "As long as *you're* waiting for me, there is."

My lips twitch. "Guess we should get cleaned up."

"Yeah," he says, rolling out of bed. "My covers are fucked."

"Well, sleep in my room tonight. You can wash them tomorrow."

"Okay." He goes to the bathroom that sits between our bedrooms, so I grab my clothes and head for the one downstairs.

"When I pass the kitchen, I swipe my phone from the counter and read the screen. I have a text from Johnny.

Where are you? I think we need to talk. Not everything is what it seems.

CHAPTER 31

"So, what happened yesterday?" I ask Javier as we sit at the table eating our breakfast.

He finishes chewing his eggs and takes a gulp of orange juice before replying. "Johnny's driver is the one that was supposed to get you the other night. We found him, and after some *encouraging* got him to spill the truth. Turns out, Johnny's ambition got the best of him. He promised the boss of the Bonetti family something that he did not get Cortez's approval on. When Cortez shot it down, Johnny was stuck between a rock and hard place. The Bonettis were promised a piece of Cortez's trafficking business, but unbeknownst to Johnny, Cortez was already in talks with the Mancini family about expanding with them. When the Bonetti family found out, they were pissed." He stops to tear off a piece of toast and pick up a pile of eggs with it before popping it into his mouth. "To sum up, the Bonettis boss—Sammy, told Johnny to do whatever was necessary to make sure they got their hands on those drugs. It's a lucrative business, and they weren't about to miss out. Johnny's plan was to work with the

Bonettis foot soldiers to have Cortez incapacitated enough that Johnny would have to step in as boss and he could change the order of business."

"Incapacitated?"

"The driver said Johnny didn't want Cortez dead, just hurt badly enough that he'd be in the hospital a while."

I shake my head, anger rolling down my back. "That..." I take a breath. "Okay, that pisses me off, but where do you come into play?"

"That's the Bonetti family as well. According to the meeting we had yesterday, the Mancinis don't care as much. As long as I'm not hired to take out anyone in their family, they won't make a fuss about it. The other family is farther out and less likely to get involved. Johnny inflated the story so Cortez wouldn't solely focus on the Bonettis."

"And Johnny revealing who I am to the Bonettis was simply what? A bargaining chip?"

"You were to be held for ransom. The assumption was that your dad would find out you were in danger and he'd rush over there and be hurt in the process."

I huff out a breath, my food forgotten as I listen. Johnny was really okay with both my dad and I being hurt or killed simply because he got ahead of himself and thought he could make boss decisions.

"Okay, so what's the plan then?"

"While Cortez is concerned about all of our lives, Alberto—the boss of the Mancinis, is concerned about the business. It benefits him to have your dad alive. They are talking to other people about how to go about taking out Sammy."

"The boss? Is that possible?"

Javier shrugs. "If you get the okay from enough of the top guys you can get away with it. It won't just be Sammy though. It'll likely be the underboss, and some of their most loyal capos. We'll have to dismantle that family to keep them in line and hope they don't try to retaliate. There's a guy who is most likely to take over, and your dad has a plan to offer him something to keep their relationship cordial. He has to talk to him and hope he doesn't tell the higher-ups what's going on."

"Sounds risky."

"Everything about this life is risky, but if your dad can take down the boss of the most vicious family, then his family gains more respect. Everyone will wonder what he's capable of, and fear is what keeps people in line."

I absorb all this information, trying to imagine how it'll all go down.

"What about Johnny?"

"We think he knows Cortez suspects him of something. Johnny isn't answering his calls. He sends him excuses via texts but avoids seeing him face to face or listening to what he has to say. I doubt he'll agree to meet up. He has to know something happened to his driver at this point."

I think about the texts Johnny sent me. I still haven't told Javier about them.

"Johnny knows my dad and I aren't close. Our relationship has been rocky for a while, so if I were to talk to Johnny and tell him—"

"No," Javier says immediately, standing up with his plate. "You are not going to see him."

I get up and follow him to the kitchen. "Listen. I can tell Johnny I don't know what's up with my dad. I can say he's been acting weird and I'm confused about what's going on, and he won't think twice about it."

"What's that gonna do, Carlo?" he asks, putting his plate down on the counter with a clatter. "He's going to lie to you and then he's going to hurt you. He'll take you to the Bonettis, and trust me, you do not want to be their captive." Javier crosses his arms over his chest. "We'll wait until we can take down the Bonetti guys. Then he won't have anyone to take you to."

"How long is that gonna take?"

"I don't know."

"And what if he leaves beforehand? There's no way my dad is going to keep up appearances with him for weeks or months. He's going to know something is wrong and he'll either run or he'll be forced to take matters in his own hands. And he cannot get away with this. He cannot! And if he kills my dad..." My chest heaves with angry breaths, but I don't finish the sentence.

Javier watches me carefully, a look in his eyes I can't quite read.

"And what is your plan?" he finally asks.

"Well, Johnny texted me last night."

Javier stands up straight, his arms dropping to his sides. "What? What did he say?"

"He asked where I was. He told me things aren't what they seemed. Said he was worried I was in danger."

He shakes his head and begins marching toward his phone. "When your dad finds out—"

"No!" I say. "Don't tell him yet." Javier stops and looks at me like I'm crazy. "I responded to him. Said I thought he was right but that I was okay. I'm keeping up appearances. I can do it better than my dad."

"Carlo." He grinds my name out through his teeth.

"We can set a trap. I can talk to him and let him think I don't know anything. I'll tell him that whatever my dad told me scared me, so I found somewhere to stay away from it all. We lure him to us."

"He could bring someone from the Bonettis with him."

"Then we can take care of them at the same time."

His lips twitch briefly. "Look, it won't be as easy as you're making it seem."

"He's dangerous. You said it yourself. Desperation isn't good."

He hesitates enough to grant me hope.

"I still have to tell your dad."

"Fine, but tell him you think it's a good idea too."

He gives me a look like he isn't quite sure it is, but then he turns around and gets his phone from the table. Instead of making the call in front of me, he goes outside.

After fifteen minutes, I peek out one of the windows and see him walking around, the phone still pressed to his ear. I decide to go to my room where I continue thinking about the decisions that need to be made, and what the outcome of those decisions could be.

Something has to be done, I know that. We won't go back to our normal lives until the situation with Johnny and the Bonettis is done.

Johnny's betrayal means death. I've come to terms with that. I don't even struggle with that fact. As a priest, I should be doing everything in my power to dissuade Javier or my father from killing him. I should preach about forgiveness and allowing God to handle it.

As Cortez's son, I know there's no such thing as forgiveness. My father plays God in this situation, and as a could-be victim, I'm having a hard time finding it within myself to let this go.

However, as I play with the crucifix that hangs from a thin chain and rests against my chest, I hear bible verses in my head.

For if you forgive other people when they sin against you, your heavenly Father will also forgive you.

The Lord our God is merciful and forgiving, even though we have rebelled against him.

"What're you thinkin' about?" Javier asks from the doorway of my bedroom. He eyes the cross between my fingers before meeting my gaze.

"Forgiveness."

He walks in and drops to his knees at the side of the bed, reaching for the cross. "Tell me a verse."

With a sigh, I stare up at the ceiling and recite one aloud.

"Be kind and compassionate to one another, forgiving each other, just as in Christ God has forgiven you."

Javier's quiet for a while, and when I turn my head to look at him, I find he's already staring at me.

"I told you when I was in the confessional that I have my own rules to abide by, and they don't fall in line with your god's rules. I'll never change my ways. I'll never be made to feel like I have to earn someone's forgiveness when it's they who should seek mine. We'll always remain on opposite sides here, Carlo. I don't believe in a god, and if there is one, he doesn't deserve my idolation. Not with the way the world looks." He drops the chain and then crawls into bed next to me. "Anyway, your dad is thinking over the plan."

My head snaps in his direction. "Really?"

"He'll get back to me on it, but that's about as much hope as you can get."

I gaze up at the ceiling. "It's not a no."

We lay side by side in silence for a while, our arms touching.

"I have to go back home tomorrow."

I turn to look at him. "For what?"

"Cortez has work to do in the city. I go where he goes."

I study his profile for a while. "You'd die for my dad, wouldn't you?"

"My job is to protect him."

"It's more than that."

"Of course it is. I do what he needs me to do, but I'm also there as his protection. If someone decides to lunge at him, I rush in to stop that from happening."

"And if someone shoots at him?"

"I get him out of the way."

"But you could get shot in the process."

"Do you want me to let him die?" he asks, turning to look at me.

I don't answer right away, but not because I want him to let my dad die, but because I'm trying to wrap my head around what I'll eventually face.

"I think I'm just now realizing that I'll lose one of you, and it'll be because of the other person."

Javier's brows furrow. "What do you mean?"

"If Dad dies, it'll be because you didn't protect him. If you die, it'll be because you were either protecting him or doing a job he sent you to do."

"Could you forgive either?" he asks after several seconds.

"I'm not sure."

He nods. "It's a cruel world, but Cortez is your dad, and the boss of the family. Who am I? I don't have a family to mourn me. There is no choice. If it's me or him, I'll save him. For you. For the people who depend on him."

My heart swells at his selflessness, but it also breaks, because he doesn't think he's worthy of life.

I slide my hand into his. "I don't want to be left to mourn you."

He runs his thumb across my skin, giving my hand a slight squeeze. "You haven't seen me in action. I'm pretty good at what I do," he says with a small smile. "I doubt I'll die."

I grin, but it's not authentic. He's trying to skirt past the topic. "Okay," I reply.

He turns to his side and brings my hand to his lips, planting a kiss on my knuckles. "We'll all be okay."

Another forced smile graces my mouth, because as much as he wants to try to give me some peace, I know it's not true. There's no way we get out of this unscathed. Even if we make it through this with our lives, someone's heart is going to be broken, and I have a feeling it'll be mine.

CHAPTER 32

I didn't realize I had fallen asleep until I open my eyes. With a stretch, I turn onto my back and find that Javier is gone. I wonder if he's already on his way to the city, and the thought of being here alone for an indefinite amount of time fills me with dread.

Getting up from the bed, I make my way to the Jack and Jill bathroom that connects mine and Javier's rooms. His door is open, and with just a quick glance, I can tell it's been emptied of his belongings.

I pull the waist of my sweatpants down and reach into them for my cock, aiming at the bowl.

"Ah, you're awake."

Javier's voice makes me jump, pee hitting the back of the toilet.

"Holy shit," I exclaim, re-aiming.

He's next to me, lingering in the doorway as his gaze lowers to watch.

"You mind?"

He grins. "I definitely don't."

I look back at the toilet to make sure I'm not making a mess, then my eyes flicker back up at him to find him still engrossed in the action.

"You got any other kinks I should know about?"

He laughs. "Plenty. You're probably not ready for them."

I finish up and flush the toilet, moving to the sink. "Does that mean you've been holding back on me?"

Javier walks in, coming to a stop at my back, his hands resting on the counter as he traps me between his arms.

Through the reflection, he stares at me. "Until recently, you hadn't had sex in years. I don't know what teenage experiences you had, but those were teenage boys. I'm not sure you're ready for me to unload all of my fantasies, fetishes, and kinks on you. Most of what I'm into is normal to me, but you might be scandalized."

I shut off the water. "You do remember the scourge, right?"

He leans in and kisses my neck. "Oh, that's right. We should put that to use soon."

I tilt my head to the side as a sign for him to keep doing it. "So, tell me something you think would scandalize me."

"There's nothing specific, *cariño*," he says, biting down on my flesh. "I'm just a little rough. Spanking, choking, hair pulling. I want to see you gag on my cock until tears stream down your face. I want to edge you until you're begging me to fuck you." His hands slide around my waist, dropping to my cock, massaging it outside my pants. "There won't be much I'll be opposed to."

"What if the roles were reversed?" I ask, arching my back and pushing my ass into him. "What if it was you who was gagging? What if I was choking you?"

He grins, his chin resting on my shoulder. "I guess you'll

have to try it out." He steps back and spanks my ass. "Now, go get packed."

"What?" I ask, turning around and drying my hands on my pants.

"Pack your stuff. We're gonna leave soon."

"I'm going with you?"

He gives me a look like he thinks I'm ridiculous for thinking otherwise. "Of course. I'm not gonna be able to be here, and you're not staying by yourself."

"Where will I stay?"

"At my house."

My brows lift. "Oh."

"It's safe and I'll get to go home to you when I'm not working."

I nod and he struts toward the door. "I'll meet you downstairs."

"Okay."

As I start gathering my belongings from the bathroom, I try not to dwell on how *I'll get to go home to you* made me feel like a jolt of electricity just ran through my body.

After double and triple checking my room and bathroom, I take my suitcase downstairs and find Javier sitting in the accent chair with his ankle resting on his knee, and a cup of coffee in one hand while his other holds his phone.

I think briefly about how domesticated he looks. A regular man drinking coffee while entertaining himself on his phone.

Then he sees me and stands up, his holster already in place, ink crawling down his muscled arms, leading to hands that are responsible for the deaths of many people. No, he's not a regular man, and I find myself glad that he's not.

"Ready?" he asks, placing his coffee mug on the table and pocketing his phone.

I start moving, my feet carrying me toward him like they have a mind of their own. He looks only slightly confused as I get closer without responding to him. I wrap my arm around his back, pushing him into me as my other hand brushes across his jaw, cradling his face as I lean in to press my lips against his.

What I thought would be a quick peck, transforms when I realize I'm not ready to pull away from him. He puts his hands on my hips, holding me tight, and I part his lips with my tongue, tasting the sweetened coffee flavor inside.

Javier moans into mouth, pulling away to say, "Keep it up and we won't be able to leave."

I smile, resting my forehead on his. "Sorry."

"Never apologize for that."

Stepping away, I say, "Yes, I'm ready."

"Okay. Let's get on the road then."

✝

AN HOUR INTO THE DRIVE, as I'm staring out the window, I feel Javier's hand land on my thigh. He gives it a squeeze, and my stomach flips, chest warming. God, he's already made me a fiend. A simple touch and I'm ready to strip down.

"You okay?" he asks.

"Yeah. Just thinking," I reply, covering his hand with mine.

"We have to see your dad first."

And any thought of stripping goes out the window.

"All right," I say.

"Before we go to my place, we can stop by yours so you can get anything else you might need."

I perk up a little. "Okay, thanks."

We're outside Crest Haven by about forty minutes, but Javier takes a left turn heading east toward the coast.

"I have a question," I say, cutting into the silence.

"Okay."

"You told me you went to St. Joseph's because of a work related thing. Now that I know what work you do, can you tell me the issue that brought you in?"

Javier's quiet for a few seconds. "I knew I was the reason your dad was getting pushback from people. And," he pauses, like he's contemplating telling me something. "Well, Cortez had mentioned in passing that he wouldn't see the issue if I did join the family."

"Wha—" I start.

"Hold on," he says, squeezing my thigh. "It wasn't a conversation. He didn't formally ask me. He was ranting about something someone said, and it felt sort of like a flippant response. It stuck with me a while, and because I knew that our exclusive working relationship was causing issues, I wondered if maybe this was something I needed to reevaluate. My proximity to him was bringing in issues he didn't need, and I was thinking maybe I could do something else. Plus, I've been lying and hiding my whole life, just like you."

"But you've dated women before, right?"

Javier glances at me. "Well, I don't date, but yes, since I'm also attracted to women, being seen with them has helped, but it also means I don't get many opportunities to explore my attraction to men."

I angle toward him in my seat. "How many men have you actually been with?"

"A few. Mostly when I leave town."

I nod. "Okay, so, you were feeling torn about working exclusively with my dad?"

"That, and because of the comment he made, I knew it had the potential to grow into a bigger issue."

"So, you were just seeking guidance?"

He glances over and grins. "I was leaving the store and walking back to my car, saw the church steeple across the street, and thought of my dad and how he would tell me that if Mami wanted to go to church, I was to go with her. He would say, 'she finds peace there. I don't have to understand it, but if she wants you to go, go.'"

I smile. "So, you went with your mom?"

"Not always, but yes. I guess at that moment, I wondered if I could also find peace there."

"I'm not sure I helped you with finding peace."

He laughs. "That's not altogether your fault, but I did end up telling Cortez I didn't have interest in having a bigger role than I already do. I told him I'd leave if it meant calming the storm, but he wouldn't hear it."

I nod, but can't help but dwell on the fact that my dad was willing to make so many changes for him. He must respect and like Javier as much as Javier respects and likes him. If he were to not only find out about Javier's sexual preferences, but also what we've been up to, I worry it would ruin their relationship. I shake my head, choosing to worry about that another time.

"Can I ask what happened to your parents? Or is that—"

"It's fine," he replies. "My mom was killed in a car accident. She was on her way to church, and a drunk driver slammed into her."

"Oh my god," I whisper. "That's awful."

"It's just another reason I question the existence of an

all-good, all-knowing, all-powerful God. Because she was a church going woman. She did nothing wrong. She left my father when she found out what he did. She took care of me and prayed every day. At meals, at night. She was the best person I've known. Why her? Why like that?"

I know he's not truly asking, and I can feel the pain in his words. A lot of people question their faith in times of tragedies. Nothing I could say would make him feel better, so I keep quiet.

He lets out a huff. "Anyway, that happened when I was thirteen. I was with my father full-time after that, and that's why I am who I am now. But, yeah, Dad lived until I was twenty-six. He was killed by a low level member of the Cattaneo family up near New York. It wasn't even work-related. They were both at the same night club, and according to witnesses, my dad stepped between him and some girl he was harassing. The man was drunk and furious because he felt he was humiliated, and then in the early morning hours, my father was found dead behind the club. No cameras were running, because it's a Cattaneo owned business, but we knew who was responsible."

"When was that?"

"Six years ago."

"But you got the guy who did it?"

"Yeah. Your dad took me out there. We didn't tell anyone. We didn't have permission. We staked out for several days, waiting and watching, following him around to know his routine. When we knew we could get him away from any witnesses, we acted."

"I'm sorry."

He shrugs. "That's life. You live, you die, and you try to have some fun between the tragedies and heartbreak."

Javier's playing it off well, but I can tell he's affected. I do him a favor and change the subject.

"I feel like I failed as a priest when it came to you."

He chuckles. "I don't think any priest would've had much luck with me."

"Not if you would have been as flirtatious and vulgar with them like you were with me."

The smile he sends me makes my heart thump in my chest. "Is that what I was doing?"

"Don't act like you don't know what you were doing."

"Well," he says, making a turn before glancing my way with a mischievous grin on his lips. "I have a confession."

I cock my head. "Oh?"

"Forgive me, Father," he teases, bringing my hand to his mouth where he plants a kiss on my fingers. "But before my second visit to the church, I looked you up."

Our connected hands come to a rest back on my thigh. "What?"

He shrugs. "I was curious. I needed to know who I'd be talking to if I went back. I saw your name on one of those brochures, so I looked you up. Found a social media page for the church which had photos and videos."

"You're a stalker," I tease.

"That's the best thing I could be," he says with a laugh.

"So, you knew what I looked like."

"Yes. And I liked what you looked like."

I bite down on a grin. "You also knew I was a priest, and didn't know I'd be into guys."

"What do I care?" he says with a shrug. "I wanted to flirt. I hardly get to with men, and I knew you couldn't say anything."

I shake my head, but a smile remains on my lips. "And

then you followed me to the bar and surmised I was gay because I didn't look at the women."

"Pretty much."

"Well, I guess I should be flattered."

We turn onto a dirt road in the middle of nowhere, and Javier pulls off onto the side. I look around, trying to figure out where a house could possibly be, but then he's tugging on my shirt, pulling me closer to him.

"Oh," I manage to get out before his lips collide into mine, his tongue sweeping into my mouth with a desperate need.

He holds the side of my face, kissing me passionately and robbing me of breath and senses. I reach for him, hating the seatbelt that's keeping me restricted. I touch his chest and then his thigh. My palm skates over his crotch and he moans into my mouth.

Javier pulls away first, then comes in for another quick peck.

"Had to do that. We're almost there and I needed it out of my system."

I touch my lips. "I think I need to get more out of my system."

He grins. "Later. At home."

My teeth sink into my bottom lip at the promise. "Okay."

We get ourselves together and then he pulls back onto the road. We travel almost two miles until he makes a turn that leads to a large house. Before we can get to the driveway, we come up to a sturdy, metal gate. He gets out and unlocks it, pulling one panel open so we can drive through. Once we're in, he closes and locks it back up.

The house sits far back on the property, giving whoever's inside enough time to see if anyone ever comes through the gate, and to prepare as needed.

When we get closer, I see several cars, and lots of powerful, scary-looking men. These guys are definitely in the family, and based on their expensive apparel, they're more than soldiers.

Javier glances at me. "He's having a meeting with his top guys. He wants to introduce you."

"Oh, God."

CHAPTER 33

We're all in the living room of my dad's safe house, which feels more like a resort than anything. It's opulent without being gaudy. It seems like it's a full-time home, but it definitely lacks warmth.

A large, flat screen TV sits inside what looks to be a custom built entertainment center that protrudes from a black wall. Two brown, leather couches and two plush, black chairs surround three of the four sides of a black, wooden coffee table.

Windows are scarce, so the light comes from lamps in different parts of the room, and the more I study the walls, the more I begin to think they're made of concrete.

I choose to sit on one of the chairs and my dad stands next to another older man with hair more white than brown. They talk quietly amongst themselves while two other men sit on each end of one of the couches. Javier lingers between the front door and a small window, keeping an eye on any oncoming vehicles.

The men on the couch don't hesitate to make me feel

unwelcome. The one in the brown suit with lines permanently etched in his forehead looks me up and down like he's judging what I'm wearing. I'm in a pair of jeans and a solid, light blue, long sleeved shirt. If I had known this meeting was going to take place, I would've chosen something different, but it's not like I'm in sweats and a stained, wrinkled Tee.

The other man in the dark gray pants and white button up has an air of haughtiness about him. He's probably the youngest out of the other guys here, but still older than me. He hardly looks my way, like he can't be bothered to show attention to someone he doesn't know. I can see both their intimidation tactics, but I'm aware of the situation, and I'm not going to let them think I'm at all uncomfortable or feel out of place, even if that might be true.

"All right," Dad says, walking toward me, slipping one hand in the pocket of his black slacks. "We all know what's going on. Johnny got too big for his britches. He thought he could play boss behind my back, got himself into some trouble, and his way of cleaning it up was to throw me in front of a bullet. He's dodging me, which leads me to believe he suspects I know something.

"We'll be working with the Mancini family to deal with the Bonetti issue, but Johnny needs to be taken care of immediately." He stops next to me, glancing down before turning to the rest of the guys in the room. "For a long time, I've kept my personal life private, because we know how this life works. Your enemies will use anyone and anything against you, but if you don't have anyone they think you care about, then they only have you to go against." His hand lands on my shoulder. "This is Giancarlo." He pauses. "Giancarlo Gallo. My son."

This gets everyone's attention, especially the haughty one. I'd bet my life that he never knew I existed.

"I haven't talked about him in years. I know a couple of you," he says, gesturing to the white-haired man and the one in the brown suit, "knew about him years ago. He was doing small jobs for me when I was still working my way up."

"I thought he died," the one in the brown suit says, studying me with a different expression now. "Never wanted to bring it up, but because you never mentioned him again, I assumed it was bad."

"I told George he was gone," Dad says, gesturing to the older man. "Which was true. He was gone from my life...*this* life. Nobody needed to know the circumstances, and you still don't," he says, glaring at everyone. "Carlo and I have family business that has nothing to do with the Esposito family. But now it's time for you to know that he's back."

"Why?" the uppity one asks, giving me a once over that has me furrowing my brow at him.

"He's going to help us with Johnny, but I don't need a fucking reason to bring my son in on the business, Elio," Dad snaps.

"Sorry, boss," Elio says, sitting back. "I was just curious."

"Again," Dad says, walking to the other corner of the living area. "There are things you don't need to know. Carlo will be as involved as I need him to be, and you'll know only what you're required to."

The older man—George, steps forward. "Cortez, I get what you're saying, but the guys should know what you told me."

Dad sighs, rubbing his forehead. "Carlo," he says, looking at me. "George is my consigliere. Elio and Dante are a couple of my capos. I nod, looking at each of them. "Once Johnny is taken care of," Dad adds, addressing everyone. "We'll need someone to take his place."

"Boss, I know you're not—" Elio begins, sitting forward.

Dad pins him with an icy glare. "I know you're not about to open your mouth to tell me you think you should get the job. You're the newest capo. You've only been in your position for six months."

"Dante's been here for years," Elio says, gesturing toward the man next to him.

"And?" Dad says.

Dante clears his throat. "I'd love to be considered for the position, Boss, but I trust you'll make the decision that makes the most sense for the family," he adds, clearly the smarter of the two.

"Johnny was my underboss for years. He was a man I thought I could trust. The one who knew about Carlo and his whereabouts this whole time. Clearly, I can't trust anyone, because he's also the one who told the Bonetti family about Carlo. When it comes to who takes his place, it will be someone I feel can do a good job and someone who will put the family's needs first. I can't have any power-hungry, self-absorbed assholes in that position."

There are things I want to question him about, but I know this isn't the time, so I sit quietly. I can tell Dante's doing the same thing. I can see the questions in his eyes as he looks at me. He wants answers but he's not dumb enough to question my father.

"Again, no offense, Boss," Elio begins.

George grumbles. "Good God, Elio."

"I'm just saying," Elio says, holding up his hands. "Your son hasn't been around. He's not even made. I'm not questioning your decisions, but I can't help but wonder how everyone else is gonna feel. We just get a new guy in a position of power that nobody knows? We don't know what he's capable of. He hasn't earned our respect or trust."

Dante's head dips in a nod, agreeing with Elio's words, but he still doesn't say anything. And as much as Elio is annoying me, he's not wrong. These are questions that'll need to be answered.

"You trusted and respected Johnny, and now look. He wants me dead. So, you'll have to respect me enough to trust that what I choose to do is what is best. If you don't agree. If anyone doesn't agree, then we can deal with that too."

The thinly veiled threat settles over everyone.

Dad exhales, running a hand through his hair.

"I didn't ask him for this," I say. "It's not something I've thought about in almost a decade, and I can understand that bothers you when it's been a goal of yours." I make sure to make eye contact with both Dante and Elio. "But don't think I'm over here begging him for something and expecting it simply because of who he is." I look at my dad. "I'm not sure I want it, because I know what it takes and I'm aware of the sacrifices. I've seen them firsthand." Staring back at the men on the couch, I continue. "You think I'm new blood and that makes you want to circle me like I'm prey, but the truth is, whether you like it or not, I was born into this. Gallo blood runs in my veins. From the time I was born until I was nineteen, I lived with him. I saw and heard plenty. This isn't new to me." I stand up, feeling myself getting worked up. "And my life is on the line here. I don't think anyone is coming after any of you." I take a breath. "I don't know what my dad's going to do, and I don't know if any of us will be happy with the decision, but know that I'll do what's necessary. I'll do what I have to save my life, and to save his. That's why I'm meeting with Johnny in order to take him out."

Nobody says anything, but my dad watches me with something akin to pride in his expression. I've never seen that look before, but I can tell he liked what he heard. When I look at the door, I spot Javier with a small grin on his lips.

CHAPTER 34

We stayed at my dad's for another half hour or so, going over our next steps. I spoke a little more with Elio and Dante, and while I'm not naive enough to think they like me, they seemed to get a little more on board with my presence.

Now, after circling the block twice, we're pulling up to my house so I can grab a few more things.

"Stay behind me," Javier says, pulling a gun from his holster and holding it close to his body.

"I doubt anyone's here."

He doesn't reply, but I follow him up the path from the driveway that leads to my front door. After he gestures to move in front of him, I take my keys and unlock it.

Javier scans the area behind us, checking the streets and growing shadows. Once I step back, he turns the knob and pushes the door open. With the gun now extended, he searches the living room and kitchen first while I stand just inside the door.

I watch as he disappears down the hall, and then remerges a couple minutes later.

Tucking his gun back in the holster, he says, "Okay, you can go pack what you need. I'll take out the trash and clear the fridge."

"You don't have to. I'll do it."

"No, you won't, because you don't need to be going outside by yourself. Just go pack."

"I'm not completely fragile or useless."

He tilts his head when he looks at me. "I'm not saying you are. I'm saying you have the bigger target on your back, and we're in the one spot where they know they can find you."

"Fine." I turn to walk down the hall, but stop and turn around. "Thank you."

Javier nods once, then makes his way to the kitchen.

In my room, I grab my black gym bag, and start gathering a few more clothing items, a couple of books, and a surprise for Javier.

I grin as I tuck it away, then I zip up the bag and head back to the living room where I find Javier walking through the front door.

"Trash is out," he says. "Your fridge is nearly bare."

"That's fine. Thanks again."

"You ready?"

"Yeah."

I hoist the bag over my shoulder and follow him through the door and to his car. The sky is darker now, the sun having hidden below the horizon.

"I liked what you said at your dad's house," Javier says as we take off down the street.

"Oh yeah? I wondered if they thought it was mostly bravado."

"Nah. You admitted to not even wanting this. Guys like that, they think everyone is out for themselves, usually because they are. Nepotism's been a problem before. Guys get their nephews, sons, or cousins involved because *they're family* and shit goes sideways because they don't actually take it seriously. You saying you'll do what's necessary was good. It takes time to earn trust and respect, but you'll get there."

My lips twitch, a smile teasing them. "And when they find out I'm a priest?"

He's quiet for a moment. "Are you?"

I gaze out the window and watch the stars twinkle like fireflies. "Technically, yes."

"But will you continue to be?"

I sigh. "I'm just trying to get through this mess first. I can't think about the future until I'm sure I'll even have one."

"If you think I'll let anyone hurt you..." he says, letting the sentence die out.

"I know," I reply. "I know I can trust you."

He glances over and gives me a small grin. "Good."

✝

Turns out Javier lives over an hour away. I chose Crest Haven because it was a quiet, small town, and it wasn't close to where I grew up with my father. Dad's work usually takes place in Boston, so it makes sense for Javier to live about half an hour away from the city.

He slows down next to a six-story building, and pulls into the underground garage. Once parked, we grab our luggage and make our way to the elevator and take it to the fifth floor.

We pass delicate furnishings and abstract art as we walk down the hall to his apartment door.

"It's not very big, but the view is nice," he says.

Inside, the floor is a light colored wood. There's a small table to the right where he drops his keys.

We turn the corner toward the left, and he starts pointing things out.

"Spare bedroom," he says, walking to the doorway and turning on a light. "There's just a daybed in there and a dresser. I don't have many guests," he says with a wry smile. "Bathroom across the hall." I spot the open door and get a glimpse of a toilet and sink. He continues walking and points straight ahead. "My room and another bathroom in there." Then we curve to the right and land in his kitchen and living room area.

It's not huge, but it looks like it costs a pretty penny. The rooms are connected, but he's got his dark gray couch separating the two spaces. The colors are a mix of black, white, and gray. The kitchen looks modern and updated, with a nice stainless steel fridge and stove, with a microwave hoisted between white cabinets.

The windows are large and take up almost the whole wall, and they definitely offer up great views.

"You hungry?" he asks.

"Definitely. And in need of a shower. We've been in the car all day."

"Go ahead and get washed up. I'll order something."

"Okay."

He leads me to his bedroom, flipping on the light. His king-sized bed is between two end tables with lamps. Another large window is on the right, and a long dresser stretches across the wall opposite the bed, a TV mounted above it.

As we turn to the left, I spot an oversized mirror resting against the wall, and next to that is the entrance to the bathroom.

"Towels are probably in the dryer," he says, pulling back a curtain to reveal a stacked washer and dryer.

"Okay. I'm just gonna unpack a few things then I'll hop in."

He turns and stops in front of me. "Food preference?"

I study his handsome face and the way his eyes skate down my body. "Hmm. Maybe something light."

He grins. "Got it."

Once he leaves the room, I take my suitcase to the bed and open it up to grab my toiletry bag. I also pull out a fresh pair of underwear, a T-shirt, and a pair of lounge pants.

I use the bathroom and then strip down and turn on the shower. As it heats up, I set all my bathroom items on a free part of the counter.

Within twenty minutes, I'm scrubbed clean, lotioned up, and in my comfortable clothes, ready to eat.

When I walk out to the living room, I spot Javier on the couch, looking at his phone. He glances up and smiles, then pats the cushion next to him.

With a grin I can't seem to fight, I walk over and settle in at his side. He leans over and nuzzles my neck, inhaling my scent before giving me a kiss under my ear.

"You smell good." Goosebumps run down my arm. "I bet you taste good, too."

A shiver runs through me. "Don't you know already?" I ask, voice breathy.

"I might need to refresh my memory," he says, licking a stripe across my neck.

"Mm," I moan. "I agree."

A knock on the door shatters the mood, breaking us apart.

I whine when he pulls away, and he chuckles on the way to the door.

Getting up, I meet him in the kitchen where he puts down a couple of bags on the counter.

"Salad and club sandwiches okay?" he asks.

"Yeah. Sounds good."

Once we grab our food, we sit back on the couch and dig in. Javier turns on the TV but the volume is low as the weatherman talks about the upcoming rain in our forecast.

I always have a dozen things running through my head, so when I speak a thought out loud, it's not out of the blue for me, but it seems to catch Javier off guard.

"How did you feel after you killed someone for the first time?"

He stops moving, his head turning toward me. "Okay, that was unexpected."

"Sorry. I was just thinking."

Javier takes a bite and chews for a while before attempting to answer. "I was scared. Mostly of being caught. That was for my first solo job, though. I had done jobs with my dad before then. But I never had anything to worry about if I was with him. When you're on your own, you wonder if you were lazy. Did someone see you? Were there cameras in the area?"

"But you didn't have a moral struggle?"

"Nah. You have to understand I was brought up very differently than most kids. I knew what my dad was doing. And while I did question it around the age of ten or so, he explained it to me in a way that I accepted. He said 'Son, you know how we have soldiers in the military? And sometimes they have to kill people because it's for the benefit of a larger picture. Soldiers kill our enemies before they can kill us. Well, we have enemies too, and we have to kill them before they kill us. They're not always good people, but in the end, it's for a larger picture that we may not fully understand.'"

"Hmm."

"Kill or be killed, in the plainest of terms," he says.

"Yeah, I get that." I take another bite and chew it up. "You never felt bad?"

He shrugs. "I haven't killed any innocent women or children. I'm killing men who signed up for a life where they knew that was a possibility." Silence stretches between us. "You'll do what's necessary, right? Only what's necessary."

"Stepping into this life means abandoning everything I've been taught and have preached to others. Sure, I can justify a death as self-defense, but to become the antithesis of all my teachings by strolling into an underworld full of crime, violence, and murder?"

"You knew this world. You said so yourself. You grew up in it. It's not new to you. You're struggling with taking that final step because it directly involves you now. You didn't care what your dad did. You didn't struggle with the knowledge that he was involved in everything you told people to fight against. I hate to break it to you, Carlo, but you've already crossed the line."

"Yeah, with you, but—"

"No, with everything. You met with a crime family to discuss murdering a man. And it's your plan."

"To save myself and my father."

"Or you could call the cops, right? Wouldn't that be another option for someone not in the life?"

His words are like a hand around my throat, robbing me

of a reply, because the truth is I never thought of that as a possibility.

"It seems you've made a decision, but you're struggling to let go of your past. But the more you talk about your struggles between right and wrong, the more I start to wonder what we're even doing together. You can't be so self-righteous and pious and also let me fuck you after I've killed a man."

Javier puts the remaining part of his sandwich in the box it came in and stands up. "I'm gonna go shower."

"Javi," I say, watching him leave.

He stops. "I like you, Carlo. Despite our differences, and maybe even because of them. But we're at a point now where you have to choose one life or the other. I won't tell you what to do. If you want to live the rest of your life dedicated to your god and church, so be it. I hope you find happiness. But I think if you choose me—" He cuts himself off and adjusts. "Or this life...I believe you'll find the freedom and excitement you've been longing for. But you can't question the morality of it every day."

"If I choose you. This darker life. I'm still in hiding, aren't I? We couldn't tell anyone about us, could we?"

He inhales, watching me carefully. "You'd be free of the shackles of guilt when we're tangled up in each other in the dark. You'd be free to love and commit your life to someone other than Jesus. You wouldn't be lonely."

Without giving me time to reply, he tosses his food on the kitchen counter and disappears into his room, leaving me with a head full of conflicts.

CHAPTER 35

J avier takes a lengthy shower, giving me time to think. He's right, though it's always easier said than done. He doesn't have the same conflicts I do, but I should make a concise decision, even though my actions would say that I have.

The truth of the matter is, regardless of my feelings on religion, I know that going back to the church and redevoting myself into the priesthood would mean saying goodbye to Javier for good, and likely cutting my dad off as well. I'd need to make a clean break to separate myself from everything they have going on. But the thought of doing that makes my heart clench.

I couldn't imagine saying goodbye to a life I always told myself I wanted. A life I resented being robbed of. It might not be a path most people take or would even want, but now I'm being offered the chance at having a family again.

I don't think about how I could leave the church and also reject my dad's offer. I could move away and start over without being a priest and without being a criminal, but that thought barely touches my brain, and when it does, I dismiss it as an option, and that alone speaks volumes.

It's time to cut ties.

I have to leave Father Carlo Gallini in the past and step into the shoes of Giancarlo Gallo—heir to a mafia crime family.

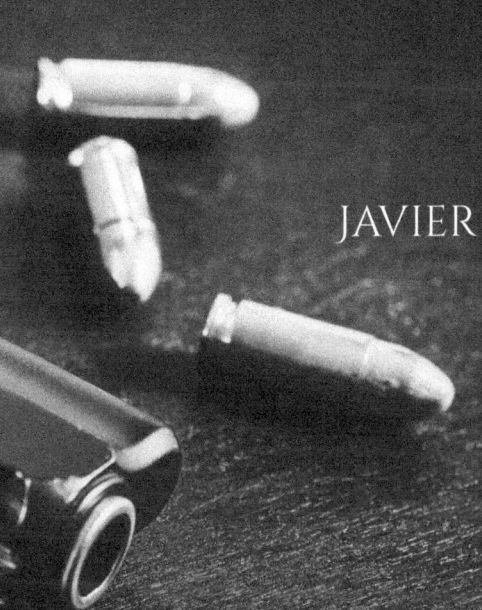

JAVIER

When I get out of the shower, I go into my bedroom with a towel wrapped around my waist as I open up drawers to find some clothes. The house is silent, and I imagine Carlo is still in the living room thinking over his life decisions.

In the shower, I questioned what I said to him. He's a grown man, and we all have to do things on our own time, but I also don't think I was wrong. We've been operating like he's not a priest. At this point, there's not much about him that screams *holy man*. I understand the switch over is stark, but to me it seems like a no brainer.

That's probably my selfishness talking. I'm not ready to be done with him yet. The fact that he's Cortez's son adds a layer of complexity I've yet to fully examine, but I know if he chooses his job, it'll be because he's sure which means no more luring him into submission.

I remember our earlier conversations, before we knew the truth about each other, where he talked about his relationship with his dad. They're not close and haven't been, but I think if he steps into this, he has the opportunity to change that. They have a lot of work to do, and it's mostly on Cortez's end, but as someone who's lost both parents, I think he'd appreciate having some sort of relationship with his father.

I like Carlo, despite having reasons I shouldn't. I want more time to get to know him, and to continue to peel back all the layers that cover him up. We've both been hiding and lying, forced to keep parts of ourselves in the dark. I guess I have layers too, but together, we can be ourselves, and that's all anybody wants, right? Comfortability.

There's more to it than that. I'm not stupid, but for a little while, before the world comes crashing in, I'd like to enjoy the time I'm able to have with him. The fact that he's even remotely interested in me doesn't quite compute in my head, but I'm not about to tell him he's wrong. He's crazy to be with me, but I hope he never comes to his senses.

I fear what he'll think when he sees me in action. It's easy to excuse or justify something that you've never witnessed, but if he sticks around long enough, he's bound to see me take a life, and I wonder if that'll change his opinion of me.

As I'm about to drop my towel to put on my boxers, Carlo steps into the room. His presence freezes me in place, not because I wasn't expecting him, but because of what he's wearing.

Decked from head to toe in black, except the white collar around his neck, my brain short circuits wondering if this is him telling me he's made his decision and he's about to leave.

The robe falls all the way to the tops of his feet, with buttons down the middle, and a rosary dangles from his clasped hands.

After looking him up and down a couple times, I wet my bottom lip with my tongue. "What—"

He holds up his hand. "I think it's time you confess all your sins."

I angle my head slightly, still unsure about the situation. "I've told you everything."

Carlo steps forward. "Have you?"

My eyes drink him in, enjoying seeing him in his priest outfit. Not sure what it is exactly, but it sets fire to my blood. My temperature rises as I study him.

"I think you need to confess your lustful thoughts." He moves even closer. "You're having them right now, aren't you?"

My lips quirk and realization settles in. He's not leaving. He's giving me what I want. "Yes, Father. I am having many, many lustful thoughts."

"I thought so. Tell me what you're thinking right now."

My eyes travel downward, tracking the buttons that hold together the black material. "I want to be under this robe, on my knees, worshiping you."

His eyes flash briefly, desire swirling in their depths. "It's wrong to bow down and worship anyone who is not God."

I bite down on my lip. "I also have the strong desire to take you into my mouth and feel you grow against the wetness of my tongue. Is that wrong?"

Carlo swallows. "Yes. You should strive for purity."

My fingers begin playing with the buttons on the robe. "There's one more thing I'm thinking about right now, Father." His brows lift. "I can't stop thinking about you fucking me while wearing this. Is there a penance for that?"

"Yes," he says, reaching down to rip the towel from my

waist, leaving me naked. "Get on the bed. On your hands and knees."

I only pause for a second, but I do what he says.

"No. Over here," he says, directing me to another spot on the bed.

I crawl over and Carlo tosses the rosary in front of me. As I study the beads, I feel his hands on my ass.

"I'm going to give you what you say you want, but your penance is that you don't get to come."

"What?" I exclaim.

"It's a punishment." He leans over me, the material of his clothes rubbing against my skin. "That's what you want, right? You want me to punish you."

A low growl vibrates in my throat. "Yes, but, Carlo, the get-back will be good."

He eases away, and a sharp smack against my right cheek reverberates into the room. "We'll see."

His hands spread me apart, and his tongue licks a path up my crease. "Oh god," I cry out.

Carlo's tongue moves up and down, circling the hole. When I lift my head, I'm met with the image of us in my oversized mirror. This is why he positioned me here.

The pure bliss of the moment has me wanting to squeeze my eyes closed, just to disappear from the world and dive into the sensation of what his mouth is doing to me, but the vision is too good to ignore. Carlo, looking every bit the pious priest in his cassock and collar, is tongue deep in my ass, and the visual heightens the experience ten-fold.

He pulls away and meets my gaze in the reflection, but his fingers replace his mouth, and he gently teases my hole.

"Did you enjoy that?"

"Yes."

"Of course you did. You're a filthy sinner."

My teeth drag across my bottom lip. "Yes, I am."

Carlo pulls his hand away and begins messing with the buttons on his cassock. "Turn around," he commands.

When I spin around in front of him, he has his cassock open from the waist down, and his pants pushed to his knees. His snug, white briefs barely contain his erection.

"Father," I say in a sing-song tone. "Looks like I'm not the only one who wants to sin."

He gazes down at me, unamused. "I believe you said you wanted to take me in your mouth."

I reach for him, my fingers dipping into the waistband and tugging the material down. His cock springs free, the tip red, veins protruding from the taut skin.

My lips part and I lick the underside of his tip before looking up at him. He's trying his best to stay stoic, so now I'm motivated to break him from this role, as much as I love it. Call me competitive.

I take him into my mouth, his hardness sliding across my tongue and reaching for the back of my throat. My right hand cups his balls, massaging them as I bob up and down on his length.

When I hear a grunt come from above, I know I'm getting to him. I move my hand to his shaft, stroking as I suck on his head. I take it all the way in again, making it nice and wet before I continue to fist his cock.

After several more seconds, his hand slides through my hair, pulling hard enough to get me to release him.

"That's enough," he says. "I think you're enjoying it too much."

I smirk at him. "You taste like heaven. Can you blame me?"

He narrows his eyes at me, then begins kicking off his shoes and removing his pants and underwear. I lie back on the bed, watching as he opens the drawers of my night stand, searching for something.

"I knew you'd have these," he says, throwing a bottle of lube and a condom onto the bed. "But what's this?"

He holds up a hard, plastic case that hides the masturbator inside.

"Take the lid off."

He unscrews the top and eyes it with disappointment. Turning it toward me, he shows me the opening that resembles a pussy.

"Disgusting," he says, throwing it back in the drawer.

"Well, Father, if you don't want me using that, I suppose you need to let me use you."

"You're the one that's about to be used," he says, reaching back into the drawer to pull out a realistic looking dildo. "Now this...this we can use."

I get up on my elbows, a mischievous smirk on my lips. "What're you gonna do with that?"

"Nothing. You're gonna show me what you do to yourself when you choose to dishonor God with your carnal nature."

He tosses it next to the lube, then turns and walks toward the corner of the room where I have a single accent chair resting near a window. He brings it to the side of the bed and sits in it. When I don't make a move, he lifts his brows and gestures to the toy that sits beside me.

I watch him for a few seconds before I reach for the dildo and lube. I begin with just my fingers, sliding the slick digits toward my entrance. After I get two fingers inside me, I pour some of the liquid on the brown skin of the silicone toy and position it at my hole.

With a glance at Carlo, I find him entranced in my movements, his hand under his robe.

I begin pushing it inside, slow and careful. The slick sounds of lube fill the room as I move it in and out. Once comfortable, I reach for my cock with my free hand while the other continues the movement.

A moan escapes my throat and I get lost in pleasure. I fuck myself with the toy, enjoying the feeling of being stretched. It's been a little while since I've used it, and even longer since I've had the real thing. It feels good, but I want more. I want him.

I turn my head, peeking over my shoulder to see Carlo jerking his cock as he watches. I bite on my lip, suppressing a moan.

"Carlo," I say, my voice breathy.

His eyes find my face. "You better not come."

I shake my head once. "I want more."

He stands, coming to kneel on the bed between my legs. He knocks my hand away from my cock and replaces it with his on the base of the toy.

"This isn't enough for you?" he questions, thrusting it deeper inside me.

I gasp. "No."

He takes my dick in his free hand. "But you're so hard. It seems like you're enjoying yourself."

"I like that you're watching me," I admit, my back arching as he manipulates the toy.

Carlo removes the dildo, tossing it aside. "Roll over."

I'm on my knees in no time, watching in the mirror as he reaches for the condom.

"We don't need it," I say, desperate to feel him without a barrier.

He cocks his head, questioning.

"You haven't had sex with anyone else in years. It's been

224

a while for me too, and my last appointment had me in the clear. Don't use it."

I watch the wheels in his head spin and then he throws the condom to the side and reaches for the lube.

Carlo pulls me back to the edge of the mattress, manipulating my body to get me at the right height before I feel the tip of his cock at my entrance.

Our eyes meet in the mirror, and as he begins to enter me, his eyes close and his head lifts to the ceiling. I'm not sure if he's reveling in the feeling of our bodies merging or if he's praying for forgiveness.

When his head lowers, he enters me fully, and his gaze is much different now. He's hungry, and I'm the only food on the table.

His hands grip my waist, and he drives into me deep and hard. I grunt, gripping the covers in my hands. His vigorous thrusts and animalistic moans have me abandoning the idea that I can keep a faithful watch on the mirror. I'm forced into closing my eyes or burying my face in the covers as I moan and grunt in pleasure.

"This is what you wanted?" he asks, breaths heavy.

"Yes. Fuck yes."

"You like watching a priest break his vow to bend you over and fuck you?"

"Yes!" I cry out, dragging out the word.

"That's why you won't be able to come. You shouldn't enjoy such a thing."

I groan as he continues to push into me. "Please."

"You'll probably love having my cum in your ass, won't you? You want to feel me throb and twitch as I release inside you."

"Oh god, yes!"

"Your ass is so fucking tight. You're strangling my cock."

"Mmm," I moan. "You feel so good."

Carlo slowly pulls back, spreading me apart to watch his cock slip free just to dip it back in.

"You're taking me so well," he croons. "Are you a cock slut, Javier? Is that another sinful secret you have?"

"Fuck," I grunt, when he buries himself deep inside me again. "I'll be whatever you want me to be."

He continues his motions, hips rocking back and forth as the black robe moves with him. My cock throbs with the need to be touched. At this point, I'm afraid a strong burst of air against it will send me over the edge.

After slowing down, he wraps an arm around my torso, pulling me up. His hand goes to my cock, giving it the gentlest of touches as he looks at me in the mirror.

"And what if I wanted you to be mine?"

My heart thumps hard in my chest. I lick my lips as I stare back at him. He's waiting for an answer, and I know what I want to say. But my wants have never been prioritized because they can't be. I've never been in a real relationship. It's never been possible, and this relationship comes with its own set of problems.

He continues to softly stroke me, his lips at my neck. "Tell me, Javier," he says quietly. "Will you ever be mine?" He traps my skin between his teeth, eliciting a hiss from my lips. "Can I be yours?"

"You sure you want to be with me?" I ask.

He releases me, pushing away from my body before getting me to my back. I spread my legs and he climbs between them, pushing his robe out of the way.

"Look at me," he says, putting his cock back at my entrance. "I'm making my decision now. It's not about a job, the mafia, or my father. I'm choosing you, because going back to a life without you isn't something I'm interested in." He slides deep inside me, his body hovering over mine. "Here's *my* confession." Thrust. "I might be obsessed with you." Thrust. "And if what we do is a sin, I never want to stop sinning." Thrust. "I don't want to be saved. I don't want to seek forgiveness for what I feel when I'm inside you."

Carlo moves a little faster, his strokes long and hard. "Tell me I can have you. Even if it's only in the dark. Even if we remain a secret. Even if it's short-lived. Tell me," he pleads, sweat shining on his forehead. "Javi," he groans.

"Yes." The word shoots from the tip of my tongue like an accidental misfire. I had no intention of saying it until my name left his lips with such need. His eyes are filled with relief. Relief mixed with surprise. "Yes," I repeat. "I'm yours."

His eyes close as the words roll over him. Then he fucks me like it's true. Like I'm his property. If I thought he was hungry before, I was mistaken. He's starved. He's a starving man and I'm the only thing that'll sustain him. He devours me in a way that's like a punishment for having been deprived in the first place, and a reverence for having something he's been craving.

"I want to come, Carlo," I say. "Please. I'm yours, let me show you what belongs to you."

He growls, eyes dark, jaw clenched as he thrusts. "Yes. Show me."

I don't even revel in the win with a grin or chuckle. I spit in my hand and fist my cock, bringing myself to bliss in no time.

"I'm so close."

"Me too," he pants. "I'm gonna fill you up."

"Good. I want to feel every drop." After a few more

strokes, as unbridled ecstasy envelops me, I say, "I'm about to come. I'm...I'm coming."

White liquid shoots from my tip, pouring over my fingers as I yell into the room, my cries of pleasures sounding like they're being ripped from the bottom of my lungs. It's a harsh, deep noise but the feeling that accompanies it can only be described as freeing.

"Oh god, oh god," Carlo cries. "Fuck!"

He falls over me, his face in my neck as his hips move. His body jerks above mine, our heavy breaths and moans forming their own symphony.

I wrap my arms around him, dragging my fingers up and down his back.

After a while, he eases away, slowly pulling out of me. He moves over, falling to his back to my left with a sigh.

I turn my head to look at him, and his eyes find mine. A small, exhausted grin touches his lips.

Reaching for his hand, I bring it to my mouth and plant a kiss on the back of it, finding myself looking forward to falling asleep with him in my arms tonight.

My eyes open and close a couple times before I reach behind me, hoping to find Carlo still there. When all I'm met with is a cold sheet, I turn over and find I'm alone in the room.

I pick up my phone from the nightstand and look at the time. It's only three minutes past eight.

As I stretch, I internally catalog every part of my body that's sore, but it puts a small smile on my lips. After we got cleaned up last night, we got back in bed together, legs tangling under the covers as we talked about nothing and everything. Carlo fell asleep first, but a few hours after I had closed my eyes, I woke up to his hand curving around my hip. He ended up going down on me, jerking himself to completion in the process. We quickly fell back into unconsciousness, and I assumed we'd both sleep in today, but since he's not here, I wonder if he's stuck in that head of his.

When I get out of bed, I pull on my boxers and head to the bathroom for my morning routine. With an empty bladder, clean teeth, and smelling of deodorant and lotion, I stroll into my living room, looking for my naughty priest.

Dressed in a pair of black slacks, a white button up with the sleeves pushed to the elbow, he stands in front of the large window with his phone pressed to his ear.

My steps get his attention, and he turns, looking me up and down, his lips curling up in a small smile.

"Yeah," he says into the phone, turning to the window again. "When will that be? I'll let him know. Sure, it's fine. Okay. Bye."

He pockets the phone and turns around to face me. "My dad."

"Ah," I say, moving forward, my fingers sliding into the front of his waistband, pulling him into me. "And what did he say?" I question, pressing a kiss to the corner of his mouth.

His hand cradles my jaw before giving me a harder, lingering kiss on the lips. "He'll be calling you soon. I guess you two have something to do today."

"I see," I reply, running my hand through his soft hair as I stare into his eyes. "I don't want you leaving here."

He flattens his lips and narrows his eyes. "Am I your prisoner?"

I smirk. "We can play that game if you want. I *am* into role playing."

"I can take care of myself."

"Listen, Carlo," I say, stepping away from him. "My job is to keep you safe. I know you're a grown man, but you don't know the people we're messing with. You're not even armed. All it'll take is for you to step outside for one second and you can be cut down like that," I say with a snap of my fingers.

"I didn't plan on leaving," he says with an exhale. "But maybe it's time I keep a gun with me."

I eye him for a few seconds, then walk over to a corner cabinet. I pull open a drawer and grab the Glock that's inside, then I grab a fully loaded magazine from another drawer and insert it.

"This has seventeen rounds," I say, handing it to him. "Safety is on. You should probably learn some basics. I'll take you somewhere when I have some time."

He nods, inspecting the gun in his hand.

My phone rings from the bedroom, and knowing it's likely Cortez, I rush toward it.

"Hello?"

"I have to meet with Aurelio today. We only have an hour before he has to meet with Sammy. This is the only time we have to convince him to keep things cordial between our families once we take out the top brass."

I suck in a deep breath. "And if he doesn't appreciate your plan to take out half his family…"

"He wants to be boss. This will be his chance, so he'd be stupid to run and tell Sammy the plan, but if he does, then we have to be prepared for what comes after that."

"And if all goes according to plan?"

"By the end of the week."

"I see."

"You think Carlo will be all right at your place?"

"Yeah. I told him he can't leave."

Cortez snorts. "I'm sure he loved that."

"It doesn't matter."

"You're right. Okay, well, I'm gonna send you the location as soon as I know it."

"Sounds good."

He ends the call and I go back into the living room, finding Carlo staring out the window again.

"Is it going to be dangerous?"

"Shouldn't be," I answer, putting my phone on the coffee table.

"But you can't anticipate what someone else will do."

"Right, but if anything happens it shouldn't be for a few more days."

He runs a hand through his hair. "I'm ready for this to be over."

"I know."

His phone dings from in his pocket, and he pulls it out and reads the screen. He turns to look at me.

"It's Johnny."

I rush forward and take the phone, reading the message myself.

Can you meet me today?

I LOOK AT HIM. "No. You're not doing anything today. We don't have a place picked out for this plan of yours yet."

"When will we know? The longer I put him off, the more suspicious he'll be."

"We can't pick a safe house he knows about. We can't do it in a public place either. If we lure him too far out, he won't go."

I watch as he chews on his bottom lip, eyebrows furrowed as he stares toward the floor.

"The rectory," he says. "It's still being worked on, but the work stops on the weekends, and we can choose a time where the church will be empty. There's no houses nearby. Only a cemetery."

"He'd probably assume you were there for work purposes, so he wouldn't think it would be weird."

"Right. I could tell him I stay there sometimes when I'm preparing for mass. Though I doubt he'll ask too many questions."

"A cemetery," I muse.

"We will not desecrate a grave," he says, and the look on his face lets me know there's no budging on that.

"I wasn't going to suggest that, but if there's a newly dug grave, and it remains unmarked..."

He nods once. "We can figure something out."

"Okay. I'll talk to Cortez when I meet him." I hand Carlo his phone. "Respond and tell him you'll let him know when you're free, but that it'll likely be this weekend. I have to get ready."

"Okay."

As I get dressed, I think about how too much is happening around the same time. We can't allow mistakes, so everything will have to be well-planned, but dealing with Johnny the same weekend we're supposed to be taking out the Bonetti family means a lot of blood will be shed. In war, anything goes, but unfortunately we can't guarantee that that won't include any of us. This could be the last week we have on this planet, but I plan on doing everything in my power to keep the Gallo men alive.

Strapped up, I go back into the living room. "I'll see you later, okay?"

Carlo comes toward me, his hand snaking around my waist as he leans in. "Be safe."

I grin. "Always."

His fingers rest over the spot where I was stabbed before, pulling at the fabric of my shirt. "Not always."

I kiss him. "I'll be back," I state with finality. "And I'll punish you for doubting my ability to keep myself alive."

His lips twitch slightly. "Okay."

Outside my apartment door, a switch flips. I have the ability to turn it on and off as needed. I can be a normal person, wanting mundane human things like love, sex, food, and entertainment, but when I'm on the clock, I shed as much humanity as possible, and I become the only thing that's kept me alive all these years—a cold-blooded killer.

CHAPTER 38

"How's he holding up?" Cortez asks me as I drive him to the meeting place.

"He's fine," I reply simply.

"Think he'll be able to handle this?"

I hesitate, careful about how I frame my response. "I believe him when he says he'll do what's necessary. He seems to care about you."

The last comment makes Cortez huff. "I don't know about that."

We sit in silence for a little bit as I turn thoughts over in my head. It's not my business, and I've never made it a habit to talk to Cortez about any of his personal issues, but now I feel entangled in it.

"He made a comment about wanting this a long time ago, but being so removed from it in his adult life..." I pause, not wanting to say he doesn't feel capable. "I don't know. His role as a priest has to be conflicting."

Cortez sighs, and I wonder if I'm pushing it too much. He's not required to tell me anything, and considering he's kept the existence of a son under wraps, he probably won't say a lot about their relationship.

"I question myself all the time, wondering if I did the right thing," he says, surprising me. I keep quiet and hope he continues talking, if only for my own curiosity. "I had every intention of bringing him into the fold. He was in it as much as he could be as a teenager. It's hard to hide the life-style, ya know? He never questioned it, because it was all he knew. But." He stops talking, looking out the passenger window.

"His sexuality?" I prompt, my heart in my throat as I wait for his response.

Cortez sucks his teeth, and I glance over at him to see his jaw is clenched.

"You know how this life is, Javier. He'd be a target. A victim."

My instinct is to defend Carlo, but I can't let on that I know him more than I should. "A target, sure, but do you think he'd allow himself to be a victim?"

"He's different," Cortez says. "He's not like me. Or you, for that matter. He's lived a different life. I'm not sure he'd be able to stand up for himself in the way he'd need to."

"He did come up with the idea to get Johnny," I offer.

"True," he says after a few seconds. "Generally, I don't care about what people do in their personal lives, as long as it doesn't affect me. This is my son, though."

The flare of hope I felt quickly fades. A lot of people say similar things. They don't care what anyone does with their life as long as it's not their kid. It's still prejudice, but they convince themselves it's not.

"But how does that affect you?"

The question is out before I can think better of it.

Cortez's head snaps in my direction, but I keep my eyes on the road.

"I just mean..." I don't know how else to phrase it, but I know I shouldn't question him, and definitely not about his son or his parenting.

"How does it affect me?" he questions, his tone stern. "He's my fucking son. You think I want to watch him—" he cuts himself off and takes a few seconds to breathe. "I won't watch him become a victim. He may not get it. Nobody has to understand," he bites, burning holes into the side of my face. "But I will protect him even if that means pushing him away."

I nod once, understanding seeping in. Cortez isn't a vulnerable or emotional man. He doesn't talk about anything except work, so I only know the version of him that he's shown me, and that's a crime boss. I've never known him as a father, but now I see what Carlo hasn't. His dad doesn't hate that he's gay because he hates gay people. He hates that his son is gay because he's afraid of what will happen to him.

"For what it's worth," I say. "I think Carlo would do anything for you, regardless of whether he understands why you've pushed him away."

"I know," Cortez says. "And I'm using that knowledge to get what I want."

He doesn't say it like he's proud of it. If anything, he sounds regretful, but it's also an admission to wanting his son to take his place.

As we approach the junkyard parking lot, I forget about their relationship issues, and start focusing on the work at hand.

"Think he'll accept your offer?"

"Let's go see."

As we get out, I scan the area, making sure Aurelio actually came alone. He's leaning against his black Cadillac, a toothpick in his mouth and one hand in his pocket.

I stay back, because I'm not in the family, so I'm not allowed to be privy to business conversations. But I'm close enough to pull my gun and shoot him dead if he makes a move. Cortez never gets too close to anyone deemed untrustworthy, and by the time they could pull a gun, the bullet from mine will already be flying.

When Aurelio pushes away from the car, I reach for the gun in my holster, unsnapping the clip that's holding it in place. He looks me up and down before turning his attention back to Cortez and removing his hand from his pocket.

He's not holding anything, but I stay ready.

Aurelio's voice rises only once, and I hear enough to know he's questioning the need to dispose of so many people in the family. Cortez begins gesturing, talking to him calmly, probably explaining how this is a good thing for him.

We stand out here for nearly forty minutes, the sun beating down on us, but Aurelio seems to at least be hearing him out, though there's a lot of backstabbing in this life, so he could very well be listening to details just to go tell his boss later.

I watch Cortez back away, nodding his head, and I know we're about to leave. I keep my eye on Aurelio while Cortez gets in the car. When he drives off, I get in the car and start it up.

"So?"

"He won't say anything. He wants it too much."

"So when does it happen?"

"A lot of them will be together this weekend at a wedding. Aurelio will make sure he's out of town."

"An after party massacre?"

"Something like that. Could end up killing more people than necessary."

When I get back on the main road, I speak up again. "Johnny reached out to Carlo again."

"What?" he exclaims. "Why the fuck am I just now hearing about this?"

"I didn't want to get you upset before your meeting with Aurelio. It just happened this morning."

"What did he say?"

"He wants to meet up with him. He asked for today, but I told him to put it off."

Cortez nods, his brows furrowed. "That fucking snake. He's hiding from me but reaching out to Carlo. I can't believe he's willing to stoop this fucking low."

"Carlo came up with an idea. He wants to get Johnny over to the rectory by his church. He shouldn't think it's unusual to need to meet there, and probably wouldn't expect anything to happen so close to St. Joseph's."

Cortez nods. "Okay. Not bad."

"There's a cemetery nearby for easy disposal."

"Good, good," he says.

"The bad news is it'll have to be this weekend."

"When?"

"Saturday."

"Fuck. That's when the wedding is."

"We may have to split up."

Cortez shakes his head. "I don't want Carlo to be alone."

"I'll be with him," I say quickly and without question. Which isn't necessarily a good thing. "But I want to be at the wedding too," I add. "Maybe they'll happen at two different times."

He's quiet for a minute. "I want to be there to confront Johnny, but I don't know how to swing both."

"We don't know a time yet for Johnny. I can talk to Carlo about when to tell him to go over. He mentioned it would have to be late enough so that nobody is at the church. Maybe it'll be after the wedding party."

"Hmm."

"I also thought maybe I need to take Carlo to a range. He might need some lessons."

"He learned when he was a kid."

My brows lift. "Oh?"

"Yeah. I always took him every weekend. He shouldn't have forgotten too much. But a refresher wouldn't be a bad thing."

I nod and make another turn into town.

"Javier," Cortez says, his tone serious. "If it comes down to it."

I'm already shaking my head. "Don't."

"Listen to me," he spits, leaving no room for argument. "We don't know what's going to happen. It may not go the way we want it to, but I want you to save my son. Keep him safe. If I go, he'll need someone, and you're the one I trust the most. Don't leave his side. Help him if and when he needs it. Tell everyone who will listen that this is what I want. I want him at the top. Make sure there's no pushback, and if there is, end it. You hear me?"

I'm still shaking my head, but I say, "Yes. But Cortez, you're not going anywhere." I look at him. "Nobody's ready for that just yet."

He claps my shoulder, giving it a squeeze. "You'll be okay. Carlo will keep you on."

I know he's not naive enough to think I'm only referring to concern over my job, but I don't expect him to be vulnerable now. He knows exactly what I mean, and that's why he's not going to touch it.

The problem is, while I understand his stance as a father and wanting to make sure his son stays alive, I couldn't imagine Cortez dying. I want them both alive for my own selfish reasons, and I'll sacrifice myself if it means keeping them both on this earth.

"Turn right here," Cortez says, gesturing to an alleyway between two buildings. "I'm meeting with—"

Glass explodes inward milliseconds after a loud bang, and it doesn't take long for me to realize a bullet has just traveled through the passenger window and out the windshield.

I slam on the brakes and shove the door open, rounding the front of the car while simultaneously pulling a gun from my holster. Small pinpricks of pain on my face let me know I've been cut by the flying shards of glass. With a glance inside the car, I see Cortez wave me away, letting me know he's fine.

There's a partially open window, but nobody is in sight, so I quickly make my way to the door that leads into the brick building.

Gun outstretched in front of me, I scan the area and make my way down a hall. The place seems abandoned, and I wonder who the hell Cortez was planning to meet here, but more importantly, who gave him up and to whom.

In the hall, there's a few closed doors, and as I inch past one, a slight noise inside gets my attention. Someone's in there.

With the gun in my right hand, I put my left on the doorknob, ready to push it open and shoot whoever is on the other side. But I don't want to kill him. Not right away anyway.

I turn the knob ever so slightly, just to disengage the latch, then I lift my foot and kick the door with ferocity. When I step in, I see a tall, skinny man to my left, a gun aimed right at me. My bullet meets his shoulder before he can pull the trigger. As his body jerks back, I rush forward, hitting him in the temple with the butt of the gun. He stumbles, body going loose as his eyes glaze over. I take his gun from him and shove it in the back of my pants before pushing him to the floor and aiming at his forehead.

"Tell me everything."

"Fuck you."

I lift my foot and bring my black boot down on his knee. He screams, reaching for his leg.

I crouch down so I can look him straight in his eyes. "This can be done in a more civilized way, but only you can control that." I reach behind me, unsnapping the button on the sheath that holds a knife along my belt.

"Man, I'm just doing what I was paid to do," he says, his eyes stuck on the sharp blade.

"Who paid you?"

He hesitates, reaching for the wound in his shoulder. "He'll kill me."

I lunge forward, putting the tip of the knife at his balls. "I'm going to fucking kill you, but I can leave you in one piece or cut you into many. It's your choice. Now tell me who the fuck paid you to shoot Cortez."

He sucks in a shuddering breath, attempting to scoot away from me, but he's already backed into a corner. "Okay, okay, okay. I wasn't paid to shoot Cortez."

I push the tip of the blade into his jeans, cutting through the material. "Fine."

"Fuck! Okay, look, I'm serious. He wasn't the target. You were."

I inhale through my nose, fury boiling in my veins. "Who paid you?"

"This guy. He didn't tell me his name. He was kinda big, you know? He was wearing a hat and glasses, but he had a gold ring on his pinky. It had the letter J stamped in black. I noticed it because he kept fucking with his disguise."

"Fucking Johnny," I seethe. "All right," I say, standing up. "You did good."

He sighs, body slumping as I sheath my knife. I take the gun and aim, shooting him right between the eyes before he's aware it's happening.

Back outside, I find Cortez standing by the car, his phone to his ear.

"Yeah, exactly. We'll be there soon. Keep an eye on him."

"He told me Johnny hired him, but it was me who was the target."

"He's trying to get me unprotected," Cortez says. "With you gone, he might feel like he has a better chance."

"I doubt Johnny will do anything himself. The Bonettis want me gone since I'm the brick wall between you and their bullets."

"Well, I thought I had an inside guy. Looks like he turned back and told the Bonettis about my meeting with him. They probably told Johnny to pay someone for the job so it wouldn't be linked to them."

"Think he'll still show up?"

He looks at his watch. "We'll see in about five minutes. Let's get inside. Park the car along the building and roll the window down. I don't want him to see that it's been shot."

"You okay?" I ask, gesturing to his shoulder.

"Just a graze. Besides messed up sleeves, my skin is only slightly burnt and bleeding is minimal."

"Good."

I get in the car and park it with the passenger side close to the building. There's shattered glass in the alley, but it's not like the road was clean before. I kick it around to spread it out before heading inside.

I watch from the window as another car slowly pulls up a few minutes later.

"He's on the phone," I whisper to Cortez who's on the other side of the hall.

"Yeah, I bet he is."

Loud vibrations start filtering in from the other room.

"Shit."

I rush to the dead man slumped in the corner and fish into his pockets to silence the phone.

"He's checking on him," Cortez says when I make it back to the window.

"He has to know he didn't get the job done."

"We still need to get him inside."

Cortez walks to the door, pulling it open and raising his uninjured arm. The man in the car sees him and lifts his chin before removing the phone from his ear. Cortez lets the door close as he comes back to stand against the wall.

"How do you wanna do this?" I ask.

"We don't really need information from him. That guy said it was Johnny, right?"

I nod. "And we know this guy is a rat."

"So, the Bonettis could be aware something is coming. I never told him details of what I was planning, but he'd know enough that they'd be on guard."

"So, we need to change our plans," I say, reaching for the gun in the back of my pants as I watch the man exit his car. "We can't wait for the wedding."

"That only leaves us tomorrow or the next day."

"If we kill him now, they'll know we know."

Cortez huffs. "I'm tired of the bullshit. We already got one man dead in there. What's another one? We'll just have to move fast."

"You sure?"

Cortez nods.

"Step back," I say, right as the door opens.

"Hey," the man greets, watching us with a careful expression.

I lift my head, arms positioned behind my back.

"Hey," Cortez greets, standing in a way that hides his torn shirt.

"So—"

He starts speaking but doesn't finish, because as soon as I hear the click of the heavy door, I extend my arm. Pulling the trigger, a bullet hits him square in the forehead, dropping him into a heap on the floor.

Cortez sighs. "Let's get out of here before my blood starts seeping through my clothes. Wipe down the knobs and meet me in the car. We have to meet up with the guys and get started on this."

"Okay." A thought hits me. "Hey, boss."

He stops and looks at me.

"If they're after me like this, maybe Carlo shouldn't be alone at my house. They could know where I stay."

His jaw clenches and he pinches the bridge of his nose. "Okay. We can get him."

"All right. I'll let him know."

Cortez walks out and I start calling Carlo while I wipe my prints from the dead man's gun and leave it next to his body.

"You okay?" he asks as soon as he answers.

"Yes, but I have to get you soon. Me and your dad will be there in half an hour."

"What's happening?"

"A lot, but I'll explain later. Stay away from windows. Don't answer the door either."

He's quiet for a second. "Okay."

"See you soon."

I push open the door and walk in to find Carlo already standing nearby, expression tense.

"Oh my God," he says, moving forward with his hands up, like he's ready to study the cuts on my face.

I give him a quick shake of my head before walking past him. Cortez enters behind me.

"What happened?" Carlo questions when he sees the scratches on his dad's face and his torn sleeve.

I take off my jacket and remove my holster before pulling my shirt over my head. I have specks of blood that don't belong to me on my clothing, because I was standing too close to the first guy when I shot him.

"Everything's fine," Cortez answers, taking off his suit jacket and unbuttoning his shirt.

"That's not what I asked," Carlo retorts. "Clearly something happened."

"We got surprised," I tell him.

"Uh huh. By?"

I glance at Cortez but he's still trying to get his shirt off.

"Someone was waiting for us at one of the meeting

spots. They shot through the window. Your dad got grazed and we both got glass in the face."

"Jesus," he breathes.

"Nope. Don't think he was there, Son," Cortez says, flinging his shirt onto the couch.

I watch Carlo's expression morph into one of annoyance before walking to his dad and inspecting the wound on his arm.

"You have anything here?" he asks me. "First-aid kit? Band-Aid?"

"Yeah. One sec."

I walk into my bathroom and grab the kit I bought after I had to have Carlo stitch me up in the rectory.

He meets my gaze when I hand it to him.

"This is a lot bigger than I expected."

I smirk at him. "I had an incident a while ago. Thought it would be smart to always be prepared."

His lips twitch slightly. "Hope you have one in your car."

"I do."

He opens it up and takes out an antiseptic wipe and some butterfly bandages, and while he helps his dad, I go to my bathroom and wash my face. The cuts are superficial and don't require anything but to be cleaned.

When I get back to the living room, he's already done patching his dad up.

"So, what's the plan?" he's asking Cortez.

"We were going to do it at the wedding reception this weekend, but now with two of their people dead, they're going to—"

"You killed them?" he asks, looking past his dad and at me.

I nod once.

"Oftentimes, there's not a choice in this game, Son."

"No, yeah," he says, processing. "It makes sense. They shot at you."

"Javier was the target," Cortez adds.

Carlo's eyes widen slightly, and once again, he's looking at me. "You?"

"They want him out of the way for a better chance at me," Cortez says. "They missed. It's fine."

"They might not always miss," Carlo says.

"Which is why we have to move fast. They could be aware of my plans, and they'll definitely be aware of the deaths of two of their guys. We can't wait for the wedding."

"It was Johnny who paid the guy to kill me," I say.

"What?" Carlo exclaims.

"Yeah, he's a real piece of shit," Cortez says. "I'm gonna use the bathroom, but then we need to go."

"Okay," I reply.

As soon as the bathroom door closes, Carlo walks toward me, inspecting my face.

"Are you okay?" he asks.

I hold his chin between my thumb and forefinger. "I'm fine." After a quick kiss on his lips, I step back to put space between us.

"I'm not gonna lie and pretend I'm not afraid about what's going to happen," he says.

"Do you think I'm never afraid?"

"You don't seem like you are."

"I suppose it's because it doesn't make a difference. I have to do what I have to do regardless of the outcome."

"You're not afraid of dying?"

"I'm afraid of dying slowly. Painfully. If it's quick, then I'm not even going to be aware."

He shakes his head like he doesn't understand. "You don't think about what you're leaving behind?"

"What am I leaving?" I question. "I told you. I don't have any family. I don't have friends. Death is only sad for those left behind, but I have nobody to leave behind."

"Nobody's dying," Cortez says as he enters the room. "Well, none of *us*. Now let's go ensure that's the case. We have some planning to do."

It takes a few seconds for Carlo to snap out of whatever daze he was caught in. "Okay. I'm ready."

✝

A LITTLE OVER AN HOUR LATER, we're at a safe house in the coastal town of Marblehead with everyone Cortez has on his side in this war. Not only are the capos here, but so are the soldiers.

As he recounts what happened to us in that alleyway, he alerts them that the Bonettis are likely more aware of our plans than we'd want them to be.

From my spot near the front of the house where I can keep an eye on any incoming traffic, my gaze continues to find Carlo. He stands amongst the group of men who've known each other for years, but doesn't allow himself to be pushed out. He talks strategy with his father, he agrees with one of the capos while disagreeing with another one's plans. He's smart and conscientious. He thinks over things in a way some of the others don't—with his moral goodness front and center. It may not make sense for someone to be morally good while planning a war, but I think he's starting to realize that this has to be done. Being a target will make you understand it's kill or be killed, and while he's not taking into consideration the lives of the people we all know need to go, he wants to ensure all of us on this end remain unharmed.

I study him in his gray slacks, white cable knit Polo, and titanium round glasses, and I can't help the grin that forms on my lips. He looks nothing like these other guys. He looks like a college professor in a room full of gangsters.

As I'm staring at him, his eyes find mine. Our gazes lock onto each other, and though it's not for long, something passes between us that makes my heart gallop. Something in his expression reminds me of the look he had at my place earlier.

Realization hits me like a bolt of lightning. He's afraid. Not just for himself. Not even only for his father. He's worried about me. I told him I had nobody to leave behind, and an expression washed over his face that I didn't understand at the time. I told him I wasn't leaving anyone behind if I died, but it's clear he's been thinking that *he'll* be left behind. He's over here with his father, drawing up a plan for a war that he knows will have us on the frontline. I can't imagine how he feels knowing what he's helping plan could very well end in the deaths of his dad, me, or both of us.

His dad doesn't want him there when it happens, so he'll be safe, but he'll be going out of his mind not knowing what's happening, or if anyone will come back to him.

I'm important enough to him for him to worry about, and I've never felt like more than an employee. Bodyguard. Killer.

I need to talk to him.

Luckily, they break apart a few minutes later, and I find that I was so stuck in my own head that I didn't pay enough attention to the plan. Cortez will fill me in later, but that's not even my concern right now. Where can I talk to Carlo without it looking suspicious?

"Javier."

I snap out of my daze and find Cortez calling me over.

"All good?" I ask.

"Yeah. We'll go over a few things later once there's less people here."

I nod. "Okay."

"This is set for tomorrow. Carlo needs to be put up in a hotel somewhere. I don't want anyone to know where that is. Get him far if you can."

"He's gonna put up a fight."

"Yeah, well, he needs to steer clear of this. If everything goes wrong, and we all die, then the family ends up in the hands of Johnny by default, and we don't have time to take care of him first."

"But the other guys know what's up with him."

"It would take time to find someone to take the lead if all of us end up dead. Carlo needs to remain alive."

I nod again. "I'll talk to him."

"Go ahead," he says. "Let him know there can be no other way."

"You wanna be involved in this conversation?"

He shakes his head. "He definitely won't wanna hear it from me."

"All right."

I glance around but don't see him in the living room, so I make my way to the kitchen, following voices and hoping to find him.

When I don't see him there, I travel through the small hall and hit the stairs. There's two bedrooms and a bathroom up there. I imagine he wanted alone time to reflect, but I have to interrupt.

I find him standing at the window that faces the back of the house, staring at birds flying from trees.

"Hey."

He turns around quickly, his expression changing from tense to relief when he sees me. "Hey."

I push the door behind me to drown out the voices and walk closer to him. "You okay?"

"Yeah," he says, going back to looking out the window. "I've known it was coming, but it's a strange feeling knowing it all goes down tomorrow."

"Yeah."

I move in front of him, perching my ass on the wide window sill. "I was wrong earlier."

He looks down at me, brows knit into a furrow. "What do you mean?"

"I do have someone I'd leave behind."

I can't explain what thoughts go through his head, but as I watch him, his body sags, like a weight was lifted from his shoulders and he can finally relax. The skin between his brows smooth out and his eyelids seem to droop slightly, like sadness is tugging on them.

He pinches the bridge of his nose in a similar fashion as his father does, but unlike Cortez, he doesn't shy away from showing any emotion. His hand falls to his side before slipping into his pocket, and he looks at me in a way I've never experienced. There's too much emotion there and I can't decipher any of it.

"I'm sorry I didn't realize earlier. For a long time, it's only been me. I respect Cortez, and he's the closest thing to family I've had since my dad died, but I'm still his employee. If I died, I'm sure he'd be upset, but he'd find someone else to do what I do.

"I've been worried about you dying and having to face

your father after the fact. I've been concerned about what his death would do to you, because if either one of you dies, I'd feel like I was to blame. I can't imagine not having your dad around, and honestly, I don't want to know what that would feel like. I'll admit that in the beginning, I was watching out for you for the sake of Cortez, but now...now I want to keep you safe because I can't imagine being without you."

He glances behind his shoulder before stepping forward and running his hand through my hair.

"I don't want to lose either of you. My relationship with my dad is not the best, but if he dies, I don't get the opportunity to even try to make it better. If you..." He doesn't finish the sentence, like he can't bring himself to even think it. "Then I don't know what I'd do. You've changed my world."

I grin. "Probably not for the best."

His hand curves around the back of my head. "It's been scary. I've been terrified for more reasons than one, but I've also never been happier. I feel free with you. Only you have made me feel that way."

I reach up and grab his hand, holding it in mine. "I want you to have the opportunity to fix the relationship with your dad, but I...and I can't believe I'm saying this, but I want the opportunity to have one with you."

His lips form a small grin. "Coming from Mr. I Don't Date...that's something."

I playfully roll my eyes. "You should feel special."

He squeezes my hand, smiling wider. "I do."

I stand up and wrap an arm around his waist, bringing us close together. "I also think you should know something. It might help with your dad."

"What's that?"

"He and I were talking, and while I know you've thought he disowned you for being gay, and kept you from his life out of hatred, I think maybe that's not the case."

Carlo pulls away, moving to the other side of the window. "What do you mean? Are you defending him to me?"

"Listen," I say, holding my hands up. "He said he would do whatever he could to protect you, even if it meant pushing you away."

Carlo shakes his head, brows furrowed. "How does that help?"

"You know your dad. He's not about to be vulnerable. What I got from what he said was that he's been worried about you. He pushed you into the priesthood to keep you from being able to be seen with another man. I'm not saying that's right or logical. In his head, though, he was keeping you from being hurt. Not just by people in the mafia, but in life. He didn't want to see you become a victim. He was angry, not at you, at the idea of you being hurt."

Carlo shakes his head. "I don't...that's not—"

"I'm not saying he did everything the right way. I know I don't know all the details, but I believe there was maybe a little more care and concern on his end than you thought. He wants to keep you safe, but he doesn't know how to express that in a way that doesn't come off hostile."

"I would never let myself be a victim."

I smile. "I know. I told him that."

"You did?"

I nod. "All that to say, I hope you have the time to figure things out."

"We'll see."

I step forward and grab his hands. "Also."

256

"Oh no."

"I have to take you and put you up in a hotel somewhere. He wants you far away."

He cocks his head then exhales. "Do I have a choice?"

"Mmm, not really. I want you safe, too."

"So, I'd have to go against you and my dad in order to be involved."

"Right."

"Well, I'm going to be directly involved in the Johnny thing."

"Yes, but I'll be with you."

"Maybe you should take me to the hotel now...so we have some time."

I grin and step forward, putting my hands on his ass as I nuzzle into his neck. "Yes, I still have to punish you for doubting my abilities. You see how I came back, mostly unscathed."

"Mm," he murmurs, hands going to my back. "Yes, I'm sorry I doubted you."

I step back and study him. "You look so prim and proper today." He glances down at his clothes. "Like a good boy who doesn't get into any trouble."

He bites into his bottom lip and the action makes me want to pounce on him right here and now.

"I am a good boy."

A growl rumbles in my throat. "I want to dirty you up."

"Then let's get out of here."

"Deal."

When I found Cortez, he seemed distracted, still talking to people, so I told him I was going to take Carlo to the hotel, and then come back so we can discuss the plan in full without anyone else here.

While I think everyone is aware that I know most details about the business, I don't voice opinions around the family. I'm an outsider, unable to be a made man. Which is fine by me, but people don't appreciate someone from the outside having a say in the politics of family business. Cortez and I have those conversations alone.

After stopping by my place to pick up Carlo's things, I drove over an hour and a half away to get him set up in a hotel that nobody should have easy access to.

It's a luxury place with security by the doors, twenty-four hour surveillance, and the need to have a key card to access the elevators or stairwell. Even if someone was able to follow me all the way here, they shouldn't be able to get to him inside.

"This seems like a little much," Carlo says as we exit the

elevator on the thirteenth floor. "I could've stayed in a cheaper hotel."

"Cheaper means less safe, and you are going to be safe here."

"Does my father pay you well?"

"Yes."

"That's good. I mean, I'd assume you'd have constant hazard pay."

"Something like that."

I unlock the door to his room and quickly re-lock it once we're inside. It's a suite that has a small kitchen area, living room, bedroom with an en-suite, and a balcony.

"Don't—" I start.

"I won't go on the balcony," he finishes. "But I am going to go to the bathroom," he says, a certain look in his eye.

"Ah."

He takes his suitcase into the bedroom and then disappears behind another door. I make my way to the half bathroom by the front door and freshen up there.

Once I'm in the living room, I start stripping down until I'm only in my undershirt and boxers.

When I hear the bathroom door open, I start heading toward the bedroom. I find Carlo wearing only his boxer-briefs, kneeling at his open luggage on the floor.

"What're you looking for in there?"

He continues rifling through before pulling out the flogger, and turning around to present it to me.

"I thought you said something about punishment."

I take the whip in my hands, fingering the leather tails. "You know, that night, when I used this on you..." I exhale, meeting his gaze. "I was harder than I've ever been. I went home and jacked off twice just thinking about it."

He sinks his teeth into his lip. "You acted unaffected."

"Oh, I was very affected," I say, stepping closer to him. "I've been affected by you since you stitched me up."

"Oh."

I grin. "Now, what are you being punished for this time? Still having sinful thoughts?"

Walking toward the mattress, I grab a pillow and throw it on the floor next to the bed. I point to it so he knows to kneel on it.

"Yes. Very much so."

"Tell me what you're thinking."

He puts his hands together in front of him on the mattress, fingers interlocked. "I think about your body." He swallows, and I walk around to the other side to be able to see his face as he speaks. "How I love the weight of it on top of me."

"Mm," I murmur. "What else?"

"I like the way your tattoos wrap around your muscles, and the way they flex when you fuck me."

Now it's my turn to swallow.

"I think about how it felt to be inside you, and how I've never experienced such pleasure before. I think about you all the time. I think about us and all the things we've done, and the things not yet done, but yearning for."

I take in a deep breath. "And are you sorry for any of those thoughts?"

He slowly shakes his head, looking at me like he wants to devour me.

I tsk at him. "Maybe you're not such a good boy."

"So punish me."

I walk around until I'm behind him. "Lust is wrong, is it not?" Before he can answer, I let the tails of the flogger hit his back.

"Oh, God," he exclaims.

"Unholy thoughts. Also wrong, am I right?"

"Yes."

I strike him again, watching his skin turn pink.

"Do you still want to fuck me?"

"Yes," he cries after the leather meets his flesh.

I tug down his boxer-briefs, exposing his round ass. He moans, arching ever so slightly.

On my knees behind him, I drop the flogger to the floor and cup one of his cheeks. "You want me more than you want forgiveness?"

"Yes."

My hand eases away before meeting his skin with a sharp smack.

"Ah!" he yelps before swaying his hips.

"You want to feel me inside here," I say, my fingers teasing his crease.

"Yes. Please," he begs.

I spank him again and revel in his cries of pleasure.

"My kinky priest."

He moans, wanton and wild. "Yes."

"You like that?" I ask, caressing his ass and thighs as I press up against him. "You like being mine?"

A full-body chill rolls over him. "Yes."

"Good. Is there anything else you'd like to confess?"

He angles his head over his shoulder. "I've never felt closer to heaven than when I'm with you."

I suck in a breath and quickly turn him around, lifting him up to the bed in a frenzy. "Fuck," I say, nuzzling into his neck where I plant kisses along the skin. "You...you mess me up, Carlo. I don't know what to do or say, but fuck if you don't know exactly how to get to me."

He shoves his underwear down his legs, and I help remove them, tossing the material to the floor. I swiftly remove my own clothing before finding my place between his legs.

"How's your back?"

"Fine," he says, pulling me even closer, and pressing his mouth to mine.

Our tongues dance to the music our moans create, and for a while, we just kiss and touch. Our cocks grind together, eliciting grunts and groans from our throats, but we don't move to do any more than this. We take our time, and I try to ignore the little voice in the back of my head that says it's because we don't know if we'll have another opportunity again.

Eventually, I move lower down his body, my lips and tongue getting to know as much of his flesh as possible. I kiss down his throat and across his collarbone. I tease and nibble on both of his nipples before covering his torso in kisses.

He arches his back as he moans, his fingers threading through my hair.

"I may not be a believer," I say, peeking up at him as I hover over his erection. "But I'll worship down here any day."

He smiles. "Show me."

I kiss down his shaft, letting my tongue touch the skin before my lips do. I lick his balls, taking turns bringing each one into my mouth.

"Oh fuck," he moans.

I hook his legs over my shoulders and continue my onslaught of attention on every part of skin I can reach. My tongue skates up the crease between his thigh and groin and then my lips encircle the tip of his cock with a gentle teasing suck.

"God, please," he begs, his body squirming as his hands hit the mattress and grab at the covers.

I continue to torture him with pleasure, bringing him to the edge of ecstasy, just to ease away again. I love seeing him turned on to the point of desperation.

With my hands under his thighs, I push up, dropping lower to my stomach. My tongue slides between my lips until I reach his entrance. Carlo sucks in a shuddering breath and I keep exploring. I prod at the hole, teasing and licking until we're both moaning and grunting. I dip it inside, going as deep as I can. One of his hands lands on my head, pushing me closer, wanting more.

I squeeze his cheeks while spreading him apart, eating him like he's my favorite dessert.

"Javi, please," he groans.

I love when he calls me Javi. I feel like the shortening of a name or any sort of nickname is a sign of comfortability and closeness.

"You ready for more, baby?" His eyes flash and he nods. "Got lube in your bag?"

"Zipper pocket."

I get to the floor and find the small bottle in his suitcase. As soon as I'm back on the bed, I coat my fingers in the liquid and begin prepping him. As my fingers slide in and out, I use my other hand to stroke his shaft.

"I want you so bad," he says in a breathy voice.

"You'll get me," I tell him. "Then you won't be able to think about anything but me for days," I say with a grin.

"Probably longer," he replies.

After a few more minutes, I reach for the lube and begin to coat my erection in it. With a little more around his hole, I settle between his legs and begin to push in.

He hitches one leg up around my hip and I slide all the way inside.

Our noises collide between us as I move slowly, making sure he has time to feel comfortable. When he starts bucking his hips, I know he's ready, so I begin to move faster.

My body thrums with need. I've felt lust before. It's always been a simple desire to fuck someone. Anyone. This, though. This is different. I crave him with an intensity that borders on obsession. The passion I feel is overwhelming. I want nothing more than to make him feel good. I don't even care about myself, because I know I'll be fulfilled by pleasing him.

I watch his face contort as I fuck him. His teeth bite into his lip as his eyes close tight. Then his mouth opens as he releases a sinful moan.

"You're so fucking sexy, you know that?" I say. His gaze meets mine, his cheeks flushed. "I love watching you come apart beneath me."

"I love having you inside me."

Lowering myself, I plant a fervid kiss on his lips, my tongue pushing through and tangling with his. My hips keep moving, fucking him with long, deep strokes as he moans into my mouth.

"So good," he whispers. "You feel so fucking good."

"*You* feel good," I tell him. "Everything about being with you feels good, and I never thought I'd know that feeling."

He closes his eyes, his head moving back as a noise rumbles in this throat. "Javi." My name is a plea...a prayer on his lips. Like he wants more but doesn't know how or even if he should request it.

Considering what we're on the eve of doing, I know fear

sits heavy in his heart, and maybe he hates hearing these things unaware if we'll have more after tomorrow.

"*Cariño*," I murmur, moving my mouth to his neck where I kiss a trail to his ear. "*Mi amor*. I will always come back to you." I plant another kiss on his heated skin.

He wraps his arms around me, holding me tight. "What if you don't?"

"Then know that I will have done everything in my power to have tried, and that you were the last thing I thought about."

I kiss his cheek, then his forehead before easing away.

"Come back to me," he says.

I nod once before sitting up on my knees and thrusting in and out. His fingers wrap around his shaft and he begins to stroke.

"Yes, baby," I whisper huskily.

My gaze goes to his hand, watching how he handles himself, but the visual heightens what I'm already feeling, and my orgasm begins to build.

"Don't come yet. I want it in my mouth."

His tongue swipes across his bottom lip and he slows his movements.

"You better hurry then."

"I never want to hurry when I'm with you."

His face softens, and one hand cups his balls while his other one continues languid strokes. "I want you to fill me up," he says in a husky voice. "I want to feel you throb and twitch inside me."

"Oh fuck."

"Come on, baby. Come for me."

And that's it. With just a few words, I'm sent over the edge. My orgasm detonates, shattering me as I empty my release deep inside him. My entire body shakes and shivers, my breath coming in deep, shuddering pants.

"Oh my God," I cry. "Fuck. Yes."

"Oh God," Carlo exclaims. "Oh God, I'm close. I'm about—"

I open my eyes and see his hand moving quickly up and down his shaft. He picked up the pace as he watched me, and now he's about to be sent over that same edge.

I pull out and drop lower, resting my weight on one forearm as I use the other hand to take over his movements.

"Fuck!" he yells, drawing the word out as his release hits my tongue.

I keep stroking, letting my mouth fill up with his cum. Even as his body rocks with the aftershocks of his orgasm, I keep moving my hand, catching every drop before I swallow it all down.

"Oh my God, yes. Fuck. Oh God," he chants.

I eventually pull away, after licking him clean, and lie on my side next to him. He turns into me, draping a leg over mine.

We're still trying to catch our breath, and though our bodies are slick with sweat, neither one of us seems to want any space between us.

With his forehead against mine, he presses his lips to my mouth, holding steady for several seconds before pulling away.

"I know it's not fully in your control," he starts, and I already know where he's going.

"I finally have someone to come back to," I say. "You better believe I'll mow over any and everyone to be able to get back to this."

His hand goes to the side of my face, and he just nods. I

can tell by his expression that he doesn't want to risk saying anything else. There's too much emotion and vulnerability behind his eyes.

When this is all over with, he'll say what he needs to say. We just have to get past tomorrow.

CARLO

CHAPTER 42

Waking up today, we do normal morning routines, but with a rain cloud over our heads. We discuss mundane topics, but in the silent stretches, the concern is deafening. There's a storm on the horizon, but we don't know how it's going to develop, or the destruction it'll leave in its wake.

Javier left to see my dad again last night, and didn't crawl back into bed until almost one in the morning. He didn't come with a whole lot of new information, but reiterated my father's request to keep me far from the action.

I hate being left here while he and my dad are in the middle of the fight. I won't be able to relax. I won't know what's going on, and if Javier never shows up, or I never hear from my dad, who do I talk to? Where do I go to find out what happened? I met my father's guys, but I don't have any contact information. Nobody will call me.

"Hey."

Javi comes to a stop next to me where I'm sitting at the table in the kitchenette and staring off into space. He runs his hands through my hair, forcing my head back so I can look up at him.

"Get out of that head of yours, huh."

I grab his hips and give him a forced smile. "I live in my head."

"I know you do." He leans down and kisses my temple.

"Can I get somebody else's number?" I ask as he walks toward the small refrigerator.

"Whose?"

"Anyone. Actually, everyone's. I don't know who's gonna be left standing, and if I don't hear back from you or my dad, I need to be able to talk to someone to find out details."

His back stiffens before he turns back to look at me. I think he's going to once again tell me that he'll be fine, and that there's nothing to worry about, but he doesn't.

"Sure. I'll get some info for you."

And that reply is like a punch in the gut.

✝

WE'RE on the couch hours later, watching TV and eating some Chinese food when a knock sounds on the door.

I glance at Javier whose brows are knitted together. He gets up and puts his food on the table before going into his bedroom and grabbing a gun.

With it down at his side, he walks to the door and looks through the peephole. Glancing back at me, he mouths, *it's your dad.*

A few seconds later, the two men walk into the living room. Javier exchanges the gun for his food and sits a little farther away from me, while Dad stands next to the other couch, his eyes glancing toward the TV.

"What's going on?" Javi asks.

"Javier, can I talk to my son for a minute?"

"Oh. Sure," he says, getting up from the couch. "I'll go grab something from my car."

I watch as he disappears into his room to get his shoes on, then promptly leaves the apartment.

Dad finally sits on the couch to my left, loosing a sigh.

"What's up?" I ask, putting my food down.

He's quiet for a bit, his eyes dancing around the room.

"You still have that box I gave you?"

"Yeah. It's at home."

He nods once. "Good."

Silence sits heavy between us, and when he doesn't say anything, I speak up.

"I told Javi..." I clear my throat. "I told Javier that I'd like some contact info for some of the guys. In case I need to reach out to someone for information."

Dad's dark eyes narrow in on me. "Someone will know to find you if that needs to be done," he says simply.

"Who?"

"Someone else who won't be there, but who I know I can trust. Well," he sighs, "who I'm pretty positive I can trust. These days, I'm not sure I can trust anyone."

I sit forward a little, running a hand through my hair. "I'm just gonna be blunt about this." He nods. "If you die, what should I expect?"

He watches me carefully, then takes a deep breath and opens his mouth. "My consigliere, George, will reach out to you. He and my top guys already know my wishes. If you choose to step in, it will happen."

"Isn't there some sort of initiation process?" I question. "Murder, for example?"

Dad shakes his head. "You stepping in will bend the rules a little, but if it comes at my demise, it'll be you who deals with any fallout. George will help you. He'll fill you in on everything you need to know, and you'll meet everyone you need to. You'll have to earn everyone's respect, and it'll take time, but I have several guys who will be there to guide you until you catch on. You're a smart kid, you'll figure it out."

"Speaking of bending rules. What about—"

He seems to know exactly where I was going. "Whatever you choose to do about that will be your own decision," he says, holding up a hand. "I'll be dead, and so will my concern. I'll warn you, as I always have, it won't be easy. Guys won't like it. It could be bad."

"So, you'd suggest keeping it a secret?"

His eyes roam over my face, an emotion behind them that's unfamiliar to me. I can't quite read it, and it's gone before I can dwell on it too much.

"I'd suggest being someone they wouldn't dare question. About anything."

I nod, and a small flutter of hope takes flight in my chest.

"Like you?"

His lips curl up slightly on one side. "I suppose."

I snort before letting some time pass. "And what if I decide it's not for me?"

Dad leans back. "Then you talk to George about that." His fingers tap on the arm of the couch. "But, Carlo, I think you could do great things with it. You're different than I am, and I don't say that as a critique. You have a good head on your shoulders. You could make changes, and with the right people on your side, you'd have an army to back you up. It'll be a slow process, but you're young. You have time."

My heart squeezes in my chest. I've never heard my dad talk to me like this before. The compliments and confidence in me has my head spinning.

I nod, swallowing down a lump of emotion.

"And Javier," he says, pointing at me. "You like him, right?"

A small amount of fear unfurls in my stomach. I want to tell him everything—that not only do I like him, but that I can't imagine living my life if Javier doesn't exist within it. However, it's not just my life, it's Javier's too. So, the truth hides in the shadows behind me as indifference runs ahead.

I shrug. "Yeah, sure."

I might've undersold it, because Dad doesn't look impressed by my answer. "He's a good guy. I mean, he's bad, but it's good to have someone like him on your side."

I choke out a laugh. "Right."

"Keep him around." He watches me, ensuring I absorb this command.

I nod. "I will."

"We'll be leaving soon," he says. "Need to meet up with George before we get things going."

I run my palms across my pants. "Okay."

He stands and I follow suit. "Be careful out there."

Dad chuckles as he aims for the front door. "I'll be fine."

I stifle a laugh, because he and Javier sound just alike. "Right."

He turns and we watch each other for a few seconds, neither one of us knowing what to do or say next. We haven't been close and he's never been affectionate. We hardly know how to have normal conversations, but now we're here, unsure if we'll see each other again.

"All right," I say, stepping forward and opening my arms. "We'll talk again soon."

He awkwardly wraps his arms around me, giving my back a couple pats. "Yeah."

When we pull away, Javier walks in, stopping short when he sees us so close to the door.

"Am I good?"

Dad nods. "I was just about to leave. Do whatever you need to do and meet me down in the garage."

"Okay."

He doesn't turn around or say anything else, and I wonder if that's the last image I'll have of my father.

"Everything okay?" Javi asks.

I nod. "Yeah."

"Well, I guess it's time for me to leave."

I step to the side and let him pass before following him into the room. From the bed, I watch him strap up, arming himself with guns in his holster and the knife on his belt. He's decked out in black—from his jeans, T-shirt, and boots, to the light jacket he always wears to hide the guns.

Once he's done, he looks at me and reaches for my hand. Our fingers touch, then he pulls me up from the bed and brings me into his arms.

"It's going to be okay," he whispers into my ear. "I'll tell you all about it when I get back."

I squeeze him tighter. "Okay."

It's hard to let him go, but eventually I pull away. He cradles my cheek and presses a kiss to my mouth.

"See you soon," he says.

"Yes. Soon."

CHAPTER 43

Seconds turn into minutes before minutes stretch into hours. I can't stop checking the time, wondering if it's started. If anyone is hurt yet. Are they dead? Is it all over?

I pace around the apartment, moving from room to room while morbid thoughts run rampant through my head. I try to sit down but my legs can't stop bouncing, so I stand again and make my way to Javier's room.

I get to my knees on the side of the bed and pray. I truly don't know if it will make a difference, but it makes me feel better. It makes me feel a little less useless.

Before I'm done, my phone trills from the other room, so I get up and rush to grab it.

"Hello?" I answer, my voice laced with fear.

"*Cariño*. I told you I'd be okay."

Javier's husky tone coming through the phone makes all the tension in my body melt away. My body sags and I drop onto the couch with an exhale.

"Thank God. How's my dad?"

"He's fine."

"Everything went well?"

He sighs. "Yes and no. I'll tell you about it later. We got a few things to do, but then I'll head home after."

"Okay. I'm glad you're alive."

Javier laughs. "Stop doubting me."

I chuckle. "I'll try to be better."

Once I get off the phone with him, I can finally breathe a little easier, so I go to the kitchen and warm up some leftover Chinese food and grab a bottle of water.

As I eat, I watch two episodes of some show that's on TV, and then I look at the clock and wonder when he'll make it back. It's nearly one-thirty when my phone dings with a message. It's from Javier.

> Won't be back for a while. Don't worry. I'll check in when I can.

THE LACK of information is what makes me worry, but at least he's still okay. I decide to take a shower before I get into bed, knowing I'll want to pounce on him the minute I realize he's back.

It's close to three before I begin falling asleep. I remember seeing 2:57 on the clock on the nightstand before I fell into unconsciousness.

When my eyes open again, I'm still facing the clock, but now the time reads 7:02.

I get up quickly, reaching for my phone and tapping on the screen. There's not a new message from him, but there is one from Johnny.

> I know we're supposed to meet tomorrow, but I need to see you today. Soon. I won't be able to tomorrow. Something's happening and your dad won't talk to me. I need you to get him a message for me. Please, kid. He'll kill me before he knows the truth.

THE PANIC in his text and the fact that he even typed out the last line without concern for anyone seeing it, makes me wonder what's going on.

My dad and Javier have told me enough to believe that Johnny can't be trusted. He's the reason all of this is happening. But now he's trying to tell me they have it all wrong.

I sit up in bed and stare at the message, trying to figure out what to do. I switch over to Javier's thread and type out a message.

> Johnny needs to meet today. Don't know if we'll have the opportunity tomorrow. Will you be able to meet me there?

WHILE I WAIT FOR JAVIER, I reply to Johnny to buy myself some time.

> I might be able to see you today. Let me move some things around and I'll get back to you. But why do you say that about him? What's going on?

I ENDED up adding the last two questions on a whim, knowing I should question what he's talking about, because I shouldn't be aware of anything. If I didn't question him, he'd be suspicious.

As I wait for text responses from either one of them, I get out of bed and start getting ready. Exhaustion still weighs me down, but I won't be able to go back to sleep now.

I'd prefer not to meet Johnny until after the sun goes down, but it definitely can't happen before three, because people will still be in the church.

When I check my phone again, I only have a message from Johnny.

> Let me know as soon as you can. Your dad hasn't told you anything?

> You know he doesn't tell me anything.

> Well I'll tell you everything when I see you.

. . .

I DON'T BOTHER REPLYING AGAIN. I'll wait until I can give him a time, but Javier never gets back to me. I send two more messages and they all remain unread. I even send one to my dad, but he doesn't answer it either.

My overthinking brain begins to imagine the worst once more. Something else could've happened between the last message Javier sent me and now. But also, maybe they're just cleaning up the scene, which I assume could take a while. It's hard to know when I'm unaware of exactly what happened or where.

It's about eleven o'clock when the front door opens and Javier walks in. I lurch from the couch and rush toward him.

"Oh my God, I was starting to worry something bad had happened."

He grins, but it doesn't quite reach his eyes. "You worry too much."

"That's probably true." I wrap my arms around him, grateful he's in one piece. "You'll have to deal with that."

His arms hang around my waist and he kisses my temple. "I need to shower and sleep, but first tell me about this text from Johnny."

I pull away and follow behind him as he makes his way to the bedroom.

"He's saying that Dad has it all wrong and that he's afraid he'll die before he can explain."

Javier's brows furrow as he begins to remove his clothes. "He's lying."

"I assume so, but he's saying that it's Dad that won't talk to him. Do you know if he's reached out to him?"

He shakes his head. "Cortez hasn't said anything like that. It's been the opposite."

I notice the dried blood on his shoes as he sits down to unlace the boots. "He seems panicked," I tell him. "Says he won't be able to meet tomorrow. That it has to be today."

"When will the church be empty?"

"It closes at three, but clergy will stick around a little longer."

Javier nods. "I'm gonna shower, sleep, then we can head over there and settle in."

"Okay."

I want to ask him about what happened, but he looks worn out, so I let him shower so he can get into bed.

While he's in the bathroom, I close the blinds and draw the curtains, trying to get the room as dark as possible. Stripping down to my underwear, I get under the covers because I could use a nap as well.

When he gets out, a small grin touches his lips when he sees me in bed. Crawling in next to me, he drapes an arm over my torso, his head near my shoulder.

Within seconds, he's out like a light.

I set an alarm on my phone before I close my eyes, but I don't fall asleep right away. I think about what's going to happen when I see Johnny.

I envision multiple scenarios, trying to imagine how it'll all play out, or what might be the best way to control the situation.

Eventually, exhaustion drags me under, and I fall asleep.

✝

"COME ON, Padre. It's time to wake up."

My eyes blink, confusion clouding my brain.

"Carlo."

"Hmm."

"We gotta go. It's already four-thirty."

My blinks come more rapidly as I try to clear the fog. "Four-thirty?"

"I made coffee," Javier says. "We need to start heading to the church. Your dad is gonna meet us there."

I roll onto my back and see Javi next to the bed, a tumbler to his lips. After taking a sip, he smiles at me. "Welcome back."

"How are you up already?"

He shrugs. "Just needed a power nap."

I stretch, shoving the covers down. "Okay, I'm up."

"I'll pour you some coffee."

"Thanks."

He walks out and I take a few more seconds to stretch before I get up and head to the bathroom. After I'm done, I go to the closet where I hung up my black slacks and shirt, and begin to put them on. I don the collar last, then I meet Javier in the kitchen.

"Oh my," he says with a small smile. "Wasn't expecting this."

"Well, he'll think I'm coming off work. I think there might be a chasuble in the rectory I can put on."

He cocks his head. "Chasuble?"

"It's an outer garment. Think poncho but better."

"Gotcha."

"I'll be able to hide a gun in my waistband without him being able to see."

He nods. "Smart." Javier hands me a tumbler of coffee. "Let's go scope the place out. Text Johnny and tell him you can meet in an hour and a half."

I take a deep breath. "Wow. That's so soon."

"It's been a long time coming."

Nerves bubble up in my stomach. "Yeah. Is my dad already on the way?"

"Yep. We're gonna get the lay of the land and find a place to hide out."

"All right. Let's do it."

CHAPTER 44

I watch through the window in the rectory as the last car drives away from the church.

"They're all gone."

My dad strolls out of the hall and into the living room. "We could be in the back room, but he might want to walk around."

"If you don't stay in the house, then you can wait just outside the back door. But the house is old and the floor creaks. He could hear you come and go."

"Don't let him search the house," Javier says. "I'm not gonna risk being outside if he tries to pull anything."

"Being in the back room won't be much better. If he shoots me, it'll be over within a second."

Javier clenches his jaw and gives me a look. He can't say what he wants to because my dad is here.

"Okay, then we just fucking ambush him as soon as he walks in," Dad says. "Grab him, subdue him, and tie him up. Then we can ask all the fucking questions we want."

Javier nods. "Sounds good to me."

I don't particularly like that idea, because I worry it'll

skew what he has to say, but at the same time, I don't like the idea of being shot either.

"What if I just bring him upstairs with the story that I have something to do in the chapel up there. He'll be put at ease if I escort him through the house, and I'll have the doors open. Just past the chapel, there's a small closet. You'll have to squeeze, but you can be in there."

"What if he shoots you the second he walks in?" Javier asks.

"He won't."

He keeps trying to send me signs of unhappiness with his eyes, but he doesn't say anything. Instead, he turns to my dad, hoping he doesn't agree with this idea either.

"This is your idea," Dad says. "We'll do it how you want, but I hope this isn't a mistake. You got the gun on you?"

I lift the chasuble. "Yes. He'll never even know I have my hand on it."

"Okay then," Dad says.

"I'll have music on to obscure any sounds. If we end up needing to go back downstairs, just quietly make your way down and hang out in the hall. He wouldn't have a need to go back that way."

"When will he be here?" Javi asks.

I look at the clock on the wall. "Soon."

"If anything seems wrong, shoot and worry about it later," Dad tells me. "We already know what we need to know."

"I just want him to tell me why," I say.

Neither one of them looks happy. I know they'd rather go about it their own way, but he's coming here thinking I'm giving him the chance to talk, and I want to hear what he has to say. Even if it's bullshit.

I look out the window again and spot a car making a turn next to the church.

"I think he's here." I turn and face the stone-faced men. "Head upstairs." They both hesitate, watching me. "I'll be okay."

Dad walks away first, and Javier turns back and looks at me, his face full of worry. I send him a forced smile and nod.

I turn on the stereo and Christian music blares from the speakers. I turn it down a little, but leave it at a volume where it could hopefully mask any creaks in the floor.

A few minutes later, there's two quick knocks on the door. I take a deep breath, relax my shoulders, and start walking.

When I pull it open, Johnny stands there with the brim of his hat low over his eyes, and sunglasses on his face.

"Hey," I say, stepping back and opening the door. "Come in."

Stepping inside, he removes the glasses and looks me up and down. "Just get off?"

"Yeah. I actually still have a few things to do, so let's go up to the chapel."

"Where's that?" he questions, his voice tense.

"Upstairs."

"Oh."

He closes the door and follows me through the living room. I do my best to move with ease, like I don't have a care in the world. Johnny's eyes scan every part of the house, his movements chock-full of nervousness.

"So, what's up?" I ask. "There's been some abnormal things going on."

Johnny scoffs. "Your father is a lunatic, that's what's going on."

My back stiffens slightly as I hit the hallway upstairs. "Well, is that new information?" I say.

"He thinks I betrayed him, kid. He's been secretive for a while—doing things without telling me."

I get to the chapel and begin putting away the vestments I haphazardly tossed across the altar earlier.

"Again, that sounds like something he'd do. And is in the position to do. I'm confused, Johnny."

He sighs, looking out the window. "I know you don't know how stuff works within the family, but I'm telling you, your father has lost it. He's doing things he shouldn't, making enemies with the wrong people, and now he got it in his head that I'm out to get him. He won't listen to me, and I've heard rumors about what he plans to do."

I glance at him. "Like what?"

"Kill me, for one. And honestly, that's all I'm worried about."

"So, what's the message you want me to get to him?"

I walk across the room to grab a broom and begin sweeping the floor just to keep myself busy and moving, that way any sounds they might make in the room next door can be masked.

"I want you to tell him it's not true. I didn't do what he thinks I did."

"What exactly does he think you did?"

Johnny huffs, taking the hat off his head to run a hand through his greasy hair before replacing it.

"Can we go downstairs? All these crosses and Jesus staring at me," he says, gesturing to the crucifix on the wall. "I can't even get comfortable in here."

"Sure," I say, hoping Javier and my dad heard. "We can go downstairs. I'll make us something to drink in the kitchen."

I add the last part so they know where we'll be. Plus it gets us farther from the hall if they decide to follow.

Leading Johnny back downstairs, we make it to the kitchen where he sits at the dining room table.

"He thinks I told another family about you," he admits.

My eyes meet his immediately. "What do you mean?"

"You've been a secret. He doesn't talk about you, you know?" I nod. "He thinks I told another family about you. To use you against him."

"Did you?"

Johnny hesitates only briefly. "No, I didn't."

"If he doesn't talk about me, who else would know I exist if not you?"

"I don't know, kid," Johnny says, slamming his hand on the table.

I finish pouring a couple glasses of lemonade, and put one in front of him before going back to the fridge to put away the pitcher.

"You told me someone was going to pick me up at my house. What was that about?"

"Your dad told me to have someone pick you up."

Leaning against the counter, I cock my head, confusion marring my face. "For what reason?"

"I try not to question him too much. He told me to have someone get you. But then you weren't there. What happened?"

I only hesitate for a second. "I was picked up. I assumed it was by the guy you said you were sending."

Johnny shakes his head. "Your dad set that up separately. He's trying to make me look like I had an ulterior motive, but he told me to get you, Carlo." He leans forward. "What happened? Where did he take you?"

Part of me wonders if there's even a small chance that

he's telling the truth. That somehow, all of this is miscommunication or a diabolical plan from my dad. But then I think about all the other stuff I know. Johnny's trying to pull information from me with his questions while also attempting to plant doubt.

"I went to some house," I say, sticking close to the truth in case he already knows. "The message was that I wasn't safe in my house that night. I questioned him about what was going on, but I didn't get much information."

Johnny rubs the stubble on his chin. "And then you left?"

"The next day. I had a work-related trip out of town and he seemed to be okay with me leaving." I shrug. "You know he never wanted me to come back here anyway."

Johnny nods. "Hmm."

I can tell he's trying to piece together information, and while I watch him, I hear the slight click of a door. I bang my knee against the cabinet to cover the noise, then I turn on the sink and wet a sponge. I keep the water running as I wipe down the counters, hoping to drown out any other creaks or steps.

"Well, I can try to talk to him, Johnny, but you know our relationship has never been great. I don't know why he'd think you'd sell me out." I stop and look at him. "You've known me my whole life. Not sure why you'd want to see me get killed."

He locks onto my gaze. "I don't. I don't, kid. Just like you said, why would I do that?"

I shrug. "You've been friends with my dad for decades. I don't know why you can't talk it out."

"Exactly. Exactly!" he says, his voice rising. "I just want the chance to talk to him without him making any rash decisions."

I nod. "Makes sense."

"But listen, I think something's wrong with Cortez. I think maybe the pressure of this job, and the fact that he had to go into hiding...I think it's getting to him. He's not as measured as he once was. His reputation is taking a hit. Hopping from safe house to safe house? Bringing in some outsider to be his right-hand man when he knows it's wrong." Johnny shakes his head. "I think it may be time for him to take a step back."

My eyes widen slightly as a lightbulb comes on. It's always been about removing my dad from power so he can claim it. He was stressed when my dad was missing, but not because he was worried about him. Because he was worried he'd come back. He was in my father's office, assuming the role of boss because it's what he's been coveting this whole time. He didn't like that I mentioned it, because if word spread, people would start looking at him a little closer.

If he can't kill my father, he wants everyone to think he's incapable of the job. If he's no longer boss, it'll be easier to kill him.

"Huh," I murmur. "Maybe."

He nods, wanting me to be on his side. "It could be good for your relationship too. Time to reconnect."

"Mmhmm." I nod again, seeing where this is going.

"If you can set up a meeting with him and I, you can sit in on it and tell him you think it's best that he steps down."

I make a face. "Since when has my father listened to me, especially when it comes to this life?"

"He loves you, kid. I think you have more pull than you think you do. But you agree, right? All these crazy thoughts he has? These bogus theories? He's out there killing people because he thinks I'm working with them. I know I'm next and I'm not ready to go yet."

It takes a few seconds to register, but it eventually hits me that he knows they just killed people in the Bonetti family. That just happened last night, and he knows about it. Someone is still communicating with him.

I go back to the sink and squeeze the sponge before turning the water up higher.

"I don't know, Johnny." I angle my head over my shoulder and see him peeking at his watch. "Like I said, I can try, but he doesn't always answer my calls."

Johnny stands up, walking up to the counter that separates us. "We can go see him now."

"Do you know where he is?" I question.

He hesitates, and I turn slightly to look at him.

"Yeah," he replies. "You'd have to go in first, obviously. To warn him not to shoot me."

Liar.

"Oh. Well, I'd have to get changed, and my clothes are at my house."

"Yeah, that's fine," he says, his voice sounding fast and higher pitched. "I can follow you there. Then we can ride together."

Something is off. He wants to get me to the Bonettis, I know it. He doesn't know where my dad is. He's luring me to the lion's den instead, but offering to follow me home is strange. I'd think he'd insist we ride together from here, but maybe this is more manipulation tactics. Let me think everything is okay just before it's not.

I see a shadow against the wall behind Johnny. Someone is walking closer.

"I'm glad we were able to talk," I tell him. "I'm lucky I have someone I can trust."

His expression falters for just a second, but then the mask is back. "Of course, kid. You know we've always been family. I'm sorry your father wasn't there for you the way he should've been."

I nod.

A snake to the end.

"Well, I guess we should go then, huh? Maybe once it's all said and done, we can get a drink."

Johnny grins, happy to be getting his way. "Of course."

I nod, seeing just how dedicated he is to this lie. How uncaring he is that he's leading me to my death.

He looks at his watch again, ready to spin around and head for the door. "I'll meet you at your place, kid."

I spot Javier round the corner, his steps quiet and calculated. I don't focus on him, instead deciding I need to further distract Johnny.

Walking toward him, I give him a smile that I hope reads as genuine. "Thanks, Johnny," I say.

He straightens up and steps away from the counter. I open my arms so he knows I'm going in for a hug. With some hesitancy, he does the same, and then I wrap my arms around him.

Javier's eyes are on mine as he approaches. He's wearing leather gloves now, and he's got something in his hands.

"You're a real piece of work, you know that?" I say in his ear.

"Huh?"

He tries to pull away, but I squeeze tighter. "You're getting exactly what you deserve."

I step back and Javier steps forward, then a wire is wrapped around Johnny's throat, cutting into his skin. His eyes widen and his fingers immediately go to his neck, trying to save himself.

"Lift his shirt," Javier says.

When I do, I find a gun tucked into his waistband. As I'm reaching for it, Johnny does the same, but I'm quicker. I take it and step back, putting it on the counter.

He attempts to talk, but all he can do is choke as Javier pulls him back to the chair he was sitting in.

My dad walks in, holding a familiar looking roll of Duct Tape. It's purple, and it's the one Father Adam bought when we needed to seal a window before the renovations started. Dad must've found it in the closet.

Moving quickly, Dad grabs Johnny's arms and brings them around the back of the chair, securing his wrists together with multiple layers of tape.

Dad attempts to tape his legs to the chair, but Johnny kicks him. Javier yanks back on the wire, and Dad lands a solid punch to Johnny's stomach.

Once his legs are taped, they both move away, leaving him with blood dripping down his neck.

"You fucks!" Johnny spits, his voice hoarse.

"I thought you wanted to talk," Dad says.

"Fuck you, Cortez."

"Why you in here telling lies, Johnny?"

"None of this would've happened if you would've just listened to me."

Dad waves his hand through the air. "I'd rather die than work with the Bonettis. Why you thought it was a good idea to make a deal with them is beyond me. Your ego knows no bounds and now you've gotten yourself in trouble."

"They want to kill me."

Dad shrugs. "And if you hadn't gone behind my back and tried to make a deal without my knowledge, I would've had your back against anyone. But this was all your doing, Johnny. You can't throw me under the bus to save your own ass. You should know me better than that. I'd never let that happen."

"You only care about yourself," he says.

"Well, that's not true," Dad says, his voice calm. "You've learned that, haven't you? You brought my son into this."

"Like you care," he spits.

Dad hauls off and lands a vicious punch to Johnny's face. "You played him like a pawn," he says, punching him again. "You didn't care if you put his life in danger."

Johnny looks at my dad, then spits blood at his feet. "He was never going to get hurt. It was to get you."

"Like they'd let him live," Dad says, landing another punch across his jaw. "Don't be stupid."

Johnny starts laughing—a hysterical sort of cackle that sets me on edge. "You've messed up, Cortez. You've really messed up."

"Nobody's gonna miss you," Dad says. "If you think the Bonettis care about you helping them, then you're even dumber than I thought. They would kill you as soon as you gave them what they wanted."

Johnny's eyes meet mine. "You're gonna regret trying to give him a chance, kid. He's going to get you killed." His eyes slide back to my dad's face. "And I hope you get to watch it happen."

Javier pulls his gun from his holster and aims at Johnny's head.

"No!" I say. "Too loud. Too messy."

Javier slides the gun back in place, his jaw tense, eyes as dark as night. With one swift motion, he pulls his knife from the sheath on his belt and steps in front of Johnny. He looks at my dad, and after he gives Javier a nod, he shoves the knife into Johnny's chest.

He makes a noise, his eyes going wide as he realizes he's going to die.

Javier twists the knife before pulling it out and doing it again.

I turn away, moving to the sink where I stare at the water going down the drain.

"I'll call the guys," Dad tells Javier. "Get some people out here to move him and clean up."

"I can start digging out in the cemetery," Javi says.

"You okay?" Dad asks me.

I nod, trying to keep the nausea at bay. "Yeah." I clear my throat. "Yeah. I'm fine."

"Javier, call George. Let him know what's going on. I'm gonna call Elio. Hopefully they can be out here within the hour. The sun will have gone down by then."

Dad walks through the living room and lingers in the hall as he makes the call. Javi stands in the center of the living room, tapping the screen of his phone.

I watch them both move, completely unaffected by the dead man taped to the chair. Unconcerned with the blood pooling on the floor.

Javier's hand is covered in blood, but his face remains stoic. He's not the same Javier right now that he is when we're alone. He's colder. I suppose it makes sense to turn off your emotions in a job like this.

I get a glimpse of Johnny, his lips parted as his wide open eyes face the ceiling.

Doing my best to not look directly at the scene, I walk closer just so I'm able to move past him and into the living room. I avoid the blood on the floor, knowing I need to start gathering cleaning supplies from upstairs.

As I'm about to pass Javier, his eyes find mine. He

switches the phone to his blood-covered hand, and holds it to his ear as he reaches out with his other.

I grab his hand briefly, aware my father could walk in at any second.

"I'm okay," I assure him. "You?"

"I'm glad you didn't have to do it."

I hear my father ending his call so I step away from Javier, moving in front of him.

"There's some cleaning supplies in the front closet," I say. "I can pull them out."

"They're on their way," Dad says, putting the phone in his pocket as he enters the living room.

"George's phone is still ringing," Javier says.

As I'm walking to the closet, the front door explodes. Wood splinters inward as people burst through. My brain short-circuits, unable to figure out what's happening.

Men with masks pulled over their faces burst in, holding guns.

CHAPTER 45

I make eye contact with one of them, and time slows down. He aims his gun at me, and I forget that I even have one tucked behind my chasuble. Fear runs down my spine.

I hear shouting, stomping, and gunshots, but I have no idea what's happening around me. All I can focus on is the dark barrel pointed directly at my chest.

His finger squeezes the trigger, and then I'm flying through the air, the sound deafening. My head bounces off the wood floor, disorienting me some more.

When I realize I'm not shot, I turn and look behind me and see Javier on his back. He's got blood gushing from his arm, but with his other one, he reaches for his weapon.

I scurry across the floor, my knees slipping on the chasuble. The man who aimed at me earlier, does the same again. Javier hastily aims and shoots, hitting him in the knee.

The man lets out a screech before collapsing.

My eyes frantically bounce around the room, and I see

my dad shoot a man in the chest at the same time another man shoots my dad in the back.

"No!" I yell.

Dad stumbles forward and Javier rushes over. The man who just shot my father aims at Javi and shoots twice.

"No!"

I can only yell the same word over and over as I process what's happening.

Javier drops.

The sound of a bullet exploding from a gun bursts through the room and the masked man goes down. When my eyes scan the area, I find my dad standing there with the gun still gripped tightly in his hand. He shot him.

I crawl across the bloody floor and get to Javier. I look over at my dad who has blood seeping from his back.

Javier's been hit in the chest and shoulder. Plus the shot in his arm when he shoved me out of the way.

Three bullet wounds. My heart sinks.

"No, no, no, no," I cry, not sure where to put my hands. "Javi, please."

He's still conscious, but barely. "I'm sorry."

"No, don't say that."

His eyes flutter open and I grab his hands. "You're stronger than this. You told me not to doubt you. You said you'd always come back."

"I'm sorry," he says again.

"No. You're fine. You're gonna be fine."

I rip the chasuble over my head and press it against the worst looking wound in his chest. Dad stumbles closer before slumping against the wall, his shirt bloodied. It looks like he wasn't only shot in the shoulder. The lower part of his shirt is wet with blood.

"Oh my God. Are you okay?"

I move closer to him to rip open his shirt and look for another wound. He puts his hand on my wrist, stopping me. His eyes move over my shoulder, staring at Javier. I follow the gaze and find Javi still conscious and looking in our direction.

"I was surprised when I overheard a conversation between you two at my safe house," Dad says, his voice weak and gravelly. "I guess there's plenty of things that happen under my nose that I'm not aware of."

"Dad," I start.

He lets go of my wrist. "I'm sorry, Son."

Tears stream from my eyes. "Don't."

"I told you before that I'd never beg for forgiveness from anyone, but I'm asking you to forgive me. I'm sorry I wasn't better. I only wanted to look out for you."

I shake my head, not ready for this conversation. Not wanting to know what it means that he feels he has to say this now.

"I need to call the cops. You both need an ambulance."

I rush to find my phone, but it was tossed around in the chaos.

"I hope he makes it," Dad says. "I hope you find happiness."

My heart shatters as I frantically search for my phone.

"Cortez." Javi's scratchy voice breaks through the silence. "I—"

"You'll take care of him. Take care of each other." His breathing becomes labored. "I didn't want to say anything. You clearly didn't want me to know."

"Where's my fucking phone?" I yell, tears pouring out of me, panic rising.

"Son," Dad says. "I love you."

I stop and look at him, my heart breaking. He could still

survive if I could get some help out here. If I could find a phone.

"I love you, too," I manage to get out through sobs.

Footsteps approach, and I'm thankful my dad made the call to the guys before all hell broke loose, but when it's only one man that walks through, the hair on the back of my neck stands up.

"Well, well, well," the man says, calmly walking through the massacre. "The almighty Cortez Gallo has fallen."

"Sammy," Dad mutters.

Recognition hits. Sammy is the boss of the Bonettis.

"Looks like Johnny did what he needed to do after all." He pauses near Johnny's body. "Guess it came with a sacrifice."

I notice he has a gun in his hand already, finger near the trigger, ready to pull.

"It's not over, Sammy," Dad says, sounding a little stronger than earlier.

Sammy, a man with hair too dark to be natural for someone of his age, has pockmarked skin, and a scar cut across his cheek. He appears to still be in good shape for someone who has to be in their early sixties.

"It will be," Sammy says simply, raising the gun and shooting my father in the head.

I can't explain what happens, but utter shock, fear, and fury like I've never felt combine together to fill me with a quiet rage. I don't scream and I hardly move—my eyes are trained at my dad's face, a bullet hole between his eyes. I almost don't believe what I'm seeing.

Javier is on the floor crying out for my father, and it gets Sammy's attention.

Without a thought, I pull the gun from my pants, turn

off the safety, and as he aims his gun at Javier, I squeeze the trigger.

His body jerks and then his eyes are on me, gun swinging in my direction. Javier screams, trying his best to reach the man's feet.

I shoot again. And again. Until he crumbles into a heap on the floor.

Before I can lower the gun, several people come rushing in with their own weapons drawn. I turn toward them, and it takes a few seconds before I recognize them as my dad's men.

"Call an ambulance," I tell them.

As they take in the scene, a couple of guys rush to Javier, and I begin to snap out of my shocked state. I drop to the floor next to my father, and take his hand in mine, leaning forward until my head is on his shoulder. Sobs wrack my body, tears falling down my cheeks and dripping from my chin.

"What happened?" someone asks. When neither Javier nor I respond, he asks again, his voice louder. "What the fuck happened?"

"They killed Johnny," I say, sitting up and leaning against the wall, still holding my dad's hand. "We thought it was over, but then people rushed in and started shooting. They both had been shot, but it was fine. It was going to be okay," I cry. "I was looking for my phone to call the police but then he came in," I say, gesturing to Sammy. "He shot my dad in the head." I swallow, hating how those words taste on my tongue. "So I killed him."

"Fuck!" one of the men yells.

"Let's get Javier to a hospital," someone says.

I crawl toward him, reaching out to touch him before I think better of it. "Is he gonna be okay?"

"Not if we don't get him to a hospital."

"Did someone call the cops?" I ask.

They each look around at the scene, and I know they're thinking about the legal fallout.

"Call the fucking cops!" I yell. "I'll figure out what to tell them, but all of this can't be swept under the rug. Call them and then leave. I'll handle the rest." I think about something. "Wait. Take Johnny. He can't be here." A few of the guys look at each other. "Hurry up and take him and call the goddamn cops!"

A guy I haven't seen before pulls a phone from his pocket. "I got my burner on me. I'll call."

Two other guys head for Johnny and start cutting the tape.

Elio and Dante look sick. Elio keeps taking glances at my father like he expects him to jump up and be fine. Dante keeps rubbing his head and cursing under his breath.

"I'm sorry, kid," Dante says. "Fuck! Let's go. We gotta talk to George."

Everyone leaves, and I hear the other guy telling the dispatcher that we're in a house near St. Joseph's church right before he walks out.

I find my way to Javier, taking his limp hand in mine. He's unconscious now, but still has a pulse.

Rocking back and forth, I bring his hand to my mouth and kiss his palm before resting my cheek in it. "Oh God, please," I cry. "Please, I can't lose them both."

After a minute of crying, reality sets in. The scene is grim. There's multiple dead bodies in here, and blood paints the walls and floors. The cops will know who my dad is. This will go down as a mob killing and I have to craft the best story I can, because all of us are responsible for murder.

They will investigate this thoroughly, so whatever I say has to save Javier and me from going to jail. That's if he survives.

With Johnny's body removed, I have a better chance at painting the best story, but I have to clean up evidence he was here. Quickly, I remove all remnants of tape and shove them in a small plastic trash bag. I grab a towel from under the sink and clean up the blood that dripped under his body while he was in the chair, and toss it in with the tape. I make sure to grab Javier's knife, sheath, guns, and holster, since I also need to get rid of those. I try not to look at his face when I turn him to strip him of his belongings, but I tell myself this is for his own good.

I run outside, finding the open grave plot and dropping the evidence inside. I grab a shovel that's nearby and dump dirt on top of it before running back into the house.

Sirens blare as cops and ambulances come barreling down the street.

Red and blue lights illuminate the night sky as they get closer. Here we go.

CHAPTER 46

"Tell us again, what happened after your father showed up?" the detective asks.

For the second time, I'm retelling the story I've told to two other detectives with my attorney at my side. I can't say I'm surprised by the continuous questioning, but it's starting to get tiring. I'm too emotionally overwhelmed to be trapped in a room for hours on end.

"We were planning on talking. Our relationship has been strained over the years, and I'm sure you can understand why," I say. "When he came, he brought his...I don't know, bodyguard?" I pretend I don't know what Javier's relationship with my father is.

"Javier Perez?" he questions.

"I guess. Anyway, after a while, Johnny—"

"Johnathan Sabatino?" the detective cuts in.

"Yes. He burst through the door, threatening my father."

"Were they not friends? As I understand it, Mr. Sabatino was your father's underboss."

I shrug, sighing. "Sir, I couldn't tell you many details

about their business or relationship. I've hardly spoken to my father in over eight years. We live different lives, you see."

He nods, writing something down. "Continue."

"The argument turned physical. Just a couple punches thrown, but then Johnny said my father would regret not listening to him. He mentioned someone by the name of Bonetti and he took off."

"The Bonetti Crime Family, yes," the detective says. "Your father just let him leave?"

"Yeah. He stormed out and Dad said he'd talk to him about it later."

"I see. What happened next?"

"Sammy walked in. He had a gun and said it was time for my dad to fall. Then several other guys came in after him. A man in a mask aimed his gun at me, but Javier shoved me to the floor and took the bullet in his arm. It was chaotic. There was so much gunfire and fighting. People were yelling, and I was face down on the floor for a minute, thinking my life had come to an end.

"When I finally flipped over, I saw a man shoot my dad in the back. When Javier saw this, he rushed toward the gunmen, but he was shot twice. Then he aimed the gun at my father again, but my dad shot him first."

"What happened to Sammy?"

"Well, I rushed to my dad, not thinking straight, and forgetting Sammy was even a threat. He had stepped back when all the shooting had happened, and at that time, I was concerned for my father."

"Even though you weren't close?"

I narrow my eyes. "Of course. He's still my dad."

He makes a face like he wants to judge who my father was, but he flattens his lips. "Keep going."

"As I'm searching for my phone to be able to call the police, Sammy shoots my father in the face."

I take a break to wipe the tears from my cheeks again, trying to get my breathing under control. "He then aimed at me and I dropped to the floor. Next to me was a discarded gun, so I picked it up and stood, hoping I'd be able to run away, but prepared to defend myself. As soon as he saw me, the gun was aimed right at my head. He was going to kill me just like he killed my father. I just started shooting," I sob. "I was so scared and I didn't want to die."

He gives me a minute before questioning me again.

"And who called the police?"

"Someone came in," I say, wiping my face. "I don't know who he was. I assume he knew my father. He took in the scene and saw me sobbing on the floor and walked back out."

"Hmm," the detective murmurs, writing something down.

"That's all you know?"

"Yes."

"All right, well, I'll be back."

Once he leaves the room, my attorney—one the family has used for years, turns to me. "You're going to be booked. It's typical, but we'll get you out on bond. This is self-defense. You shot Sammy out of fear for your own life. Considering who he is, it won't be hard for people to believe that he was in fact out to kill you. You shot, not with the intention to kill, but to keep from being killed. He just happened to die." I nod. "Everyone else there is not your problem. They all shot each other. Your father, God rest his soul, is gone. What he may or may not have done isn't relevant."

"What about Javier?"

"We're waiting for him to get out of the woods. Police are outside his hospital room. I'll let you know what happens."

I nod again. "Thanks."

"You'll be okay, kid," he says, putting a hand on my shoulder. "It'll be okay."

I'm not sure I believe him, but I don't say that. The detective comes back in and tells me I'm being booked.

As I'm escorted out of the interrogation room and through a brightly lit hallway, I can't help but think about the clergymen at the church and what they'll think when they find out what happened. And how I was involved. There's no way I'll be allowed to work there after the news breaks, even if I wanted to.

"Father," a detective says, getting my attention.

"Giancarlo is fine."

✝

A WEEK AFTER EVERYTHING HAPPENED, I knew it was time to face Bishop Charles. We have a lot to discuss, and there's no point in putting it off.

When I arrive at St. Joseph's, I stand before the stage, staring up at the stained glass window. For the last time, I appreciate the beauty and opulence this place has, then I pass the confessional booth that started it all and head toward the office where Charles waits.

After a couple knocks, I hear his voice say, "Come in."

I push open the door and walk inside.

He greets me with a kind smile, gesturing to the chair in front of his desk.

"Thanks for meeting with me," I say.

He puts down his pen and folds his hands in his lap. "Of course. I'm sorry to hear about your loss. My prayers are with you."

I nod, appreciating his concern even after finding out who my father is. *Was*. Though, now, I can understand the way others might've felt when I had offered them prayers while they were in the darkest depths of grief, because it doesn't help. I believe Charles has prayed for me, more so than any other random person who says I'm in their prayers. But regardless of whether it's true or not, it doesn't help. I don't feel better. It doesn't take the heartache and pain away. It doesn't rewind time and keep me from reliving what I saw and did. I still feel shattered in a way that doesn't feel fixable. Guilt sits heavy in my stomach for numerous reasons, and neither his prayers, nor mine, will do anything to fix that. They're simply empty words dropped in an empty heart.

"I'm sorry I didn't tell you who my father was. We had been estranged. I changed my name for distance and never thought I'd have to tell anyone about our connection."

Charles nods, his lips downturning, creating more wrinkles around his mouth. "We can't help who our family is, nor what they do."

"I can pay for the cleanup of the rectory."

He waves a hand in the air. "We have insurance."

"I hate that I brought a negative light to the church."

"I wouldn't say it's negative. It was a tragedy. Lives were lost. Lives taken." His expression changes slightly. "Lives changed. I'm sure you did what you had to do, and I'm glad you made it out alive. A bloodbath like that, you could say it was a miracle."

I flatten my lips because I know the truth. There was no miracle that night. There was only murder.

"I know I was on sabbatical. I told you I was already struggling with my place in life, and whether this was something I wanted to do forever. I'm thankful you allowed me the break, but now, after all of this, I think it's best that I step away. The attention would be too much. Everyone knows who I am now and my involvement that night. I can't continue to preach about right and wrong. Nobody would take me seriously knowing what they know now."

Charles is already nodding, so I know I'm not going to get any pushback on this.

"I understand, and I agree that it might be the best decision. We can start the process, but it can take a while for any dispensation."

I nod, knowing it doesn't matter. I've already broken the rules. They can choose to make me endure the vow of celibacy, even if they reduce me to the lay state, but it's not like I'm going to abide by that.

"That's fine," I say, standing up. "I appreciate everything you've done for me."

Charles shakes my hand. "You take care of yourself."

"You too."

When I walk out of the church, I look up toward the sky and feel a little bit lighter. There's plenty of weight left on my shoulders, but at least this is one thing I don't have to worry about anymore. It's time to move on.

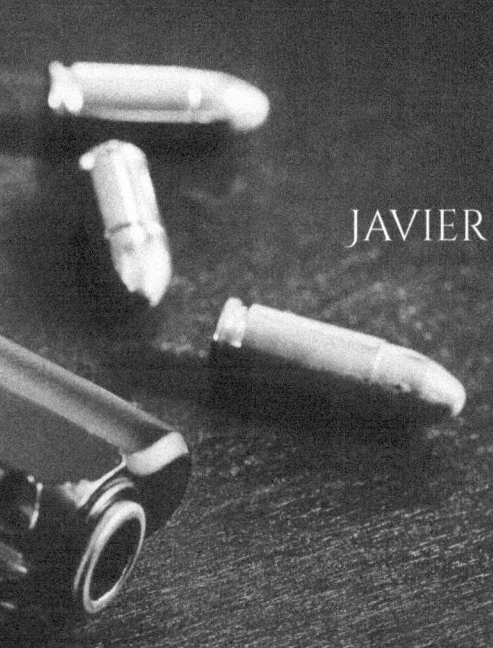

JAVIER

CHAPTER 17

I'm staring at the TV on the wall, watching the images without paying attention to what's happening. I've been in this zombified state for at least two weeks now, and I'm about ready to rip everything out of my arms and escape this torture chamber.

I'm aware of—and thankful for— their lifesaving measures, but at this point, I'm going crazy. I haven't seen almost anybody except doctors and nurses, barring a single visit from my attorney a few days ago.

"Good morning, Javier," Nurse Lisa says as she enters my room. "How you feelin' today?"

"Like I'm ready to leave."

She sends me a look. "Well, we're not ready to let you go just yet."

I sigh. "I didn't know you were in the kidnapping game."

"You're no kid," she teases. "And you just had a bullet removed from your chest after experiencing major blood loss. You're lucky to be alive."

"Lucky. Yes," I deadpan.

She doesn't say anything while she checks my vitals and updates my chart. Once she's done, she puts her hands in the pockets of her scrubs and looks at me. Her strawberry blonde hair is up in a ponytail, and her green eyes bore into me.

"Cops are gone."

"They finally realized I was only a victim," I say.

"That lawyer of yours is kinda scary."

I snort. "That's when you know you got a good one."

"The doctor will be in to check on you later today. Maybe you'll get the green light to be discharged."

"I'll keep my fingers crossed."

A light knock on the door gets our attention. Lisa turns around, and just past her arm, I spot a man in the doorway.

"Am I interrupting?"

It's Carlo.

I immediately try to sit up a little straighter, peeking around Lisa's body.

"I was just leaving," she says, glancing back at me before walking out of the room.

Carlo stands there in a black, V-neck lightweight sweater. The sleeves are pushed up to his elbows, and his gray slacks look freshly pressed. He's wearing his glasses, but they don't hide the sadness in his eyes as he looks at me.

Suddenly, I'm aware of how awful I probably look. I've been rotting in bed for way too long, unshaven, and only washed via spongebath.

He strolls closer, taking my left hand since it's the arm free of IVs.

"You're alive."

I stare at him, studying every inch of his face, trying to read each twitch of his brow or twist of his lips.

"I am."

"I knew that," he says, looking down at my hand as he runs his thumb over my fingers. "I was checking in, and getting information from anyone I could, but I wanted to see you for myself."

"Took you long enough."

He meets my gaze and I give him a small smile.

"They weren't letting anyone in for a while."

"I know. Something about me being unconscious."

"And something about the cops not wanting you to talk to anyone."

"Right. That too."

He smiles, but it's small and doesn't reach his eyes. His despair is evident.

"Javier—"

I cut him off, afraid of what he's going to say. "Wait. Let me...can I tell you something?"

He nods, and I cycle through everything I've thought about since I've been clear-headed enough to think.

"I don't know which to say first, because both seem to be of high priority, so don't think one means more than the other." I swallow. "I want to say I'm sorry, and also thank you." He continues to stare down at me, his eyes empty of their usual life. "Cortez was—" Carlo shifts, and pulls his hand away from mine as he nervously scratches at his face. "He was like family to me," I finish. "Watching him...seeing that..." I trail off, feeling my own discomfort while watching Carlo's appear on his face. "I'll never forgive myself for not doing more. For not stopping it from happening. I'm sorry I didn't do my job."

Carlo shifts his feet, rubbing at the corner of his eye while avoiding my gaze.

"But I also want to thank you, because I know you saved my life."

He scoffs, looking up at the ceiling. "I didn't do anything. I didn't help anyone."

I reach for his hands and grab two of his fingers. "Hey. That's bullshit. You saved me."

"*You* saved *me*," he says, emotion altering his voice. "You took a bullet meant to kill me."

"Listen," I say quietly. "You kept me from going to jail. I know what you said. Your attorney is my attorney. Every death was blamed on your father as well as Sammy and his people. You painted me as a hero. You saved me, Carlo, even after I didn't do what I—"

He shakes his head. "You couldn't have prevented that from happening," he says. "You tried, and you got shot for it."

I go quiet for a minute, closing my eyes as I see the image of Cortez slumped against the wall. "I'm so fucking mad, Carlo. So fucking mad at the whole situation."

"I know," he says quietly. "Me too."

"What happened with your case?" I ask, looking up at him. "Hugo didn't mention much. For a mob attorney, he's a stickler for rules."

"He told me about *your* case," he says, a pinprick of humor in his tone.

"Yeah, well, you probably used your choir boy charm on him."

He chuckles. "Maybe I'm just more likable."

"I don't doubt that," I say. "He says I'm too pushy and—"

"Abrasive?" he finishes for me.

"Hey."

Carlo shrugs. "I might've thought the same thing before."

"Yeah, well."

"My case was dismissed. There was reasonable belief that I was in imminent danger and had no choice but to shoot."

I nod. "Good, good. It's true. He was going to kill you."

Carlo doesn't respond immediately. In fact, he looks away, his thoughts taking him somewhere else. When he speaks again, I'm not sure I expect what he says.

"It wasn't self defense. He was going to shoot *you*."

I swallow, trying to remember that night. A lot of moments are blurred together, overpowered by the image of Cortez being killed. I don't remember Sammy aiming for me.

"He would've shot you after," I say. "You had no choice."

"I could've run down the hall behind me. Went out the back door." He looks at me. "And even if I had a choice, I'd do it again for what he did."

I nod, understanding.

"How was the funeral?" I ask, not necessarily wanting to talk about it, but needing to know.

Carlo cocks his head slightly. "We haven't had one yet."

"What? Why?"

"I told them to wait. I knew you'd want to be there."

My facial expressions freeze. "What?"

"I know how much he meant to you. You deserve to say goodbye, too."

"Carlo," I say, my voice breaking.

He bends down and puts his hand on my head, kissing me on the forehead. "He loved you."

I break down, and as Carlo comforts me, I feel his own tears falling onto my skin as he, too, begins to weep.

Together, we grieve a man who meant a lot to both of us, regardless of the differences in our relationships with him. We mourn his loss while finding comfort in each other, and I can finally breathe a little easier knowing Carlo doesn't blame or hate me for what happened.

T wo days after Carlo visited me in the hospital, I'm officially discharged and getting ready for Cortez's funeral.

"Let me help," Carlo says, finding me standing in front of his floor length mirror, struggling to tie my tie.

"Not being able to use my arm is going to be the death of me."

He stands in front of me, taking the two strips of material and weaving them around each other. "I'm pretty sure if three bullets couldn't take you down, a tie isn't going to do it."

I snort. "Thanks."

"You don't have to thank me," he says, looking into my eyes when he finishes.

I nod. "When do we need to leave?"

Carlo looks at the watch on his wrist. "Now. We'll be meeting everyone at the funeral home, then take the limos to the cemetery."

I don't question the lack of church service. Cortez wasn't a church going man. And considering what happened at the rectory next to St. Joseph's, I doubt any church in a two hundred mile radius would want to hold his funeral.

Since I got out of the hospital yesterday, we haven't talked much about what's to come. He took me home and helped pack a bag, then brought me to his house, telling me I'd need help for a little while. I hate that he's right, because being helpless isn't something I'm used to, but it is nice to not be alone right now.

Everything feels different and yet unchanged, stuck in limbo as Carlo decides what he wants to do.

In the car, I contemplate mentioning it, but that's not the way I normally operate. I'm used to just blurting things out, but now I care about how it could affect him. This is a little more personal, so I play it over in my head in multiple ways, hoping I don't come off insensitive.

"Have you thought about..." I pause, mulling it over, "whether you want to step in or..." I let it hang there, knowing he'll pick it up.

He's quiet for a while, focused on the road. When I think he's going to ignore the question completely, he speaks up.

"It's almost all I've been thinking about. It's a complicated situation."

I nod. "Of course."

"I have to meet with George soon. Make a decision one way or another. They have to figure out how to move on."

"Yeah."

We pull into the funeral home, and I come to the decision that I won't bring it up again. He's going to figure it out for himself, and when I need to know, I'll know. I'll have to figure out what I'm going to do after the fact.

I'm a few steps behind Carlo as he greets the men that

worked for his father. They shake hands, whispering condolences. Everyone looks solemn, but not broken. And that's the sad truth about life. Death is final, leaving behind broken hearts and a disrupted routine, but we piece ourselves together and adapt to a new normal because the world keeps spinning even if we feel entrenched in grief.

The limos are already lined up behind the hearse, and after Carlo speaks to the funeral director, he says something to George, who then disperses the message, and everyone starts getting into the waiting cars.

Only Carlo and I ride in the first limo, both of us quiet in our own thoughts for most of the journey.

When we see the cemetery, everything starts to feel real. I've been aware of Cortez's absence in this world. A man like that, you can't help but feel when he's no longer around, but putting him into the ground makes my chest cave in a little, and I can't begin to imagine how Carlo feels.

I reach over and grab his hand, grateful he's sitting on my good side. He looks at me, fighting off what has to be an overwhelming amount of emotion. He swallows, his eyes shiny. Clenching his jaw, he nods once. "I can't say anything right now."

"Okay," I say, understanding.

Sometimes just a single statement will open the floodgates.

He brings my hand to his mouth and kisses my knuckles before staring out the window.

When we come to a stop, he takes a breath and opens the door.

My injuries don't allow for me to be a pallbearer, but Carlo arranged to have me walk behind the casket, while he, some capos, and George all take the weight of Cortez, and carry him to his final resting place.

After everyone's seated, it's Carlo who stands at the podium. He's wearing a black suit paired with a black tie and shirt. His hair is perfectly combed, his facial hair trimmed low and neat, but he hides his eyes behind dark sunglasses.

"Thank you for being here today," he starts, his head held high. "My father was a complicated man. He was hard to love most days, especially as I grew older. I'm sure all of us have varying feelings regarding Cortez Gallo, but I think it's safe to say that we all can understand how he became who he was. He was tough, fearless, and wasn't afraid to hurt anyone's feelings if it meant doing something he thought was best. Oftentimes, he was right in his decision-making, even if we didn't agree with how he went about it.

"He was a smart man, and while we definitely had our differences, and though we butted heads on more than one occasion, I always looked up to him. He was my hero when I was a boy—someone I felt would always be around. He had a larger than life personality, and all I wanted was to be just like him. Things didn't turn out how either one of us thought they would. I always thought it was because we were too different, but some days I wonder if it was because we were too similar. Both of us were always ready to fight— needing to have the last word. Stubborn beyond belief, thinking we were always right." He chuckles slightly before sniffing. Shaking his head, he continues. "Yes, we're different, but his blood runs in my veins, whether I like it or not. His words, not mine." This garners a few laughs. "I can't say he was a good man or a great father, but he was never selfish and always honest. I think I've realized that recently, especially getting to talk to some of you. This family was always a priority."

He takes several seconds to look into the crowd, eventually removing his glasses. I watch his face, trying to read his expression. The wheels are turning in his head, but I have no idea what he's thinking. He puts his shoulders back, meets my gaze, then starts talking again.

"With my father gone, I think we're all looking for someone to fill his shoes. I'm not sure anyone could do that, if I'm being honest, but I think I'm willing to give it a try."

A few murmurs emerge from around me, coming from the people who know what he means. My lips quirk just slightly, and I watch as he bows his head and says a silent prayer before turning to lay a hand on his father's casket.

CHAPTER 49

I t didn't take long for people to start talking.

They say a priest killed the Bonetti boss. A man of the cloth, so set on vengeance that he was unafraid of God's wrath. How can he fear anyone if he doesn't even fear the God he believes in.

It sparked unintended trepidation amongst the criminal underground. The stories grew tendrils of untruths and exaggerations—tales of a priest walking the streets with an assault rifle under his robes, wreaking havoc.

The truth, even without all of the dramatization, is still something to fear. I'm not sure Carlo understands what he did by killing Sammy. To him, he stopped a man who killed his father, and who was going to kill me. To everyone in the underground, he brought down one of the most ruthless crime bosses to exist. The Bonetti Family is responsible for a lot of people's downfall, and the deaths of countless loved ones.

Almost everyone wanted them gone, but nobody had the army to get it done, nor the balls to even try. Johnny handed Cortez a grenade, because I'm not sure he would've started this war with the Bonettis if he didn't have to. With his and his son's life at risk, he took that grenade and pulled the pin. While what Cortez and I did inflicted damage, it was Carlo who launched it, toppling the most important man in that family. Bosses are notoriously untouchable, but he did it. And he got away with it.

Whispers are growing into screams, and slowly everyone is wondering what they can expect when Cortez Gallo's son takes the reins.

We pull up to George's house where he and Carlo are due to have an important conversation about the future. I do my best to keep my questions to myself, because it's not my place to be aware. I'll know what I need to know, and I'll support him regardless. I assume he's going to say yes, based on his speech at his father's funeral, but he didn't confirm it for me.

Inside, George leads us through his expansive living room and offers us a drink.

"I'm okay," Carlo says.

"I'm fine," I say.

"Okay, well, if you're ready, we can go into my office," George tells him.

"Actually," Carlo says. "Javier is going to be a part of this conversation."

My brows lift slightly, surprised at this news. George's expression mimics my own.

"Oh. Your father didn't—"

"I'm not my father," Carlo says simply. "Javier will be a part of this conversation."

He leaves no room for compromise, so I sit down on the couch and make myself comfortable. George glances at me before sitting across from us. Carlo sits last.

"I'm not sure what all my father told you about me or why our relationship was estranged."

"He alluded to some differences, but said your absence was what was best."

Carlo nods. "Right, well, I'm going to be honest with you, because I feel like you deserve that. If I'm going to take over for my father, then I have to trust you completely. And with everything. Your role is to advise me, right? To act as a mediator between me and the others if any conflicts arise, yes?"

George nods. "That's right."

"Then you will know everything, and once I have your reaction, I will determine whether I want you to stay in this role."

I can't control my expression as my eyes slide over to George's face, wondering how he's going to take this news.

He shifts slightly, stiffening his back. "Okay then."

"I'm gay. I realize that's not an easily accepted thing in this life, but I'm not capable of changing who I am."

I fight to keep my own shock off my face, because he did not tell me he was going to come out to George like this. To his credit, George hardly reacts.

"Okay," he replies. "I will tell you that you will likely run into some issues."

"That's fine," Carlo says. "I'll handle them as they come."

I shift slightly so I can have a better view of him, finding myself getting turned on at an inopportune time.

"Are you going to tell everyone?" George questions.

"I haven't decided how to inform everyone. I find myself struggling with the fact that it's nobody's business, but also understanding the business I find myself in. They'll know eventually, because I refuse to hide any longer, but if they have a problem with it, then they can talk to me about it, and we can figure out how they want to deal with their issues."

I bite down on my lip, hiding my smile. George's eyes flash to my face before looking back at Carlo.

"You can't possibly think you can remove everyone from the family if they don't like it. The truth is, a lot of them won't."

Carlo cocks his head. "As boss, my authority is absolute. I can promote and demote whoever I want."

George dips his head in acknowledgement. "I just think it might be hard to replace some of these guys."

"Well, hopefully it doesn't come to that. Do *you* have an issue?"

"No. My concern is with the business. As long as whatever you have going on doesn't affect the business, I don't care."

"Good. We'll need to discuss an underboss, but again, they will be vetted, because I will not work with someone who cannot respect me, especially if it's based on who I find attractive. Also," he turns toward me now, "Javier will continue in the same role my father had him in. Javier is family, regardless of whether he's made or not. If I want him to be privy to certain conversations, he will be, because the truth of the matter is he's always known. My father told him everything, and I will do the same. So he's going to be allowed to be with me in meetings I want him to be in, and he will not be treated as an outsider."

George sighs, but he doesn't argue. "Okay."

"Is there any news on anyone left from the Bonetti Family?"

"Your father and Javier got rid of four of eight capos,

and maybe a dozen soldiers. You got Sammy, so that leaves four more capos and a couple hundred soldiers."

"My dad talked to Aurelio prior to everything going down. He was to take over and make sure our relationship stayed cordial."

George sways his head back and forth. "Yeah, but we have to see how it all actually plays out. Aurelio will talk to the remaining three capos and see if they have interest in higher positions, but they could hold onto some anger and not want this to go over smoothly. And that's not counting the sheer amount of soldiers that could also be holding grudges."

"Do I need to do something about this? Send another message that informs them they better not think to reengage in this war?"

George shrugs. "Not as of now. I'll talk to some people."

"Set up a meeting with Aurelio as well."

"I take it this means you are in fact taking over?"

Carlo's quiet for a few seconds. "Yes. And it's not because I believe I owe it to my father, but because I owe it to myself. This is what I wanted when I was growing up, and I need to prove to myself that I'm capable of it."

"And your last job?" he questions.

"I've already begun the process of laicization. It will take time, and the pope makes the final decision, but considering the circumstances—the murder of my father in the rectory of my church and my self-defense case, they are okay letting me live as a layperson."

George stands up and Carlo follows. "Okay, then." He extends his hand. "I will organize the initiation ritual, then you can make any announcements afterward. Everyone will know this is an unusual way to get a new boss, but we'll deal with any questions at the ceremony."

Carlo nods, shaking his hand. "All right. Let me know where to be and when and I'll be there."

I stand and dip my head to George, then together, Carlo and I leave the house and get into his car.

"Well," I say, once we're seated. "That was fun to watch."

Carlo smirks, looking at me as he puts the car in reverse. "We'll have to discuss if we ever want to let people know about us."

"I think it's going to be hard for me to keep my hands off you if you're gonna keep talking like that when I'm around. I wanted to pounce on you, George be damned."

Carlo laughs. "You're turned on by everything."

"Nah. Just you."

He reaches over and takes my hand, giving it a small squeeze while he sends me a wink.

"So, I think I'm healed enough to have sex now."

He laughs. "Oh yeah?"

"You may have to do most of the work, but I'm willing to try it out."

"Luckily for you, I already made plans for us tonight."

"Naughty ones?" I question, wiggling my brows.

He grins. "You'll see."

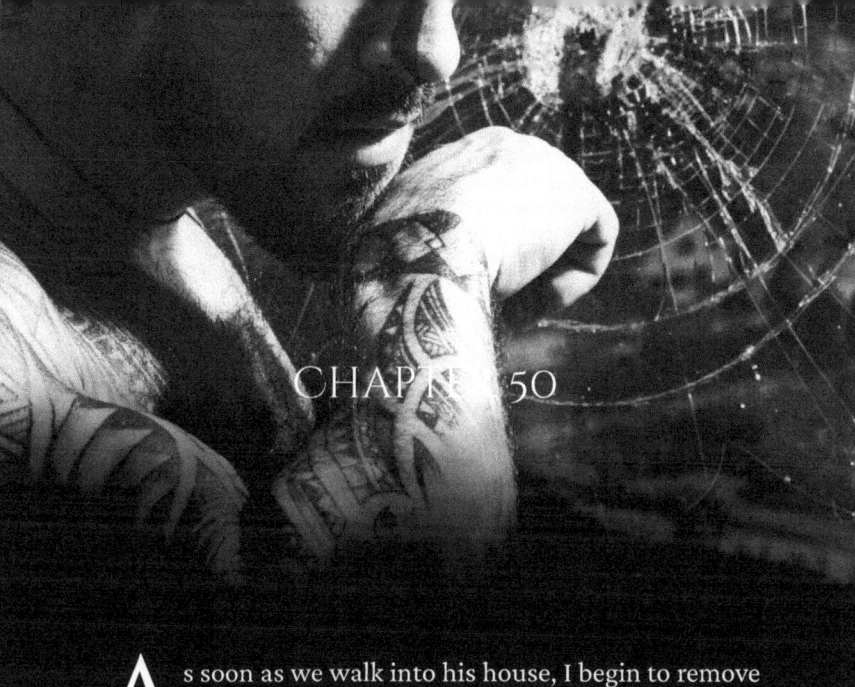

As soon as we walk into his house, I begin to remove my shoes and jacket, leaving myself in a pair of black jeans and a black tank. Carlo turns and looks at me, a grin tugging on his lips.

"Impatient?"

"It's been a month. Of course I'm impatient. I'm gonna use your bathroom and then I'll meet you in the room."

Carlo laughs. "Okay."

I wasn't thinking about sex when I was in the hospital, too focused on the pain in my arm and chest. I've been out a week now, and spending every day with Carlo, so the desire has come roaring back. I'm not a hundred percent, but I feel the best I have in a while, and if he makes me wait any longer I might lose it.

After I use the bathroom, I take time to clean up and get myself as prepared as possible. I keep on my boxers and tank top, then make my way into his bedroom. He's removed the crucifix that hung over the bed, and replaced it with a landscape picture. I didn't question him when I first noticed it, and I won't now. I can only assume he felt uncomfortable having it up.

I'm disappointed when I don't see him in bed, naked, waiting for me, but he quickly changes my mood when he strolls in, wearing only his boxer-briefs.

"I used the other bathroom to freshen up."

My eyes take in his flawless body, free of scars left by knives or bullets. He's ink-free, lean and toned, his broad shoulders and small waist giving him the appearance of a swimmer.

I step forward, but he stops me. "Lie down."

I cock my head. "Carlo, don't piss me off. If you tell me we're just going to sleep, I swear to—"

His brow lifts and he moves closer. "Just lie down."

Begrudgingly, I do what he says, getting on top of the covers and lying on my back. He slowly makes his way over, resting on his arm as he sidles up next to me. He traces his finger over the curve of my jaw, clasping my chin between his fingers before planting a kiss on my mouth.

"We haven't had much time to talk," he starts.

"Carlo," I grumble.

He smiles and kisses me again. Damn him.

"A lot has happened," he continues. "This transition has been and will continue to be tough for me. I straddle the line of thinking I can do it and feeling woefully unprepared. I want this, I do, but I want you with me."

"I'll be there," I tell him. "Always. I owe you—"

"No," he says, cutting me off. "I don't want you there because you feel like you owe me something. I don't want you at my side because of what happened to my dad and your need to fulfill a duty you think you failed at before."

"It's not that," I say. "It's hard. I do feel..." I shake my head, running a hand over my face. "I feel awful. Guilty.

Responsible, even. I hate myself for not preventing that, and I never want anything to happen to you. I want to protect you and keep you safe, but not just because I want a second chance to prove myself. I want you safe because..." I stare into his eyes, and feel a quite different dose of fear. "I don't want to be without you."

They weren't the words that first came to mind, but I suppose I *am* afraid of something—being vulnerable and then getting rejected.

"I trust you, Javi," he says. "My dad said you were the only man he trusted, and I know why. What happened hasn't altered my trust in you. It was a devastating and awful situation. You literally put your body between me and a bullet, and you attempted the same with my dad. You are not a failure. You're brave and fearless."

I shake my head. "I thought I was. Maybe I was before, but now...now I'm afraid of losing you, too."

"Dad wanted us to take care of each other. Do you remember hearing that? He knew about us, Javi."

My brows dip, my memory hazy. "He knew?"

"He found out when we were at his safe house. He must've overheard our conversation when we were in the room. He never acted differently around you?"

I shake my head. "No. But I think I remember him saying to take care of you."

"He said we'd take care of each other. That he hoped I found happiness."

I run a hand over my face. "I hate that we didn't get to talk to him about it."

"The fact that he didn't blow up means something."

I nod. "I think you'll be a great leader."

He smiles. "And if I'm not, I have you to convince people that I am."

"Convince with my gun or…"

Carlo laughs. "I love you."

He stops short, his laughter coming to an end as his eyes widen. He didn't mean to say it. They're three tiny words. Only eight letters. But together, they hold so much weight and meaning. That they fell from his tongue so easily means the thought's been there. Right? It's been in his head and it came out naturally.

My heart thumps in my chest, because the thought's been in my head too. I've never known this feeling. It scares me in a way I've never experienced. I didn't want to say it because I was afraid I was in over my head. I've been worried this wouldn't work out after his father died. I've talked myself out of believing it to even be true, because how could it be? But it is.

"I love you, too," I say back.

I watch the relief pour over him, his eyes softening and shoulders dropping. His lips pull into a smile, growing wider and wider.

"Is this weird?" he asks, a small amount of laughter breaking into the question.

"Probably. But weird is good."

He leans in and kisses me. "I didn't expect this to happen."

I kiss him again. "I knew you'd fall for my charm at some point."

Carlo rolls his eyes. "Yes, your vulgarity and violent nature."

"Hey, you like it. Who should really be judged here?"

"I do like it," he says, leaning in to kiss my neck. "I like a lot about you."

"Mm," I moan, tilting my head to the side to give him more access. "Did we already revert back to *like*?"

Carlo removes his underwear before pulling mine down. I lift my hips and he drags them down my legs and tosses them away.

"Let me show you just how much I *love* every part of you."

"Better."

He pushes my tank top up a little higher, but doesn't attempt to remove it. The action would probably hurt too much anyway, so I'm appreciative of that.

He kisses my stomach, moving lower and lower while his hands gently curve around my hips. Teasing me, he bypasses my erection, choosing to kiss and lick my inner thighs before barely brushing his fingers over my shaft.

"Carlo," I groan.

His lips replace his touch, leaving soft pecks along my shaft before his tongue swirls around my head.

"Yes," I hiss, closing my eyes.

The warmth of his mouth envelops me when he wraps his lips around my tip, taking me across his tongue.

I squeeze the blanket in my fists as my hips lift, seeking to reach the back of his throat with my cock.

Carlo moans at my greediness, taking me deep, his hand and mouth following each other as he moves up and down.

He grunts and groans, the blowjob turning wet and sloppy, just the way I like it. He gags slightly, then strokes as his tongue flickers along the underside of my head.

"It's too good," I tell him. "It's been too long."

He pulls away slowly, then gets off the bed and goes to the dresser to grab some lube. While he sits between my legs, he coats his fingers with the liquid and reaches behind himself, sliding a finger or two inside his hole.

His eyes flutter closed, and I watch as he strokes himself

with one hand, while prepping himself with the other. This image alone is enough to send me over the edge, so I don't dare touch myself.

After a while, he grabs the lube and coats my cock, moving up to my waist where he straddles my hips and slowly guides me inside of him.

"I've been waiting for this," he says in a husky tone, biting down on his lip as I slip a little deeper.

I reach for his waist with my uninjured arm, squeezing the flesh. "Me too."

"God, you feel good," he says, rotating his hips once he's fully seated.

"You're so fucking sexy."

His tongue swipes across his bottom lip as he rocks his hips back and forth, further proving just how sexy he is. The way his muscles dance with each movement he makes has my cock growing even harder.

He takes his dick in his hand, stroking while bouncing up and down on mine. He switches up the rhythm, digging his knees into the bed when he wants to take me deep, grinding down on me.

"Fuck, you're so big. So deep," he says, voice like gravel.

"I love the way you take it," I reply, squeezing his thigh. "Such a greedy boy."

His head drops back as he moans. "Yes."

I reach up and grab his throat, bringing him lower. "You missed this, didn't you?"

His eyes fly open as he puts his hands on either side of me, keeping himself from rubbing against my chest, his head nodding frantically.

I squeeze tighter before moving my hand up to his jaw and putting my thumb against his bottom lip.

Carlo sucks it into his mouth, his tongue swirling around it as he begins to move his hips again.

"There you go," I say. "Take it. Use me."

He moans, his movements quickening. When he releases my thumb from his mouth, he brings my hand back to his throat.

"Fuck," I groan, squeezing the sides of his neck.

His skin turns red, and his hand goes to his shaft, moving up and down as he rides me. His muscles flex, and his breathing changes, and I know he's close to coming.

"Javi," he moans. "Oh God, Javi. So good. So...good."

"Come for me," I demand. "Let me see that mess, baby."

"I'm so close." His voice is almost a whisper.

I squeeze his throat before gripping his jaw. He releases a sinful noise that lets me know just how much he likes it. Without much thought, I remove my hand and then let it smack against his cheek. Not too hard, but enough to garner a gasp.

His eyes open and meet mine, pupils completely blown. "Yes, yes," he chants, hips rocking faster.

He loves it.

I do it again, just a little harder this time. "Come for me, Carlo."

"Ah, ah," he moans. "I'm coming. I'm coming."

His release shoots from his cock, landing on my stomach in ribbons. His breathless whimpers stoke the fire that's already burning inside me.

I grip his waist in one hand, squeezing his thigh with the other. I lift my hips to go deeper, and feel a slight twinge of pain in my chest as my muscles flex. I ignore it, focusing more on the pleasure I feel being deep inside him. I watch as he continues to slowly stroke himself, the cum dripping from his fingers as he mewls and shakes.

"I'm gonna come," I tell him.

"Yes," he cries. "Fill me up."

"Oh fuck."

I thrust deep, a month of built-up desire and yearning culminating into the most intense orgasm I've felt in a long time. My cock twitches and throbs, and Carlo moves up and down as I roar into the room.

"Oh yes. Oh fuck yes, it feels so good," he says.

"Baby." My voice cracks, disrupted by a full-body shiver.

"Mmm."

Carlo slowly lifts up, getting off me and stretching alongside me with a sigh.

He kisses my shoulder. "I love you."

I turn my head to look at him. "I love you."

"Let's lay here for a few minutes, then get in the shower. I'll help clean you up."

"Sounds good."

We lie together, his leg slung over mine, our fingers intertwined as they rest on my stomach, and at this moment, I've never been happier. It overshadows the grief and anger that have taken up residence in my heart lately, and I'm grateful to have him pull me out of those feelings for a reprieve, and hope that I do the same for him.

"We can tell people," I say. "When you talk to everyone, you can let them know we're together. I don't want there to ever be a time where I have to hide how I feel about you."

He shifts, lifting up to look at me. "You sure?"

"About you I am."

His smile sends warmth through me, and I know it's the right plan. Regardless of how it goes down, I won't regret this.

CARLO

CHAPTER 51

While Javier sleeps, I sneak into the living room and start going through the box my dad gave me. After I got it initially, I barely went through it, confused by why he was giving me a box of memories. Since his death, I've been thinking about it more and more, but a little hesitant to subject myself to photos of us at a time when things were still good. However, something continues to play over and over in my head. When we were at Javier's house and Dad asked to speak to me alone, he once again questioned whether I had that box. He didn't say anything else, but it feels important, and now it's time to dive into it.

At first, it's mostly photos I see, some framed, most not. There's a few certificates from when I was in school—honor roll, first place in the science fair, and a character trait award.

I put them on the coffee table as I continue to search for something I feel like my father wanted me to find. There's a large manila envelope, but when I open it up and peek inside, it's mostly old art projects from school. Sketches, paintings—a talent I long forgot about when I was forced in a different direction.

I find my birth certificate, photos of me and my mom when I was a newborn, and pictures of them together, looking happy and in love. Mom died when I was one, so I never knew her, and Dad never talked about her. I sometimes wonder if things would've been different if she had lived.

As I empty the box, I begin to think maybe there wasn't a secret message. Perhaps he just knew his time could come to an end and he thought I'd like to have these. I fall back into the couch with a sigh, running a hand through my hair.

"Hey," Javier says, appearing through the hall.

"Hey," I reply with a smile.

"What's goin' on in here?" he questions, looking at the mess all around me.

"My dad left me this box. Well, it was before. When he went to the safe house for the first time. Johnny had me pick it up."

Javier sits next to me, wearing only his black tank and boxers. "This is why you were at The Kat that one time?"

"Yeah."

"What is it?"

"Photos, school stuff, my birth certificate. I thought he wanted me to find something specific, but maybe not. I guess he just wanted me to have these."

"What's in here?" he asks, grabbing the manila envelope.

"Art. Stuff I created in high school."

"Oh, right. I forgot you were an artist."

I snort. "Not sure about that."

Javier pulls out a few pages, flipping through them. One

is a lighthouse amongst a rocky water shoreline with the sun setting in the background. Another is a black and white sketch of a guy's face.

"Who's this?" he asks.

"A guy in my art class. I might've had a crush."

"What's his first and last name?" Javier deadpans.

I choke out a laugh. "Oh stop."

The other paper is more abstract, random objects melting and twisting amongst a rainbow of colors.

"Well, I don't know much about art, but you were pretty good." He reaches into the envelope again. "I'm not gonna pull out more photos of boys you were crushing on, am I?"

"I'm not sure," I say with a laugh.

He makes an unamused face but pulls out a few more papers. "It's nice that your dad kept all of this, maybe—"

A group of folded up papers falls from between the art, landing on the floor.

I reach down and pick it up, unfolding them to see what they are.

As soon as I see the writing, I know it's my dad's.

"It's a letter from my dad," I say quietly, scanning the words before fully absorbing them.

Javier puts the artwork down and sits back.

I begin reading.

> Giancarlo,
> Living this life means always straddling the line between life and death. I've known it from the beginning, but lately it feels like I'm tilting closer to

death's side, and I don't want to go without you knowing a few things.

Don't trust Johnny. I won't go into it now, but if my death comes before his, don't believe anything he says. Steer clear.

You and I didn't have the best relationship, and that's not news to either of us. I've had plenty of moments to reflect and wonder if I could've done things differently, and while I'm sure there was a better option, I don't regret keeping you safe. I regret not getting to know you as you grew into a man.

I never told you this, because I held a lot of guilt about it, and because I was afraid it would turn you astray. Ironic, considering later, I'd want to do just that. However, your mother was killed because of what I do. It wasn't an accident, though it was made to look like one. She was taken from us as a warning to me. I was already in deep and I had crossed a line I shouldn't have. Her death kept me in line for a while. I was no longer the guy willing to push the buttons and bend the rules. Doing that meant death, and not for me, but for those I loved.

When you were growing up, I was so happy to have a son. A man who would grow up in the life just as I had—someone to follow in my steps. I wanted this for you, and considering everything I know and have done, I'm not sure that makes me a great father. You have to understand, I know nothing different.

Because I wanted this for you, I didn't want to scare you off with the truth about your mother. However, when I found out your truth, I was terrified. Disappointed and angry, yes, but not for the reasons you may think. I was losing the son that would take the reins. Our relationship was going to die because I didn't want you to. I couldn't bring you in and break the rules. They wouldn't stand for that. They'd kill you. Maybe me too.

A boss in the nineties was killed after the family heard he had been with both men and women. They said nobody will respect a homosexual crime boss. I feared for your safety in the life, I feared for it in the world in general. You're my son, and I only want you to be protected.

I'm sorry I didn't think about you being happy. It came second to your life. Becoming a priest felt like a saving grace, and please excuse the irony there. You'd be away at school for a while, you wouldn't be caught with another man, and I hoped you'd stay far away from this life. It was then I wished I had told you the truth about your mother, but you were already so stubborn, wanting to stick around, wanting to be like me. It wouldn't have worked, and this was the only way I could think of to keep you safe.

I'm sorry, Carlo. I should've done more. I should've at least talked to you and not let you think

I hated you for who you are. I assumed it would help in keeping you away from me, but I've lived with the consequences my whole life. I've missed my son.

I'm going to ask you to do something I never thought I'd do. The tides are coming in and I'm stuck in the sand. I need you to take over. I need you to do better than I did. I can't have this family fall into Johnny's hands. I know I can trust you to do the best you can. Hopefully it doesn't come down to this. Maybe you'll find this letter and I'll still be alive and you'll wonder what the hell I was even worried about. Hopefully, if that's the case, we can rebuild our relationship.

If not, know you can trust George. He's old school, but he's been loyal to me a long time. He'll listen to you and he'll show you the ropes. Javier is my right hand. I've had a good relationship with him and his father before him. He'll do whatever he can to keep you safe, and that'll be my main concern. If you step into this, you'll need to be prepared for what'll be thrown at you. You'll be forced to grow up, thicken your skin, and lay down the fucking law. You will be boss. You tell them how it is. Don't let anyone intimidate you. You are a Gallo. You are capable of anything.

I love you, Son.
Stay safe.

Tears fill my eyes but they don't spill over. I stare at the writing, scribbled in a hurry based on the sloppiness. Probably written last minute, when he knew Johnny was up to something, and thrown into boring personal effects that Johnny wouldn't think twice about.

He thought he'd die when he went into hiding. He made it out, to Johnny's dismay, I'm sure. He knew I hadn't found the letter, and brought it up before thinking he could die again. He survived once more, only to die in front of me.

"Okay?" Javier asks, his hand resting on my back.

I nod, swallowing down the lump in my throat. I lift the papers. "Reiterating his wishes." I swallow again, clearing my throat. "Told me the truth about my mom, which fueled his need to protect me by sending me away."

Javier rubs my back, scratching lightly. "Was it bad?"

I look at him. "She was killed. They killed her as a warning to him. He said he was pushing too many buttons. Breaking rules."

He scratches at his jaw, shaking his head. "I'm sorry."

I twist my lips to the side, fighting off a cocktail of emotions. "He said he didn't hate me for who I was, but hated that he had to lose me to protect me." I rub my forehead. "I thought maybe I could come in and run things a little differently. I thought I could hold on to my morality in some way."

Javier nods along, humoring me if anything.

"But if I thought I could be myself and be with you..." I shake my head. "They won't have it, will they? They'll doubt me at every turn. They'll undermine me, make jokes, and do everything they can to push me out of a role that my father wanted for me. Did you know they killed a sitting boss for suspecting he was bisexual?"

Javier nods. "Yeah."

"So, what do I do?"

He's quiet for a little while. "We don't have to tell anyone. I'm used to keeping my personal shit to myself."

I watch him, studying his handsome face while thinking over what to do.

"I'm gonna talk to George," I say. "When do you think you'll be healed enough for...anything that might come our way?"

His brows lift. "I can be ready whenever you need me to be."

I put my hand on his thigh and squeeze. "Good."

CHAPTER 52

I t takes a week to get a meeting set up with the family to have the initiation ritual. There's nearly fifty people here, ready to watch as I'm sworn in. I'm told the rules and expectations, and I bleed on a card with a depiction of St. Michael, the archangel.

A lot of mafia members are Catholics, going to church on holidays, wearing pendants and making the sign of the cross, all while living a lifestyle the church condemns. I find it interesting that they cling to Catholicism so tightly, and in talking to a good amount of them, I realized they appreciate that I was a priest. Hypocrisy runs rampant.

The event goes on for a little while, strictly for made men only, so Javier isn't here. I talk to everyone, even if it's just briefly, and most everyone gives me their condolences. There's several I can tell don't like that I'm their new boss. It's written on their faces, expressed by their snarls and furrowed brows.

Once the secretive side of things is over, I announce that I'm opening it up to others, giving them time to invite their wives or girlfriends, or to call the associates to see if they'd like to attend.

The family consists of hundreds of members, so this is a risky move I'm about to make, but a necessary one, and since Javier is right outside, he'll be here before anyone else.

Once I send him a message, he strolls in, wearing his signature black. Though it can't be seen, I know he's got his new holster and guns underneath his jacket.

"How'd it go?" he asks when he sidles up next to me.

I take a sip of my drink. "Good. It's official."

"Boss," he says with a dip of his head.

I grin. "Ready?"

He takes my glass and downs the rest of the drink. "Ready."

"Everyone!" I announce, raising my voice amongst the crowd.

Javier puts his fingers in his mouth and lets loose a loud whistle. "Turn that music down."

The music quiets as does the chatter, and all eyes are on me.

"I heard the rules earlier, as you've all heard countless times before. Respect women. Don't engage with the woman of another member, or their sisters, unless your motives are serious. Stay loyal, don't interfere with anyone else's interests. Don't talk to the cops. Don't engage in a battle you can't win. You know, all of that," I say with a tight smile. "Lots of rules. Old traditions. Which I can understand. Though, I won't go into the fact that twenty-nine years ago, members of this family killed my mother." I wave my hand in the air as people murmur.

"Well, now that I've been sworn in as the new boss, I'm not here to lie and say I'll be just like my father. While we have similarities, we also have plenty of differences. I'm ready to hear anybody out. If you need to talk to me, let me know and we'll make it happen. My ego isn't too big to not listen to anybody's ideas for this family. I'm the boss, but we are a family, and I want it to feel that way.

"Having said that, there's something you all should know. It goes against everything the mafia has been known for." Javier shifts, and George moves closer to my side. "But it doesn't change the rules that were mentioned tonight. You're all aware that I came into this in an unusual way. You're also aware I spent many years as a priest. Everything about me being the boss goes against the grain, so while this might be surprising, it will not be the only thing that's different about me." I take a breath and look into the eyes of the crowd, sensing concern and confusion. "I'll never take a wife, nor any of yours," I say with a wry grin, garnering a few laughs. "Your sisters are safe, because I'm not attracted to women."

With the bomb thrown, the room goes quiet, waiting to see what happens next.

I shrug. "It doesn't change the fundamentals of who I am. I—"

"No, fuck that. What are you saying?" someone says from the crowd. "We ain't havin' a gay boss."

Murmurs and chatter pick up, people looking to each other, searching for a way to react.

"Well, you do," I say simply, trying to find the guy who said it. "What does it matter to you? To anyone?"

"Nobody's gonna take us seriously. How are we going to be intimidating with a fucking cocksucker at the helm."

I tilt my head, noticing Javier bristling with rage at my side.

"He killed Sammy," George announces. "He came up

with the plan to get rid of Johnny. He lied to the cops to keep our people out of trouble."

I notice a few people nodding along, but plenty still look angry and disturbed.

"You can feel how you feel," I say, "But you will respect this family and me as the boss." I pause. "Or, we can start revealing who is breaking rules and how." I start looking around the room, searching for the faces I've already done research on. "People who are sleeping with member's sisters." I make eye contact with at least three people I know of for sure. "Or how about someone whose brother just married someone in law enforcement? How are those family dinners going?" I look at a man named Joseph when I say that one. "Or the guy who recently hooked up with a female detective." I glance around the room. "As far as I know we don't have any women on the payroll. Oh, and I do believe someone is sleeping with someone's soon-to-be wife. Is that right?" I ask, looking at George who nods once.

"Now that last rule I mentioned. Not engaging in a battle you can't win." I smile. "I have a lot of information on a lot of you."

"Fuck that. I'm not fucking anyone's mom, sister, or nothin'. I'm not talking to the cops or any other shit. And I am not okay with this." He plows through the crowd, angry and red-faced. "This is embarrassing and I will not tolerate it."

I lift my brows. "Yeah?" He stops a few feet away from me. "You seem to know the rules then."

"Yeah, I fucking know 'em. And even though it's not explicitly said in the fucking ceremony, we don't allow..." He looks me up and down, disgust etched on his face, "this bullshit in."

I nod, my lips downturning slightly. "Got it. Okay,

what's one of the last things we say in the ceremony?" He doesn't reply right away, instead his eyes search the room, hoping for someone to join him. "Anyone?" I ask, looking into the crowd. I turn to look at this guy who decided this meant enough to him to speak up. "We live by the gun and we die by the gun. You don't get to quit."

He inhales deeply, his nostrils flaring. "I will not listen to a fa—" Javier steps up next to me, but I put my hand on his arm. Turning, I reach into his jacket, finding his gun. Our eyes meet and I unsnap the leather and pull the gun free. Turning back, I aim it at him. "Say it again."

His feet shift, and I see the fear in his eyes.

"This ain't right," someone says, coming through the crowd. "George," he pleads. "Come on, you know this ain't the way we do things."

George takes his gun out from the waist of his pants and holds it at his side. "This is a new era, Liam."

"Cortez would have never—"

"My father knew," I say, staring him in the eyes. "And he chose me for this anyway. Don't mention his name again. Not in relation to this."

With the gun still aimed at the first guy's forehead, I wave my other hand in the air. "All right, anyone who agrees with these guys, come on up."

Everyone hesitates, fear wrapping around their legs. However, a few more men step forward with their chests puffed up and noses in the air.

Javier pulls out his other gun, and then Elio and Dante make their way to my side, forming a line in front of the crowd.

"Last chance to change your mind. You're either in this family, with me as boss, or you want out, and there's only one way to go."

They stand there, holding on to their egos and pride, unwilling to open their minds to a hint of something different. But I know now this is how it's going to be. I've made my decision, and though I know it's a sin, it has to be done. I have to do what's necessary for my survival in this world. Hopefully this will be just another tale to add to the one that's already floating around about Sammy. Maybe people will know not to question me or my dedication to this family. The mafia thrives on death and violence. How else do I prove that I'm not one to fuck with if I don't show them the consequences of their behavior?

"You ready?" I ask the man my gun is aimed at.

He spits at my feet, and my finger squeezes the trigger. The loud boom is followed by several more in quick succession, and soon, the line of people who walked up are now crumpled on the floor.

I gaze around the room again. "I gave them a choice. I give you all the same one. If you leave this room, I will believe it's because you don't have an issue. If I hear even a whisper of a rumor that you're saying anything about me behind my back, you will join your friends," I say, gesturing to the bodies. "I will not work with people who do not have my back a hundred percent. I don't need you to agree with the way I live, but I need to know I can trust you to keep your mouth closed about things that don't concern you. What I got going on will not cause issues within the family, but fucking fiancés, sisters, and cops is a problem, and those will be handled soon."

When nobody says anything else, I hand the gun back to Javier. "Are we good?"

Nods and murmurs of agreement spread through the room. "All right. Wait a little while. Let everyone see this before we get it cleaned up. Tell them why it happened and that it can happen again. Enjoy your night."

George snaps at some of the guys and begins giving them instructions. I turn away and look at Javier. "Ready to go home?"

He smirks. "Who's gonna be boss when we get there?"

I laugh, putting a hand on his back as we walk out.

CHAPTER 53

He slams me against the wall as soon as we get home, his mouth attacking mine in a vicious kiss. I grab his wrists and turn him around, backing him into the wall as I assault his neck, biting on the flesh before covering it with my lips, kissing the sting away.

Javier moans, grabbing my hair and tugging on the strands.

I undo the buttons on his pants and just get the zipper down before he shoves my hands away, focusing on stripping me of my suit jacket and ripping the dress shirt apart at the buttons, sending them flying.

We fight for dominance, both wanting to consume the other. We bump into the furniture as we each start reaching for clothing, pulling and throwing while also attempting to get out of our shoes in a timely manner. Mine are easier to kick off, whereas Javier has his laced up combat boots on.

"Sit," I tell him, shoving him into an accent chair in my living room.

I get to my knees and loosen the laces, peering up at

him as he stares down at me with an animalistic hunger in his eyes.

"Hurry up," he commands when he notices I've slowed my pace.

"I'm your boss," I tell him. "You can't talk to me like that."

He reaches down and removes the second boot before grabbing me by the throat, leaning over me.

"I'm not a member of the family, remember?"

"I sign your paycheck now," I reply, putting my hands on his thighs.

He licks his lips, his thumb tracing my jaw line before he tightens his grip around my neck and yanks me up. A moan escapes my mouth and lights a fire in his eyes.

"I think you want me to be the boss right now." He leans down and lets his tongue dance across the seam of my lips. "Don't you?"

My breath leaves my lungs in a rush—a low, desperate whine intertwined with it. "No." The word isn't convincing to either one of us, and he knows it.

Javier releases my throat, standing up and looming over me. "No?" he asks with a tilt of his head.

I remove my glasses, putting them on the table next to me before standing up and saying, "No."

Turning, I head to the hall, making my way to the bedroom. His low chuckle sends chills down my spine.

I don't hear his steps until I'm in my room, and my pulse spikes as I wait to see what's coming. Facing the bed, I remove my pants and toss them along the bottom of the mattress.

"Where's the flogger?" he asks, striding into the room with a mission.

"Want me to whip you?" I question.

He pulls open drawers, searching for what he knows I keep in here.

"We both know it's you who likes the pain."

Javier shuts me up with that one, because he's right. I drop to my knees and reach under my mattress, producing the scourge. When he notices it, he grins, walking over to pluck it from my hand.

"Such a dirty, dirty boy."

"Mm," I hum quietly.

"Strip down and get on your knees on the bed. Hold onto the headboard."

I stare at him for a few seconds, being stubborn. He cocks an eyebrow, stepping closer to hold me by the chin. "You know you want to, *mi amor*." His hand skates down my body before curving around my hip and squeezing my ass. With his lips by my ear, he continues, "You know you love how I handle your body."

A shiver rolls down the middle of my back, and without saying anything, I turn and do what he says.

Naked and on my knees, I grip the wooden headboard, my eyes on the wall in front of me. He moves around the room, probably just to keep me waiting, but I don't search for him.

After what feels like an hour, the bed dips behind me, and anticipation floods my veins. I wait for a hard smack, wondering where he'll start.

His rough hands move around my hips, dropping low on my stomach as his lips plant a soft kiss under my right ear. "I love you," he whispers.

My body relaxes and I angle my head. "I love you."

Javier eases away, and then the strips of leather land across the back of my left shoulder.

With a hiss, I squeeze the wood in my hands.

He hits me again, this time on the other shoulder. I drop my head forward, a moan leaving my lips.

The next strike lands across my ass, making me jerk before a wave of desire rolls over me.

Javier presses against my back with his chest, his hand finding my erection, giving it a slow and languid stroke.

"You like when I hurt you?"

I lean back against him, a rumble in my throat. "Yes."

"I do it because it makes you feel good. Because it makes your dick weep for me. But I'd never hurt you without your consent. You know that, don't you, *mi amor*?"

I nod. "Yes. I know."

Javier gently bites down on my earlobe. "What would they think of their boss being a masochistic slut for me?" he teases.

"I don't care what they think."

With one hand on my cock, the other climbs up my throat, grabbing me tight. "I believe you. I'm proud of what you did today."

"Are you gonna praise me or fuck me?"

His grip tightens around my throat. "I see. Because you're the big boss now, you're feeling a little testy."

"Fuck me, Javier. Fuck me or—"

He releases me, moving to my side to stare at me. "Or you'll what?"

I grin at him, letting my tongue glide over my bottom lip.

A low rumble in his throat is followed by him shoving me backwards. I land on my ass but immediately lie down on my back, spreading my legs while I reach for my cock.

"You want to ravage me, don't you?" I ask. "I can see it in your eyes. You want to leave your mark, claiming me... ruining me for anyone else."

"If you think you'll get the chance at being anyone else's, you're not as smart as I thought."

Javier grabs a bottle of lube he must've brought to the bed earlier, pouring the liquid in his hand.

"It's a good thing I only want you then."

"Let me remind you what you'll lose if you ever think otherwise."

Bending over me, his mouth encircles my cock while his slick fingers slide into my ass.

"Oh my God," I say as a breath leaves my lungs.

He moans around me, taking me deep into his warm mouth. His tongue glides around my head before he swallows me down once more. His touch is magical, transporting me to a land of euphoria in an instant. In this moment, he holds all power over me, because I'd do anything he wanted as long as I was able to continue being on the receiving end of his skillful hands and mouth.

When he pulls away, he instantly coats his cock with the lube. Between my legs, he hooks one of them over his arm as he positions himself at my entrance, slowly pushing in.

Once he's all the way inside, he grabs my other leg and begins rocking his hips back and forth.

I bite down on my lip, loving the way his body is silhouetted by the nightlight coming in from the hall.

"So fucking hot," I murmur.

A growl leaves his throat and he thrusts deeper. "You're mine, Carlo. Now. Forever."

I nod. "Yes. Yours."

The pure, raw need in his gaze has my body trembling. Everything about Javier makes me feel like a different person, though perhaps it's just that he's the only one who's been able to reach the real me, pulling me out of the shell I've been in for so long.

He drops lower over my body, keeping just one of my legs up high on his arm as he fucks me deep and rough.

"You get me so hard," he growls into my ear. "My cock aches for you all fucking day."

"Mm," I moan. "You could use me whenever you want."

"Fuck," he grunts.

"Use me now," I say quietly. "Don't fuck me like you love me. Fuck me like you want to break me."

A rough, gravelly noise rumbles in his throat, sending goosebumps down my arms. Javier pulls out, flipping me around and yanking me up until I'm on my hands and knees.

I let out a wanton moan, and then he's sliding back inside with a vicious thrust. His fingers dig into my skin, leaving what I know will be bruises by tomorrow. His hips slam into my ass as he does exactly what I wanted him to do.

I spread my legs wider, dropping my chest to the bed as I squeeze the covers in my fists.

"God, the way your ass moves," he says before slapping a cheek with his palm. "Sinful."

He fucks with an animalistic nature. This is pure carnality, and I revel in it. My cock thickens, throbbing with the need to release, but I don't dare touch myself.

Javier pushes me flat on my stomach, planting his foot over my leg, somehow getting even deeper with each thrust.

My cock begins getting friction against the covers, and I begin to beg.

"Yes, please. Please."

"Please, what?" he asks, his fingers threading through my hair, pulling the strands.

I don't even know what I want. "Anything. Everything. More. Harder. I want it all."

His hand frees my hair and then his body heat is gone and he lifts my hips off the mattress, pulling me to the edge of the bed so he can stand on the floor.

When he pushes back in, he doesn't move, instead reaching around my waist, touching my cock.

"Oh God," I moan.

"You're so fucking hard," he says, rubbing my pre-cum around my head. "So wet."

"Yes," I cry. "Oh God, please."

He releases me, giving my ass another spanking before gripping my hips and beginning his thrusts.

With my arms outstretched in front of me, I rest my cheek on the mattress, clenching and unclenching the covers as I cry out, begging and praising him.

"Yes. Fuck yes. Oh God, Javier. So good. Please don't stop."

I feel wetness on my thighs and peek underneath me, noticing a stream of pre-cum dripping from my cock.

My orgasm is close and I know one stroke on my shaft will have me exploding all over the mattress.

"I'm about to come," Javier says. "I'm gonna come inside you. Fill you up and watch it drip out."

"Oh yes. Yes," I cry. "Fill me up."

"Oh God, baby. Oh God." He grunts, his hold on me painful and exhilarating.

Javier cries out, the sound booming.

When his cock twitches and throbs inside me, it sends my orgasm hurtling over the edge.

"Oh fuck," I exclaim, surprised at the sudden and overwhelming pleasure that rolls over me. "Oh fuck, oh shit. I'm coming."

I don't even have to touch myself, as it's already pouring out of me, but after a few seconds, I reach down and give myself a few strokes anyway, back bowing as I shake and cry out.

"Oh yes," he murmurs, "Oh, baby. Yes. Come apart for me," he says.

My breath comes in loud pants as I tremble and whine, my muscles giving out on me.

Javier pulls out slowly, but his hands stay on my ass, doing what he said he would and watching the cum drip from me.

When my legs shake, he takes a hold of my waist and lowers me to the bed while moving me up farther on the mattress.

Spooning me, he nuzzles his face into my neck, our sweat mixing together.

"You're so fucking perfect for me."

After several seconds, I say, "I was thinking." I take a couple more deep breaths. "We should move in together. We haven't spent a day apart since you got out of the hospital anyway, and it probably—"

"You don't have to convince me. I'm already down."

I chuckle. "Oh okay. Good."

"I love you."

I turn in his arms, facing him. "I love you."

EPILOGUE

JAVIER

He pulls the trigger, the bullet flying from the chamber and crossing the room to meet its target.

Dead.

When I glance to my left, I watch as he slowly lowers his arm to his side. His gaze finds mine.

Murderer. Sinner.

I see nothing behind his eyes. No guilt. No remorse.

He's different from when I first met him, but it doesn't matter if he's a priest or mafia boss. He's Carlo, and that's enough for me.

I spin around, aiming my gun at another man before squeezing the trigger.

It's been six months since Carlo took over, and we've had minimal problems, but problems nonetheless. Some of the Bonetti Family still take issue with Carlo killing Sammy, justified or not. Aurelio's done his best to keep them under control, but it's not enough.

Carlo's put up with threats, sabotage of his drug trafficking route, and more. He told Aurelio it was his job to fix things within his family, but we found out about a group of six Bonetti soldiers who were dead-set on ruining Carlo's reign.

I told Carlo he could steer clear of the violence and let me handle it, but he refuses to be left behind while I fight his wars for him. His words, not mine. I'd fight any and all wars for him if it meant keeping him safe, but I guess he feels the same way about me.

We hear movement outside the old junk yard office, and Carlo gestures with his head for me to stand to the left of the door while he stays in perfect view.

When the door flies open, the man spots him immediately, but he doesn't see me. I hold up my gun and send a bullet into the back of his head. As he falls, another man rushes in, but Carlo's already firing, hitting him twice in the chest before he can lift his arm to aim at me.

"That's four," Carlo says.

"Two more somewhere around here."

"The junk yard is huge. If they're smart and they've already heard the shots, they'd be leaving." Carlo looks at his watch. "We need to find them fast. It's already seven-forty."

"They're not that smart. They formed this rogue team that's going against their own boss's wishes. Dante said they get high in an old rail car out here. We just gotta find it."

Carlo sighs. "Let's go."

Outside, the sun is already setting, casting shadows everywhere. We maneuver through a maze of rusted and broken cars, heading toward a tree line along the back that has several old shipping freights.

We quietly walk past them, stopping when we hear voices inside.

Carlo looks around, picking up a brick. "You ready?"

"Always," I say with a smirk.

The brick flies through the air, smacking into the next car over, the sound echoing through the yard.

"What the fuck?"

"What was that?"

Confused voices followed by the scurrying of feet come from inside the car. They slide open the door, emerging with scowls on their faces and guns in hand. Fortunately for us, they appear to be high, therefore their reaction time is slow.

Two quick shots drop them to the ground, but they're still alive. I walk a little closer and finish them off.

Carlo tucks his gun into his pants and sighs. "I'll let Aurelio know."

"Aurelio should've got them himself, but—" I hold up my hands.

"He'll owe me. I like when people owe me favors."

I step up to him and put my hand around his lower back. "You owe me something."

He leans in and kisses my cheek. "I do, indeed. That's why we need to leave now. Do I have blood on me?" he asks, looking down at his button up.

I check him out. "I don't see anything, but it's also getting dark. I might have something on me from the guy in the office. I was a little close."

He wipes a spot off my forehead with his thumb. "I have wipes in the car. And another shirt if you need one."

"We'll see."

We walk through the junk yard, heading back to the car. He pulls his phone from his pocket and calls his underboss.

"Hey, yeah, it's done. Call Aurelio and set up a meeting for him and I to have a conversation. Oh, and Dante? Get in touch with Khalid King, will you? It's time for us to talk. Yeah. Okay."

He ends the call and puts the phone away as we get to the car. I unlock it and climb into the driver's side before I start talking.

"King? The Kinmore Family?"

I nod. "They're a different kind of mafia family. I like their diversity."

"Well, yeah, but they don't really seem to like the Italians."

"That's because Italians have always stuck to a code that goes against everything the Kinmore family is about. They have a Black boss, Hispanic underboss, and even more variety within their ranks. Rumor has it, a couple of them are queer."

"Who told you this rumor?"

"I sent someone out there to check in on things. He saw one of the capos with a man in a club."

"Huh. And what's the point of this meeting?"

"I want to extend an olive branch. Maybe we can work together. We're doing things differently here, and perhaps they'll be more willing to talk to me now." He goes quiet for a while. "They have a sex club out there. We could go visit it."

"Ah, now I'm interested."

He chuckles. "Of course you are. They also have a casino. I'm thinking we could do something like that in Boston. Anyway, just a meeting to see how to expand our legal businesses while being able to utilize them for cleaning money."

"Gotcha."

He looks at his watch again. "Hurry. We're gonna be late."

I press down on the gas, taking us toward the city.

EPILOGUE PART TWO
CARLO

"Get out here," Javier says. "I'll park and meet you in a minute."

I push open the door and reach into the backseat to grab my suit jacket, sliding my arms through the sleeves as I approach the restaurant door.

"Mr. Gallo." The manager greets me as soon as I step inside. "We're honored you chose our restaurant."

I nod. "Thank you, Francesco. I heard my father was a fan of this place."

"He was, sir. The place is as you requested," he says, gesturing to the empty restaurant.

"Thank you."

"I'll be in my office if you need me, but the waitress will be with you shortly."

I nod again and watch as he walks away.

A few minutes later, Javier pulls open the door and struts inside, his expression showing his confusion.

"Are they closed?"

I smile, sliding my hands into my pants pockets. "No. They're open. Just for us."

He grins. "Oh, I see."

"I feel bad I wasn't able to make our date on your birthday, so here's a belated celebration."

"All of this wasn't necessary," he says. "I understood."

"I know you did, but I want to celebrate your existence in the world. Come."

I turn and lead us to our seats in the center of the room. The lights are dim, with candles and flowers on every table, including ours. Javier's not a romantic. Not in the traditional sense. He would never ask for or expect candles and flowers, but based on the look on his face, I can tell he's appreciative of the thought.

"I'd think you were in love with me or something," he teases.

I pull out his chair, kissing his lips before making my way to my side. "A little."

The both of us remove our suit jackets, and before we can hang them over our seats, a woman is there with a smile on her face, her hands outstretched.

"I'll take those for you."

"Thank you," we say at the same time.

We sit, scooting closer to the table that already has a bottle of wine sitting in a bucket of ice.

"You're crazy," Javier says with a laugh, shaking his head.

"I didn't want any interruptions. We have this whole place all to ourselves, and I got a room in a hotel just down the street."

"So you're just trying to get me drunk so you can take advantage of me."

I laugh. "Exactly."

He smirks. "Ah, I'm pretty easy."

The waitress comes back with ice water, and then opens the wine for us. "Appetizers will be out soon."

She disappears and Javier raises his brows at me. "You preordered the food?"

"I know what you like."

He reaches across the table, and my hand meets his. "Who knew a random stop in a church would lead to this?"

I snort. "Well, I never thought I'd be here, that's for sure." I squeeze his hand. "But I wouldn't want it any other way."

Most everyone knows about Javier and me now. We went through another wave of shock at people finding out about Javier being bisexual, and then the fact that we were together. We've had to clear out a few more members, but everything's calmed down the last few months.

Other families know about my sexuality now, but it hasn't brought up any issues. Not since also finding out that I've had members of my own family killed for saying anything negative about it.

They may not agree, or even like it, but business is king, and they want the business I include them in, so they'll deal with it. I care less about them talking shit, because I expect that, and until they use it as a reason to try to take me out, I won't worry about what they have to say. My priority is my own family and trusting that they have my back so if the time comes that another family wants to do something about it, I know I have a loyal army behind me.

We moved into a house together last month—one a few hours from Boston that we use as a retreat when we need to get away. Javier kept his apartment near the city so we stay there a good amount of time too.

"I'm glad you got over your concern about going to Hell," Javier says with a smirk.

"Well, the people I love will be there, too. Why would I want to be alone?"

Javi winks at me and takes a sip of his wine. He's still not a believer. To him, there's no Heaven, no Hell. No God, no Satan. We live on this earth, we die, and that's where it ends.

I sometimes wish I had gone through life with that thought process. It would've saved me a lot of guilt and fear.

Whether there's a God that brought Javier into my life, be it to test me or test him, I don't know. We both failed, if that were the case. He didn't become a believer, and I turned away from the church.

There could be a higher power, but choosing to believe means knowing I won't ever reach Heaven's gates. So, I try not to dwell on it so much these days. I've made my decision to be with Javier and to run the Esposito family. No amount of prayers will change either of those things.

Perhaps all life is just luck and happenstance. Regardless of what it was, I'm grateful for whatever brought Javier into my church that day.

I never felt authentic in my cassock and collar. I feel like my true self when I'm with him. If I don't make it to Heaven, I'm going to enjoy the heaven I have on earth here with him.

Acknowledgments

Well, if you got this far, I want to thank you for reading. I hope you enjoyed Carlo and Javier's story.

Huge thanks to Kate Farlow for designing the model and discreet version of this book. And thanks to Tal Lewin for designing the illustrated cover. It's hard to pick a favorite when they're all so good!

Thank you to my beta readers, ARC and street team members, and any and everyone who shared their excitement over this book.

Massive thanks to all the bloggers, reviewers, and influencers who make teasers and videos and spread the love. I appreciate you all so much.

Thanks to my husband for being there to listen to me rant and run questions by him. For reading this and offering his opinions and editing advice. And for being the absolute best.

This book took a long time to come to fruition. After struggling for months, and starting and tossing several other ideas, someone posted a picture in my reader group. Leeann R, if you're reading this, I can't thank you enough for posting that photo and asking for their story. If it weren't for you, this probably wouldn't exist.

A priest's story was never in my box of ideas, and then when I started, I didn't expect it to have any mafia elements. Alas, here we are. Sometimes, you go where the characters take you. (Most times, honestly) I love this story. I love these two guys, and though I don't know what's coming next, I hope it fills me with as much joy as these two did.

About the Author

Isabel Lucero is a bestselling author, finding joy in giving readers books for every mood.

Born in a small town in New Mexico, Isabel was lucky enough to escape and travel the world thanks to her husband's career in the Air Force. She and her husband have three kids and two dogs together, and currently reside in Delaware. When Isabel isn't on mommy duty or writing her next book, she can be found reading, or binging a TV show she's already seen three times.

Isabel loves connecting with her readers and fans of books in general. Keep in touch!

Sign up for my newsletter.

Join my reading group.

ALSO BY

<u>Dysfunctional</u>

Think Again

Darkness Within

His Secret

Lights, Camera, Passion

Splintered

Dysfunctional Short Stories

Twisted Valentine

Until Death Parts Us

The Kingston Brothers Series

On the Rocks

Truth or Dare

Against the Rules

Risking it All

South River University Series

Stealing Ronan

Tasting Innocence

Breaking Free

Tempting Him